ZACHARY JEFFRIES

The Unseen Curse

First edition

ISBN: 978-1-957079-04-2

This book was professionally typeset on Reedsy.
Find out more at reedsy.com

Contents

Author's Note

Dear Reader,

Please don't keep this book a secret! Feel free to let your friends, family, loved ones, and strangers know what you're reading. Post about it on social media. Spread the word on social media! Every book is an investment of hundreds of hours and thousands of dollars. Every moment you can spare helping this book find the right readers is appreciated more than you know.

Sincerely,

-Z

Content warnings

Adult language

Animal abuse

Antisemitism

Blood

Bullying

Car accident

Homophobia

intense action

Loss of a loved one

Racism

Chapter One: October 28th, ril ril late

The fire on the hill cast an eerie, nearly magical orange glow onto the entire town. The soft, warm light on the hodgepodge of impossibly old building facades almost made this town look like more than the useless hole in the ground June resented. Almost.

She sped up and ran a couple stop signs. It was the middle of the night, anyway. Besides, even if he didn't command that much respect, her dad was Deputy Mayor and should be able to get her out of a ticket. And she had to get up the hill before all the fun ended. She had to learn what this fire was all about. It was literally the most interesting thing to happen in Miridical since she and Dad moved there. So, sorry, stop signs, June had somewhere to be, a delicious mystery up on that hill just waiting for her. Magical lighting be damned.

Dad got picked up by the mayor about fifteen minutes ago, and those two never work outside of business hours. But it was nearly midnight then, and the whole town slept in the orange glow.

From the right angle, a tire fire can add a magic glow to any crappy boondock town that looks absolutely enchanting.

Even a grosshole as basic as Miridical. The smell of burning tire was not as enchanting. The ancient buildings of the town square below, normally lit by moonlight, tonight shone orange, punctuated by strobes of the emergency vehicles. The V where the Providence River split around Miridical twinkled in yellowy firelight. Beautiful. But looks were deceiving, and June would rather have eaten the window of the tiny roller-skate-of-a-car than live another year here.

After who knows how long, June snapped out of the unsettling hypnotic power of the fire. It was small, under control. Just like whoever the sheriff put in charge of investigating the accident would be. Seeing the Miridical Fire Department do their job well got a rise out of June, knowing how wicked dumb the town's sheriff's patrol was.

Eventually, the firefighters put out the flames on the overturned vehicle, piled back into their trucks, and snaked back down the hill. The ambulance left before June arrived on the scene; June didn't know if it carried anyone — a driver, or maybe a pedestrian. Probably not a pedestrian this late. The pack of lounging cops and the smell of burnt tire remained.

And of course, no one was actually investigating, piecing together what had happened, or corroborating the driver's account, whoever they were. Instead, they lounged on their hoods in the red and blue strobe of the three cruisers, laughing and goofing off.

As June pulled up in the town's Mini Cooper, road flares lit Dad's angry, flashing eyes. For a moment, she realized what a bad idea this was and considered driving past, around the hill, and back home, but she had to find out about the wreck.

"What are you doing here?" He whispered angrily, though trying not to lose his cool in front of the cops.

Technically, she shouldn't have been driving alone at all, considering she only had her learner's permit. But cops didn't keep track of every kid in town.

"I'm here to figure out what happened," she answered simply, putting the car in park. "It's not like those guys will."

Ahead, one of the officers tripped over a road flare and sent it skidding down the hill face below.

Dad rolled his eyes and tried to calm himself again. "Can I at least ask you to stay in the car?"

Instead of looking up at him, June turned her attention to her phone and said, "You can ask."

He stared her down, but she didn't budge. "Will you stay in the car, please, Juniper?"

"Will you stand up for yourself if the cops are wicked dicks to you?"

"And you wonder why I ask you to stay in the car."

"I know exactly why you ask me to stay in the car. I'll say something to piss the cops off and it puts you in a bad work position, but you can't control me."

He almost replied, then gave up with a sigh. "Please stay in the car, Junebug."

"Please don't refer to me as an insect."

Straightening his too-short tie, he re-tucked in his shirt (gross) and re-approached the police.

Loud enough for the khaki-clad officers on the scene to hear, June called out to her father, "Tell the pigs I say hi!"

Stooping, he shot a fiery look back at June before storming off. Like he could stay mad. June laughed. Dad could stay mad at her like Mom could rise from the dead; wasn't going to happen.

She wanted to keep quiet; she really did. Instead of immediately inserting herself into whatever the situation with the car accident was, she texted Connor again. Nothing. She checked the school social media group, just to be reminded the queer kids didn't invite her or Connor out to the movies... again. June tried to care about all of this high school BS, but wouldn't lower her intellect enough to do so effectively.

So it was back to the car wreck. Some vehicle had turned on its side and skidded into the ditch. Lucky for them, the car slid in toward the steep hill, and not off the side of the hill to roll down. Three of Miridical's finest lounged on their cruisers along a smoky red line of road flares as they scratched their heads and their asses, probably trying to figure out what caused the wreck. But they were way too close. Obviously, the car must have been moving fast in order to tip, which meant whatever caused the accident was farther back down the road. June didn't know the math, but she knew something went wrong in that car way back behind the parked green Mini Cooper.

From here, she couldn't identify the car, but saw the under-carriage and wheels. Two of the tires, the ones on the ground, were off-kilter, but the top ones were straight, so June figured the car had tipped onto its side but hadn't tumbled. In the strobing lights, June traced the skid on the old asphalt from its finish in the ditch, back down the winding hill road, under the Miridical Township Mini Cooper, and to the rumple in the road behind them, the pothole they'd just hit.

June's top left canine tooth stuck out a little, leaving a pocket of fleshy gum behind it that June sucked on, making a squirrel noise, while she looked into the blue and red flashing night. Behind the Mini Cooper, in the root of a Boston oak tree pushing up the blacktop, a divot had formed and filled with water from a cold rain that afternoon. At the skid, June followed the action from the puddle up to the overturned car and back. Whoever was driving hit the bump in the road too fast with the wheel turned, veered nearly off the hill, and panicked, steering too far to overcompensate. The car fish-tailed then tipped over, sliding into the ditch.

Obviously.

But why'd the driver cut the wheel so hard in the first place?

In the road ahead, one of the officers talked into her CB radio. Dad nodded and smiled politely as the other three hooted and laughed, one doubled over.

June's jaw set tight. They were mocking him, like always. And Dad was too nice, too laid back to stand up for himself. Not that June ever stood up for herself, but who cared what those idiots at school said? Dad was different; even if he was the mayor's errand boy, the officers could pretend to have an ounce of respect for the guy. She heard one of them laugh at that awful nickname, "Shitty Szmydtty," and then the interior of the car was suddenly hot, her skin itchy, and she was all kinds of agitated.

THWACK. A pale palm smacked the driver's side window, and June screamed. A dark face, shiny sweat giving away creased wrinkles, one near-black eye looking down the road, the other trained on June. Holy blood-thundering crap. Evens Bonhomme. Snapping in bursts of deep breaths to slow her heart, June slumped back against the passenger door, laughing at herself for being so jumpy.

The Bonhommes owned land on the other side of Fortune Hill, which was technically still in Miridical, although they barely ever came into Miridical. Evens was the exception, who worked in the courthouse. But did he walk home every day? That would've been a pretty serious commute.

So what was Evens doing all the way up Fortune Hill? Necktie askew, dress shirt partially unbuttoned and untucked, Evens Bonhomme held onto his briefcase, walking along the red flare-smoked road toward the wreck. Was he in the wreck? One of the sheriff's patrolmen intercepted the guy, joking around with him in the middle of the street. Evens wasn't the driver — just a guy walking the long way home. Real long. He sauntered away into the night.

Again tracing the skid, June looked back to the puddle in the road. Why had the driver swerved? In the intervals between the red and blue strobes, when the woods of Fortune Hill had instances of darkness, she saw them. Eyes. Staring back at her.

Her breath caught. Animal eyes, glowing green in the black night, not wild, but thoughtful. The animal wasn't simply looking at her, it held eye contact. All the flesh in her body turned cold. June couldn't look away from the shiny disks cowering in the dark. Two creatures sharing a moment in the night. But something was wrong and June knew it. Why would a wild animal keep so close? Why didn't the people and lights and the fire scare it away?

The eyes didn't move from the Mini Cooper like they could see through the glass to June. Like they could communicate with her. June experienced a sensation, electric, magical. She felt connected.

This was no ordinary wild animal. This wasn't just a simple car wreck. Something was up. What's the word? Afoot. Something was afoot as hell.

June opened the passenger door of the Mini Cooper and stepped out. Attempting to whisper at her father, June couldn't raise her voice loud enough to gain his attention without spooking the creature. Dad laughed off some insult. "Still,

I've got to do my job. Told the mayor I'd keep an eye on things here, so why don't you catch me up on what happened?"

She didn't turn from the animal to see which dumb bro cop answered. "Pretty straightforward — car swerved, turned, skidded. Nobody hurt, case closed."

"And you let him walk away?"

"Dad?" she croaked dryly. Slowly stepping from the Mini Cooper, June kept her eyes trained on the creature. The shiny green disks called to her from the dark, somehow communicating that though it was wild, the animal wasn't a threat. It wasn't dangerous. It needed something; must have been hurt. Needed help. Needed her help.

"C'mon, Shitty, Mayor said so."

"What were we supposed to do?" the bro cops spoke over her whispers.

The creature elicited a low rumble and June couldn't help but shake, but still stepped closer. Her voice grew stronger as she grew braver. "Dad? Officer Cops?"

But Dad didn't hear. "Was he drunk?"

"I don't think so."

"Probably just hydroplaned, lost control, Shitty."

Eyes still locked with the animal, June yelled over her shoulder with her woofing big-boy voice she made that time she had to scare away a swan, "There's not enough water to hydroplane!"

That got their attention and didn't scare off the creature. The sight of June at yet another crime scene elicited a groan from several of the officers, one bemoaning, "Great, the detective is here..." June even thought she heard a muttering of "Nancy Jew."

"Juniper!" Dad scolded.

"What? Arrest me. But first, check out WTF that is."

A heavy hand gripped June's elbow. "Young lady, I asked you to stay in the car!"

She tugged her arm free from her dad. "They didn't hydroplane, they swerved to miss that creature."

And she pointed at the glowing green shimmer of eyes. A whimper came from the dark behind the oak.

"What in Hell...?" one cop asked.

"Is that a..." another said something garbled, June didn't quite hear until the word, "hound?"

The officers stayed back from the animal, safe behind the Mini Cooper.

"We should call animal control."

"It'll be long gone by then," another officer said, drawing his gun.

"Put that away; you'll hurt yourself!" the only woman officer said.

But instead of staying in the safety behind the tiny car, June was drawn to the creature. It was hurting, and she had to help. Dad tried holding her back by the shoulders, but she just wriggled out of her puffy jacket into the crisp, cold autumn air, walking deliberately toward the whimpering eyes.

"Juniper!" her dad pleaded in a whisper. She waved him off as she tiptoed toward the animal.

"Shitty, get a hold of your daughter!" a cop yelled.

"Quiet, you'll spook it," the woman officer whispered.

June's oxblood Doc Martens didn't make a sound softly stepping, one in front of the other, closer and closer when the creature's whimper changed to a growl, a row of yellow-white teeth glinting through the shadows. Her steps paused. Her heartbeat thrummed in her ears. Behind her, one of the officers pumped a shotgun.

The growl rumbled louder, culminating in a desperate, high-pitched bark. In the shadow of the oak, the creature rose to its feet, a hulking figure, almost as tall as her — impossible for an animal on all fours. June forced another foot forward, another step toward the growling beast, her heartbeat an out-of-control drum solo against her ribcage. The animal bristled, seemingly growing larger at her approach, a great blob of shadow at the wood's edge, beady green eyes not looking away from June's.

With a click, one of the police cruiser's searchlight cut into the dark, and an oval beam lit up the glimmering puddle in the road. June stopped. The spotlight swept across the skidded asphalt, past June, over the trunk of the enormous Boston Oak, then settling down into the brush to reveal a dog, small and black.

Letting out a steamy breath, June dropped the tension from her shoulders. The dog was tiny, laid down in a ditch, ears pinned back, whimpering in fear or pain. Its front paw swiped at its face as it squinted from the bright light.

"Holy shit, she was right," one officer said.

"It is a..." another garbled word June didn't catch, "hound."

But it wasn't a hound; it was a mutt. Like a miniature black lab, but not a puppy. The officers kept their distance, but June and her father approached the poor thing, hiding a bloody back paw.

Dad threw his jacket over the dog's head to keep it from biting, then he scooped his hands underneath and lifted. He grunted under the surprising weight that he couldn't budge. June gasped. Dad was built like her, thick with strong legs, but even he couldn't get the little dog off the oak's roots.

"Give me a hand, would you?" Dad asked the cops.

They replied with a litany of excuses. Protocol was to wait for animal control. Someone had to drive Evens back. One officer was allergic.

"Fine, assholes." The only policewoman, who happened to be the only cop not bullying Dad, pulled plastic gloves from her belt and snapped them on before squatting down to join him as they got their hands under the little guy.

"How's he so heavy?" she grunted. It couldn't have been but two feet tall, despite the monstrous shadow it'd cast.

They awkwardly took turns attempting to lead the animal into the backseat of the Mini Cooper, spinning around, trying to give each other directions, laughing and wincing at the weight and awkwardness. Finally, the officer climbed in backward.

Beyond the little green car with the seal of the township of Miridical was the view of the Miridical township, specifically the square. This curve in the road was just below Prayer Point where tons of the straight high school kids went to make-out and/or beg each other for sex. As the officer and Dad embarrassed themselves, June's eyes wandered down to the library clock tower sticking up from the town square, noticing among the boughs of the giant thick-trunked trees spotted in yellow-orange leaves something caught the light from the police cars, some bit of white or silver reflected the strobing red and blue. June squinted and could almost make out a sparkling object, like a little line, stuck in a tree farther down the hill.

Whatever the shiny object dangling in the branch was, June couldn't take her eyes off it.

Bright light swept across her vision, headlights blinding her momentarily. A murmur spread across the officers and they all stood up straighter with unease. Blinking hard, June made out another sheriff's patrol cruiser sideways on the road. The window rolled down, revealing a pale face, square jaw, and grey goatee.

There's all kinds of tough-looking people, from muscly dudes to unafraid women, folks with scars or people who are just aggro. Sheriff Marrock was scary like Clint Eastwood; he'd seen some messed up stuff and lived through it, so even though he was completely relaxed, hanging elbow-first out of his window, his sneer still made June want to run. But there was a scar, too. June only noticed when Marrock wore his sheriff's hat, pushing back his brown and silver shag to reveal a notch cut out of the top of one ear.

The rumor was Marrock lost a chunk of ear the second time he got shot in the head, but nobody believed that. As mean as the sheriff was, most folks figured there was some scorned ex-Mrs. Marrock, who took a souvenir earring the night she left him.

"Serious situation. We've got another Garrison incident on our hands." His gravelly voice was like the tip of a knife pressed into flesh. "All the boys come with me. Azantian, stay on this scene for the tow. Mr. Szmydt..." His voice lowered, as if Marrock leaned into the flesh-dimpling knife. Gave June the willies.

"What brings you out?" the sheriff said, more of a warning than a question.

"The mayor. The mayor sent me."

"Well, he just left."

"That's what I understand."

"And did you get what you came for?" The sheriff's eyes flashed at Dad and June's shoulders tensed like she was caught between a couple animals in the wild.

The dog, now sitting up in the Mini Cooper's back seat, set his teeth and growled at the sheriff. Dad nodded toward the dog. "Yep."

"I imagine you'll be taking him out of town to a vet or animal control? Mayor's orders."

Dad took his time answering, and impressing June by how tough he looked. "Imagine so."

"He's a good boss, Mr. Mayor. Already home by now. Drive safe, Mr. Szmydt. Boys." He let out a sharp, piercing whistle.

The policemen jumped to their cars like trained dogs, leaving the policewoman behind the Mini Cooper, splotched in dog blood and shaking her head at cruisers driving away. June didn't relax until the sheriff's car had rounded the corner. Dad seemed to be wound just as tight, his shoulders and fists flexed.

"Bug?" Dad's voice made June jump. "You okay?"

She waved him off, annoyed. "Yeah, fine."

"Well, can we get going? I'll need your help getting this guy to the vet."

As June and Dad got into the Mini Cooper, Officer Azantian leaned in. "Where you taking her? Pawtucket? New Salem?"

"Headed for the animal hospital."

"The mayor said to keep this out of Miridical. Even the tow's from next town over," Azantian said as she came around the other side of the Mini Cooper.

"I'm no vet, but that animal's hurt. He'll need medical attention fast." Dad buckled up.

"You ain't afraid of Sheriff Marrock? The mayor?"

"I don't work for Sheriff Marrock, Officer. And I disappoint the mayor all the time." And they drove off. It was actually pretty smooth. For Dad. June would have given him credit for standing up for himself if she didn't suspect it was a show to impress Officer Azantian.

June wondered what a 'Garrison incident' was. And whatever the shiny object in the tree was.

She wouldn't find out until second period the next day about the murder.

Chapter Two: October 29th, morning

"Juniper Szmydt, seen late last night at the Miridical Animal Hospital, everyone wants to know," Connor Spellman ran to catch up with June between first and second period, holding a hairbrush to her face. "Did you finally birth that calf?"

June suppressed a laugh. "No, your Mom did, though. Mazel Tov, you've got a baby brother."

Stopping in his tracks, Connor let out a theatrical gasp that the other students buzzing about the halls ignored, lucky for June. "Never in my life have I been so insulted!"

"Then you haven't been listening to me, Connor."

They talked trash without looking at each other, relegated to the margins of the hallway. The students of Miridical Prep, with their matching maroon and black plaid jumpers, skirts, and jackets, almost fit in with the ancient building if it weren't for their phones, bags, and hair colors. Most kids said they liked it, that the old building made them feel like they were orphaned superheroes learning in a mansion. June and Connor thought the gray lockers against smooth stone made the whole school look cheap. For real - rich wooden rooms filled with flimsy plastic desks? And they wondered why no one sat with them at lunch (they didn't).

Checking himself in his phone's camera, Connor pushed his curly, faded-blue hair out of his eyes. "And what did the vet say about poochie?"

"We find out this afternoon. He should live."

"Alright," he stopped and held out a hand. "Show me the dumb pictures of the stupid cute puppy."

"There are none."

"Sad face," he pouted.

"He was bleeding all over the backseat, Connor." June started walking again; he always set their pace while he kept up. "It didn't seem like a good time to scroll filters."

"And the mayor ran over him? Was he drunk?"

"The mayor wasn't driving, I don't think."

"He wasn't?"

"I don't think so."

"Who was?"
June shrugged.

"But the mayor was there?"
June nodded.

"Why?"

"No idea."

"But you have a theory, right? June, you're nothing but a stack of theories in a trench coat back-talking adults." They laughed.

"No theories yet. But there was something I saw at the scene."

"What?"

"I don't know. Stuck in a tree halfway up the hill. It... changed. Like it looked different in my periphery and when I looked directly at it, it... changed."

"WTF does that mean?" When Connor tilted his thin, pale face and rolled his eyes, June thought he resembled the Joker. His now-greenish hair color didn't help.

She shrugged again.

"Okay, bitch, figure it out and let me know. I'm off to math." he punched at her hand in solidarity before moping off.

"Bye, bitch." June grew a little anxious whenever Connor left her alone with the student body. Like swimming in the open ocean without a life preserver... or a shark cage.

A crowd in the hall slowed traffic, but not like normal loitering before first period. This was students trying to keep their laughter down, eyes darting to avoid hers. This was trouble. A semicircle around June's locker. People tittering and laughing. Laughter and tittering that stopped as soon as she walked up, replaced by quieter snickering and stares as the crowd dispersed. The attention made her skin crawl. She wished she had something to cover her face.

What is it this time? The kids lingering around her locker parted, and June saw the trouble. Written on the black locker in silver magic-marker letters were the words, "Juniper Szmydt can't even..." and then the letters broke down into jumbled nonsense.

June's shoulders tightened at the thought of everyone laughing. She didn't give two thoughts about most of the jerks at this school; why'd they have to care enough to laugh at her? What was the graffiti even supposed to mean? She thumbed the ink, but it was permanent. June had been the subject of plenty of ridicule at school, usually more clever than this. But she knew better than to give the culprit any satisfaction. Even though her fists clenched on her backpack straps until her knuckles turned white, she wouldn't show any emotion. That's when what Connor referred to as her "resting bitch face" came in handy.

With the most disinterest she could muster, she opened her locker and grabbed books for third period. It took a lot for her to close and not to slam her locker shut. And then the graffiti stared her in the face again. Was the jumbled nonsense at the bottom scratched out? She'd have to look closer some other time...like maybe when she wasn't bright freaking red with the whole sophomore class staring at her.

"Juniper Szmydt can't even..."

Can't even what?

She turned and almost ran into Hailey Daley, aggressive matriarch of the rich girl clique. And, of course, she was flanked by the bougie, nondescript girls in matching hairstyles, matching expensive puffy coats, and matching punchable smirks.

But there, among the girls, was a face that always threw June off. Like 'off' the freaking planet before she slammed back into her Doc Martens.

Chelsea Goddamned Blackstone. Nobody liked her anyway. Well, everyone liked her, but that was besides the point; June hated her. With all her name-brand clothes that were always the latest style. With her wicked good grades. And ugh, that disgustingly perfect pale skin with a natural blush on those gorgeous high cheekbones. And all that silken blonde hair that came down past her shoulders and always shined in the light, cascading perfectly without a strand out of place, like some commercial for expensive conditioner. Plus, her flawless smile with made-for-tv teeth that got June blushing, her ears burning, and gave her a tingly feeling in her downstairs.

Yeah, Juniper Szmydt hated Chelsea Blackstone.

Little Miss Popular Blackstone kept her focus on a phone she wildly swiped and tapped, carelessly holding beef jerky in her free hand. The rest of the smirkers cocked a hip, falling behind Hailey, who smirked so hard, she looked like she was moving a lozenge around in her cheek.

Eyes to the white marble floor, June braced for more embarrassment. One of the rich girls definitely defaced her locker, and now they were here to gloat.

"What happened to your locker?" one of them asked innocently.

"It's really a waste of parents' tuition money, defacing property like that." Hailey shook her head with her arms folded. Such a bad actress.

"Good thing you don't pay tuition," another one pointed out.

June's fists clenched tight even though she couldn't hit a person even if she had to. And if she had to speak in front of so many students, her voice would crack, or she'd start crying...

"Good thing you spend most of your time perving in the girls' locker rooms."

Only a couple kids laughed in the crowded hall, but June's shoulders knotted up and her cheeks flare.

It took a lot of chutzpah to make fun of June's sexuality; all of Hailey's little clique claimed they were pansexual (if you believed their Instagram profiles that changed when they all got back from Burning Man last year, which June didn't).

"When we heard you were up on the hill last night, we were so worried." Eyes batted along with Hailey's faux whisper.

"So worried," one of the other girls parroted. They did that a lot.

"So. Worried."

Chelsea Blackstone didn't look worried; she didn't even look up from her phone or beef jerky. Like she was too good to even lower herself to laugh at June. Too good twice over to even look in June's direction.

"Why?" June asked, addressing the tile floor halfway between her and Chelsea. Pulling her eyes up to Chelsea's face would have been too embarrassing. June wasn't sure her own face wouldn't give her complicated feelings away.

Hailey made a disgusted face. "Didn't you read what Chels said on group chat?"

Well, that's just trolling. The only Miridical group chats June was on was the gay clique, not that they ever invited her to anything. In her periphery, June saw that Chelsea wasn't taking the bait. But down here on the lowest part of the food chain where June resided, a little critter like her would get picked at until she answered. So June mumbled, "I'm not in your group chat."

"Oh yeah," Hailey scoffed, "that's right."

Another girl squawked, "She didn't hear what you said about her hair, Chels."

"Oh, yeah, we decided that you'd look much better with straight hair. Chelsea volunteered to do it herself, didn't you, Chels?"

"Shut up, Hailey." Chelsea shot the de facto clique-leader a look.

June had had enough. Whatever was going on between Hailey and Chelsea was their business, but also maybe a window to get the focus off June, who pushed past Hailey and one of her stick figure minions.

"You better watch it, Juniper Shit," barked Hailey. "You think I'm afraid to fight? That nose of yours is big now, wait til

I break it." Eyes went wide and hands covered mouths as gasps and "oooooh" surrounded them. June stopped in her tracks and immediately regretted the attention it drew.

Everyone knew June's nose was nothing worth noticing, but everyone in town also knew the Szmydts were the one Jewish family. She'd run into snide antisemitic comments before, back in Massachusetts, but this was blatant. Probably something to say to get Hailey a reaction from the crowd. If it wasn't a Jewish joke, it'd be another gay joke. Or a fat joke. Embarrassment was embarrassment.

Tensed in anger or uncertainty, June stood wide-legged, bag straps wound tight around her hand like she would wield her backpack as a weapon. She was saved from needing one when the PA speakers crackled and hissed to life, "Attention students. Due to recent events, classes for the rest of the day have been canceled. Please-" The pandemonium of students darting in all directions, their squeals of glee drowned out the rest of the announcement. What was going on?

Using the instant chaos, June retreated from the standoff, catching Chelsea's eye for just a moment. The skinny blond girl looked heated, though whether at June or Hailey was anyone's guess. Seeing Chelsea like that only stoked the fire hotter in June, who tried to shake the image of those pissed-off baby blues when she ran nose-first into a Miridical Prep logo stitched onto a blazer.

"Watch where you're going, NipSlip," Connor smiled.

"What's going on? Why're classes canceled?"

"Um... because Mrs. Carlisle's husband was murdered?"

June stopped in her tracks, almost dropping the books in her arms. Her jaw hung loose for a second, then she shook her head and marched with purpose against the wild throng of students back to her locker.

"What are you doing?" Connor followed and asked.

"If there's been a murder," June said, not turning or slowing down...in fact, she gained speed, "Dad'll need me."

####

Predictably, all of Miridical Prep had relocated to the Del's Italian Ice in the old ShopWay parking lot; there was nothing else to do. So it wasn't surprising to see the old photomat kiosk swarming with students. Even Connor ducked off to get his fix. What was surprising was Sam approaching June in the overgrown corner of the unkempt parking lot.

"Your dad needs to get a clue. Anyway, I just feel bad for him." Sam cringed visibly as she spoke in monotone. Sam was cute, but to be honest, she never seemed like she felt bad for anyone. She seemed like she never felt anything for anyone. Under a tussle of short-cropped black hair, Sam's eyes were in a permanent squint - not a the-sun-is-too-bright squint, but the kind of squint made when someone said something wicked stupid, and squinting silently at them was the only course of action.

But despite Sam's eyeballing, it was the nicest anyone from the gay clique ever was to June. Even if it was bad news.

At the same time that the entirety of Miridical Prep formed a line at Del's Italian Ice, June's dad, who the school knew as Deputy Mayor Daryl Szmydt, answered his phone crossing the street while carrying a tray of hot coffees and a bag of hanging dry-cleaning. Then dropped his phone right onto the double yellow line and squatted to pick it up. His pants split.

"Don't worry; he didn't notice," Sam dead-panned.

Great. Dad never caught on to what a hundred-odd of June's classmates were laughing at. Thank God she wasn't there when it happened. At least the burning embarrassment was second hand.

"And then, before he dropped all four hot coffees on himself and the laundry, he screamed into the phone. Not like he was mad, but like...like when old people think it helps you hear better?"

Between the five kids in the misfit group, there were only two names among them, variants of (Ch, C)Kris and Sam(mi). They meant well, always cordial to June. Heck, one of the Sams was even on her soccer team. But when it came to sleepovers, school functions, or, dare she say it, dates, June was always left out. People were only willing to be friends with June in environments that wouldn't give them away as friends.

"Yeah, he does that."

Hands shoved into the pockets of her jean jacket with wool lining, Sam rhythmically kicked at a scrap of chain link fence gathering fallen leaves in the corner of the parking lot. "Anyway, he yelled something about he'd be in the way anyways and he'd work the phones from home."

"He went back home? Why? We were headed to the Mayor's office to catch him."

"I don't know." Sam shrugged, all elbows and bony shoulders. "But it sounded like your dad didn't understand, either."

"There's a lot he doesn't understand," June grumbled. "Thanks for telling me, Sam."

"No problemo," Sam said in monotone before turning and heading back to her misfit friends. "Hey, June?"

She was scouring the parking lot for Connor's pale, acned face. "Yeah, Sam?"

"Are you going to insert yourself into police business like you did with the fire and the robbery and the cheating scandal and the insurance scam?"

June was about ninety percent certain Sam was on the autism spectrum, which led to honest questions like this. June didn't mind; she loved honesty. TBH, she wouldn't mind hanging out with Sam more often. But maybe because June was the girl who inserted herself into police business, she wasn't a good friendship prospect.

June shrugged. "Yeah, I guess I am."

"Okay. Be careful, though, anyways."

The Sams and the Chrises, aka the gay clique, had always been so distant or wary of June. Seeing Sam like this, not quite smiling, but also almost awkwardly flinching, June found herself staring a little. Sam was pretty, sharply cut hair showing off her strong chin and eyes that might just be secretly kind. And for a second, June forgot how much she hated this hellhole of a town.

But then she remembered and said, "I promise nothing, Sam. If you hear anything that could help my investigation out, let me know." And then marched off back toward her house.

Catching up to her while scooping frozen lemonade from his cup, Connor spoke like he was continuing a previous conversation, "So does Mrs. Carlisle even have it in her? And for what, money? Jealousy? He wasn't smashing around town. And how much money could they have? Didn't Mr. Carlisle have to sell the funeral home because they were broke?"

June posited, "How could she do it, anyway? Mrs. Carlisle is so sweet."

"I heard he got thrown into a wood chipper."

June had to laugh at the Miridical rumor mill. "Who in this town has a wood chipper?"

"Perhaps she rented a wood chipper."

"Where would someone rent a wood chipper, Connor?"

"I don't know, I'm not the murderer." He gasped. "Unless I am the murderer. What if I'm under hypnotic influence? Or I'm a somnambulist and I slept-walked to the base of Fortune Hill to commit my grisly deeds. Do you think they're onto me? Would your dad give me a heads-up if I were a suspect?"

June had texted her dad several times with no answer. Either he was too busy with work to respond, or he was working from home and his phone was charging in another room. Considering the mayor and everyone who worked for Miridical treated Dad like shit and wouldn't trust him with a cup of coffee, June figured they were keeping him at home, far away from the murder investigation. Without a ride from Dad in what Connor called the "Mini Pooper," the fastest way home was to cut through the woods.

"Ew. I hate the woods," Connor whined.

"Well I hate dick, but I put up with you."

"Touche."

"You're pronouncing it wrong." She grinned as they made their way onto the town square, passing the enormous old library with a clock tower that looked like it would house old European monks inside, not books.

"Oh, Nipslip, it's too bad you're Jewish and Jesus is in charge of giving all the little girls their senses of humor..."

June liked having Connor around because she could pretty much talk out loud and he'd just listen and chime in with snark. And she needed snark to lighten the mood while heading through Dabbit's Forest. Past the town square, the roads either opened up to Miridical residences or dove into the lush forests pouring off of Fortune Hill. The bright colors of early autumn faded from expressive reds to drabber browns, and jagged gray branches of maples and oaks jutted out from the naked trees, like knobby fingers pointing visitors away or undead arms clawing with desperation. Scary AF.

June shook off a shiver. "So are you ditching me here or are we cutting through the woods?"

"Let's cut through the woods until I feel like ditching you."

June was no good in the woods, taking her time stepping over logs, daintily pulling back branches and thorns, and generally slowing down Connor, who'd been raised next to these woods. He could just trudge along, ducking underbrush, stepping on logs, powering through the overgrown scrub, and, of course, making fun of how slow June was.

"I don't get what the big deal is," Connor said, somehow not out of breath, "What does a murder have to do with the deputy mayor? It's not like he's expected to solve the crime. Unless. Unless you think it was the mayor and if your dad can prove it, then he'll take over as mayor!"

"That's not how it works Connor. If anything, the mayor appointed my dad, so if he committed any crime, Dad would lose his job, too. But the mayor is a boring asshole; he didn't murder anybody."

"So why's it matter to Papa Bear?"

"Connor, do you remember the last murder in Miridical?"

"No…"

"Yeah, neither do I. I've never heard of one. The mayor hasn't had to deal with one before, so he's going to be freaking out.

And that means he'll take it out on Dad."

"Unless your dad finds the killer?"

"It wouldn't hurt if he did. So who's a suspect? Who was around Fortune Hill at the time?"

"Mr. Carlisle."

"Obvi." June ducked under an enormous English Oak branch. "Also, whoever drove that overturned car, Evens Bonhomme, and who else?"

"Creepy sexy Sheriff Marrock."

"Sheriff Marrock's sexy?"

"Is he not?"

She shrugged.

"And of course," Connor arched an eyebrow on his sharp, angular face, "the Szmydts!"

"Excuse me?"

"The Szmydts were in the area at the time," he chirped curtly. June rolled her eyes.

"They only have each other for an alibi..."

"Connor, this is serious." She was getting annoyed, slowing down to wait on him to make his way through thicket and take her own investigation seriously.

"Father-Daughter serial killers, moving from town to town..."

She lowered her voice, gloved hands in fists. "We need to figure out who had a reason to kill Mr. Carlisle. A motive."

"... Leaving a trail of dead bodies in their wake."

"Fucking stop, Connor." She punched him in the arm.

"OMG." Connor stopped, hands out in anticipation of danger. June froze. "What is it?"

"I'm going to be on a true-crime podcast one day. 'She was always nice to me, but...you know...a little off.'"

"Fuck off, Connor." She continued crunching steps ahead of him into the thick of the woods. "You think Marrock and all his cousins are going to crack the case? We get to solve a murder."

"Who wants to solve a murder, you weirdo?"

"I do. Of course, I do. Everyone treats my dad and me like we're idiots when we're smarter than everyone."

"You treat your dad like an idiot."

"That's different. I'm his daughter; that's my job."

"Well, yeah. But if it gets too hairy, I'm ghosting."

"Of course you are," June said. Ghosting when things got hairy was practically Connor's superpower. June's was either solving crime or getting really really embarrassed.

Connor sighed in forfeit and asked earnestly, "So how do we do this?"

"Dad has access to things. And we can get the gossip he can't. We have to... I don't know... figure it out. Carlisle. Vernon Carlisle. Old white guy. In his, what, seventies? Drove a hearse for a long time but now drives that ugly silver thing. Or he used to drive it. Lived over on Washington. Married for a thousand years to Emma Carlisle. Retired funeral home director. What does he do now?"

"What everyone else does in Miridical."

"Commutes to Providence," they said in unison. June laughed. Connor gasped.

"Shh!"

His hand clamped over June's mouth and the two of them hit the leafy forest floor, crouched behind a rotting log. Ahead, in a small clearing, a flash of white stood out against the natural autumnal scene. A puffy coat on a slender figure seated on a tree stump. June's eyes widened and she gasped as she realized the identity of the figure, seated cross-legged in an expensive-looking down jacket, reading a book.

Chelsea Goddamned Blackstone.

June was so low to the ground she smelled the rot, practically felt the heat coming off the decomposing leaves. What was Blackstone doing in the middle of Dabbitt's Forest? June had never seen the popular blond girl outside of her gaggle of bourgeoisie. Alone, Little Miss Popular seemed... small. A very different look for one of the girls who owned the hallways of Miridical Prep.

In her expensive puffy coat, the girl sat perched on the stump, an over-sized hardback book taking up most of her lap. Then she removed a plastic baggie from a pocket, the bag full of something reddish-brown. Without taking her eyes off the opened book, she reached into the baggie and withdrew something smaller than a business card, tan with a big splotch of that rusty muddy color.

June squinted to see.

It wasn't a business card, but... GROSS. A used Band-Aid. From a baggie full of used Band-Aids.

In the middle of the woods, Chelsea Blackstone read something out of a book to a gross old Band-Aid.

Chapter Three: October 29th, still morning

"What is she doing?" June whispered in shock, staring along as Chelsea Blackstone sang a song from her book to a gross used Band-Aid. If June had eaten a frozen lemonade, she would have chucked it up. "Is she worshiping it?"

That's when June realized she was alone. That was so like Connor. Whenever June needed him, he'd vanish. So she lay by herself on Dabbitt's Forest's leafy floor behind a log watching the hot girl from her Bio class engaged in some ritual. More than fascinated, June wished she was just at home, hashing out murder details with Dad. To June, this was much grosser. And even though June found the whole thing totally disgusting, she couldn't look away. Whatever Chelsea was doing with that old bandage, it made the hairs all over June's skin stand on end. And with a hairy Jewish girl, that was a lot of goose pimples.

A rustling of crushing leaves to June's right made her jump. It was close, not twenty feet away, but June couldn't see what made the noise. Then she smelled it. A wild animal stench, unclean fur and ammoniated urine.

The smell hadn't hit Chelsea, or she was too focused on the Band-Aid to notice.

Holding her breath, June squinted towards where the sound originated. Nothing but oaks, elms, and pines striping the orange and yellow-leaved forest floor. But then there it was. June blinked hard to make sure she wasn't seeing things: a big cat. Like a mountain lion, or a puma, or whatever an ocelot was - any wild cat that June couldn't identify. Still as the trees surrounding it. Tan with white tufts of fur sprouting from its chest, ears, and tail. Black smudges on its face. But somehow, near-invisible against the backdrop of fall colors. Feline and taut and deadly.

A sickly freezing sensation overtook June's joints, pinning her wrists, clenching her knees, restraining her. Her whole body was so tense behind that log, wound so tight, she thought she'd be able to spring ten feet up a tree to safety. Silently, she screamed at herself, railed against her own instincts to stay still, crouched behind the log, not a stone's throw away from a predator as big as she was. Sweat poured down her face, and she was burning up within her coat.

Clumsily tipping this way and that with each step, the cat moved towards Chelsea. The popular girl was still in deep thought, dangling the first aid product above the tome of a book she sang off-key. Another of the big cat's steps and June's body rebelled, vision cloudy from crying, sweating, even her nose began to run. Her heartbeat pounding within her ears, June could no longer hear the crush of the leaves under the heavy claw-laden paws.

One step after another, the cat closed in on its prey, Chelsea still oblivious. Half of June wanted to flee, the other half wanted to stay, and then a statistically negligible percentage wanted to help Chelsea Blackstone. But Chelsea was BFFs with the girls who'd made June's life a living Hell. Chelsea had walked around with her nose up, knowing she was the hottest girl in school, and had probably changed her profile to pansexual just to drive the queers wild, June included. Walking by Chelsea, being laughed at by her, merely existing at the same school as Chelsea Blackstone was torturous. Chelsea was a big reason why June hated high school, why she hated this town, why June couldn't wait to get away. But did that mean Chelsea deserved to die?

The cat took another step, the fur on its shoulders puffed out, its whiskers pivoting forward aiming like cross-hairs. It crouched down, legs compressing like a coiled spring, ready to explode forward and preparing to pounce.

"Over here, jerk!" June couldn't believe the words coming from her own mouth.

Two heads whipped around to her - Chelsea's and the cat's.

Eyes wide and mouth agape, Chelsea stood, dropping the Band-Aid and book to the forest floor.

The cat leapt, breaking into a gallop right for June.

She screamed and ran away, pumping her arms, sprinting, bounding and bouncing, through brush and over logs. Branches and twigs whipping her face as June cut a sharp turn to avoid a ravine, sliding along the wet leaves. She peeked behind her, the cat pursuing, closing in, running in an awkward gallop. There was no feline grace, no nature-video precision of movement. This animal hopped and leapt and jerked after June. And as she glanced back, breath searing, pulse pounding, her wide eyes saw the animal as something different, something beastly and bigger. But when she looked back at it, all she saw was the big cat gaining on her. She cut through thin bushes the cat easily hurdled. Ducking, she crawled through a canopy of saplings and dead tree trunks, only to come out the other side to see that the cat had circumnavigated the wood, even closer, not five feet away.

All June could do was run. Out of breath, muscles burning, tears streaming down her face. She'd never been fast, but as a goalie she was quick. Turning constantly, she curved around rocks and big trees. Then sliding on the leaves and loam to a stop, she came upon a split in a deep ravine. Nowhere to turn without turning back toward the cat.

Behind her, a hiss and a roar. The cat, pacing ten feet from its cornered prey, seemed even bigger. Bigger than June. Bigger than Dad. Muscle and fur and finger-length white teeth. Another roar elicited a whimper from June.

She fell to her knees and prayed. Not that she was even religious, but she prayed. She recited the beginning of the Channukah prayer that trailed off to the part she stopped remembering. Prayed to God and the Universe and Science. Even to Jesus. Another step closer and another roar, the force, the power of it, knocking June back onto her ass. Her hand barely caught a root at the ravine's edge.

This was it. This was how June was going to die. As fucking cat food. And never even got to make out with a hot girl. In an instant, the cat crouched and leapt talon-like claws first, enormous maw gaping. Flinching, June curled up and closed her eyes.

Then came a crash. A cacophony so loud, it shook the forest floor.

Instead of claws, June was hit with a rush of wind and leaves.

As June sat, eyes scrunched shut, the quiet forest sounds of birds and insects and rustling grew to fill the air.

Once she was positive she hadn't died, June opened her eyes. The cat lay a couple feet away, the thick trunk of a pine tree laying across its bloody body. The beast's ferocious and surprised face frozen in still death.

June struggled to her feet, taking a step back, almost stepping into the ravine behind her. Her body numb, her fingers tingly, her breath coming back to her in gulps, she looked to the source of the fallen tree. Eyes and mouth also wide, Chelsea stood, looking as if pleading to June. They looked in mirror of each other, tear-streaked, out of breath, clothing and hair askew.

Instinct took control of June's body and she ran to the shiksa girl, their weight crashing into one other in desperate forfeit, the hug of victims sharing survival. Choking with sobs, June buried her face in Chelsea's white down jacket, curling up into her blond hair. Their burning-hot cheeks touched.

At the same time, they both said, "You saved me."

Then before June could even laugh in relief or the ridiculousness of the situation, Chelsea's mouth was on hers. Shock at first, June bristled and almost pushed her away. Instead, she surrendered, kissing back. Pushing her soft lips onto Chelsea's, hands still holding each other tight, was such a rush. It wasn't cinematic, it wasn't perfect. June tilted her head awkwardly, and she didn't know when to counter Chelsea's face, so their teeth bumped slightly. June felt a small giggle escape, moving back from her lips into Chelsea's mouth. Chelsea kissed harder back into the giggle, eliciting a tiny moan from June.

The rush might have lasted forever if June wasn't sure the kiss had ended, the absence of warm, firm lips a shock of cold loneliness to her face. They stood, arms still around one another, foreheads touching, sniffing back tears that wouldn't stop. They laughed together. They kissed again. They didn't let go.

"Why was it after you?" Chelsea asked, addressing June for the first time without some cruel nickname or dig.

"After me? It was after you," June managed in a laugh, in some shocked ecstasy in the arms of the girl she had wanted for longer than she could remember.

"June, I don't know why, but that... thing was following the scent of your blood."

In automatic response, June smiled and almost laughed until it sunk in and June's face went suddenly confused. The idea didn't make sense until it did, and her stomach turned.

"That Band-Aid?" June asked, hoping she was wrong.

Shaking her head like it was the most obvious thing in the world, Chelsea answered, "Well, yeah."

It was all too much. She'd almost died, then was saved by... a girl who'd stolen her used Band-Aids? Who must have rummaged in the garbage to find them? For what, another way to embarrass her? Was the kiss just another humiliation, the rich beautiful girl putting the unpopular fat Jew in her place? It turned June's stomach.

With seething anger, she pushed Chelsea away, fell to her knees and retched. Nothing came up, only a burning dry heave. She stumbled to her feet in a clumsy run, Chelsea's hand covering her own mouth as if she could stop this disgusting truth from coming out. June had to get away. From the woods, from Chelsea. From the idea of whatever Chelsea was doing in the woods.

Past the body of the cat under the fallen pine, back through the woods, she ran toward the safety of home, where there was Dad and the investigation and things she had a handle on, things she understood, things she could control.

Behind her, Chelsea called out, "June!"

But June wouldn't stop, couldn't stop as Chelsea filled the autumn air of Dabbitt's Forest behind her, echoing. "Ju-ni-per!!!"

Chapter Four: October 29th, how is it still morning?

That numb buzzing from running too hard vibrated through June's lungs. Walking when her thighs and calves were simultaneously stiff and jiggly gave her a zombie quality, and she shambled the rest of the way home and into their little house with the vertical brown siding. She'd barely pushed all the way through the front door before Dad came stomping in from the kitchen with his angry parent voice. "Juniper Laurel Szmydt! Why didn't you answer your phone? I've been driving all over town..."

But then he saw her and his brow relaxed and his tense posture melted. June must have looked worse than she'd figured to make Dad go all my-poor-baby-girl. Before she knew it, she was pressed into his soft chest, his big hairy paws stroking her hair, and suddenly June wasn't motivated enough to be embarrassed by Dad, curling into his big bear hug.

"Junebug," he said softly into her mess of springy hair, "what happened?"

Hoarse and livid, she spoke in low tones, "There was an animal in the woods. I ran. Daddy, I don't want to talk about it." She pushed away from him, pissed that she'd let her guard down enough to call him that. Mad that he was treating her like some little girl from years ago when they had their perfect little life. Furious at Chelsea for literally everything else.

"Why are you home? Why aren't you at the police station or helping the mayor?"

"Bug, I am helping the mayor. He needed calls made, and his office is a zoo right now."

"Dad, they're keeping you out of the way."

"Bug, I want to be out of the way. What do I know about a murder investigation?"

"What does anyone in Miridical know about a murder investigation?" She pulled out a rubber band and set to taming her thick brown mane into a new tight ponytail. June composed herself; the edge to her words was back, and despite her coloring, her demeanor changed back to giving him crap and taking control. "Is the state sending anyone to help?"

"Not if it's an isolated crime just in Miridical."

"So?" She pulled her pony tight and twisted it into a bun, usually reserved for soccer or heavy yard work. "Did you lie?"

"Lie? No."

"Well, where's the mayor now?" she asked, walking past him into the kitchen.

"At the office, I guess." He followed her.

"And who's running the crime scene?"

"I don't know. The sheriff?"

"We need to make sure we know who's where so we won't get chased off."

"No, Bug. We can't do this. Burglaries and car accidents are one thing, but there's a murderer out there on the streets. I won't let you butt in on this one."

They stood in silence for a moment, their similar brown eyes locked, hers a shade deeper and more clever, his brighter and wilder, their breathing synced. Jaws flexed. Stubborn. "You know you can't stop me from doing this. It just means I'll do it without you."

"This is dangerous."

What Dad said as a warning felt like fun to June. "Then come with me. Let's go get a clue. Or at least learn what the pigs know."

"And how are you going to do that when you're calling them pigs?"

She thought about it, then smiled coyly. "That's where you come in. Buddy up to them? We crack this, you get the credit? Share it with the force?"

"I don't know if you've realized this, but you've alienated the entire sheriff's office, June."

"That's why we need someone from the state to work with."

"I told you, I called and the RIBI aren't sending anyone. Besides, agents don't work with high schoolers."

Instead of getting angry, June took a big breath and looked her dad deep in his dark eyes. "I don't know why you're pretending like something can keep me out of this."

Even though she thought she was stating the obvious, it seemed to catch Dad a little off guard. "Watch it, Bug," he warned.

"Don't call me that," she said matter-of-factly. Then, with a death stare, she sent him a psychic message only a daughter can send a parent: I'm not backing down.

Dad groaned, rolled his eyes, and gave up. "Fine. Go shower and change; I'll make sandwiches for the ride."

"I'm ready to go now. The longer we wait, the harder the

murder gets to solve." She popped his coffee mug into their ancient microwave, started it, and pulled milk and Autocrat coffee syrup from the faux-woodgrain fridge. "We need to find out who's where, then head to where nobody's going to tell you to piss off."

The microwave dinged, and she handed Dad the hot mug. "Chug," she commanded as she loaded up two travel mugs with coffee milk. She made his extra sweet."You call the mayor and I'll call the lieutenant governor." She looked at him expectantly. "Put your coat on!"

He automatically obliged, heading for the hall closet. "Where are we going?"

She grabbed his phone off the counter and read an incoming text. "First stop, the diner. I've got your phone."

June shed her shredded coat and tossed it in the hamper in the hall before ducking into the closet. Again, Dad followed. From the hanging coats, she asked, "What does the mayor mean when he says, 'Forget about the blind man?'"

"June, my texts are my personal business." He tried to use the dad voice, but June was immune. Now in a hooded black peacoat and matching knit maroon hat, gloves, and scarf, she popped back out of the closet to hand him his phone. "This would be so cute without all this-" Dad tapped one of the plastic skull buttons on her coat.

June's glare stopped Dad's sentence. Guiltily, he steered the conversation back, following June out the front door of the little brown vertical-siding house. "I asked the mayor about something I overheard at Town Hall this morning, people whispering, obviously didn't want to be overheard, something about the murder and a blind guy. But I must have heard it wrong. Why the diner?"

"Whoever found the crime scene will be downing dough-nuts and telling tales." She held up a hand to catch as he grabbed his car keys. "I'm driving."

Winding up to throw the keys, he froze mid-motion, then smirked at his 15-year-old daughter's attempt.

She grumbled, "Fine, but this is how I fail my driving exam."

He sighed, his broad shoulders slouching. "Now, what was this wild animal that attacked you?"

"Don't want to talk about it. What exactly did you hear about a blind man at the Town Hall?"

"Don't want to talk about it."

Sitting shotgun in the township's Mini Cooper, June did her best Rhode Island accent (like Boston, but lower and slower) on the phone with the Lieutenant Governor's office. She couldn't tell if Ralph was buying it or not. "What I'm saying, Ralph... can I call you Ralph? Ralph, what I'm saying is that I don't know if this shooting is connected to the violence last weekend in Providence, but all these reporters showing up from the Providence Journal sure think so."

The lie elicited a "Hey!" from Dad, but June put out a hand to shush him, pressing poor Ralph instead. "My only problem is, Ralph, we employ nothing but small-potato cops here, thirsty for attention, and if a journalist shows any interest, they're gonna spin a yarn long enough to catch fish with!"

"Is that even a saying?" Dad asked in a whisper as he drove.

"Ralph, you do what you gotta do. I don't want you to put your job at risk, but realize that I'm not going to be able to keep a lid on this much longer. The faster we can get the support we need to solve this murder, the better it will be for both our offices. My name? Uh...you got a pen? Officer Azantian. Badge number? Three point one four one five nine two six."

She hung up quickly, uncertain what law she must have just broken. "They're not going to help. Is the mayor answering?"

"No dice."

"Who was driving the overturned car last night?"

"We're not telling anyone, but... Reverend LaChance. You can't tell–"

"LaChance the lush?"

"Yeah."

"Then why didn't he get a DUI? Why didn't he spend the night in the drunk tank? Why was the mayor so concerned about his car accident?"

"You got me, Bug."

"Any chance the blind man the folks at town hall were talking about was our dear reverend being 'blind stinking drunk'?"

"I don't think it's common knowledge that LaChance was driving," Dad said, pulling into the diner, which was abnormally busy for an early lunch. "I don't think anyone was talking about the car accident after Carlisle was found, though."

June had been right; the cops who'd found the body were now local celebrities holding court in the corner booth of the Miridical Diner. The cute little restaurant was 50s Americana chic, like a time capsule right from black-and-white tv, all big curved angles, boomerangs and starbursts, primary colors, and chrome accents everywhere.

The front door jingled open, letting in the Szmydts and out a uniform chuckle like a sitcom laugh track. At the far end of the restaurant, past the barstools and the glass case of cakes, twenty or so Miridicaliens (which wasn't what they were officially known as, but June called them that) faced the three smug officers, all uptight and square-jawed like Marrock. One of them, hair especially clipped brown, jaw especially pointy, sat on the table with his boots up on the seat of the booth, his hands ahead of him, painting the picture for his audience. "But I say to him, 'You've been staring at fires all night, old guy, you aren't seeing right. That ain't no deer carcass, that guy's a guy, guy!'"

This got some laughter plus some oohs and ahs.

"Excuse me, cheese sticks and two cabinets to go?" Dad said to a skinny pale waitress, most likely one of Connor's many cousins. Dad paid, then with a string of "Excuse mes," he made his way toward the corner booth, past the people sitting on the mushroom barstools turned with their legs in the way, snaking around folks who pulled chairs up to hear the officers, but the citizenry was too thick to navigate.

Back at the edge of the seated crowd, June spotted one of the Chrises. Kris, she was pretty sure. Kris was all apple cheeks, glasses, and grey-brown hair. Next to her in the booth was a carbon-copy Mom. Crouching by their bench seats, June whispered, "How long have they been talking?"

"Since before we got here."

"How long was that?"

Kris's mom, who was married to one of the mayor's nephews, leaned over her daughter and whispered threateningly, "Hello, Juniper. Nice to see you."

"Nice to see you, too, Mrs. M. Do you guys know where the mayor and sheriff are? Dad's looking for them and they aren't answering their phones."

"Sh!" Kris's mom shushed at the girls.

The officers in the corner of the diner kept on. "So I said,

'Get out of the way, you pansies, I'll move the damned thing,' and I crawled under the thicket and turned the body over to see Old Carlisle's mug, pale and slack-jawed, staring up at nothing. I felt the breath of the angel of death."

June rolled her eyes so hard she was careful not to knock a glass off Kris's table. She tried again. "Has anyone seen Bumpy? Was he the firefighter who was there?"

"Junebug Szmydt, the Mayor and the Sheriff are at Town Hall. Go bug them."

June couldn't stand that nickname from her dad, but another adult using it for the evil purposes of a pun was beyond aggravating. It was a pretty predictable attitude that the adults of Miridical had for teens, but June always felt it was worse somehow when directed at her. Nodding without speaking, she left Kris and found her dad halfway across the diner. With inevitable embarrassment, June waved and whisper-yelled to get his attention. Unfortunately, the heroes of the day noticed. "Hey, Shitty! We found a murder for you to solve!"

This elicited a laugh from the other officers, which cued their audience to join in. Burning in humiliation, June weighed standing up for her dad against public speaking and stayed quiet. But not Dad; he chuckled right along with everyone, laughing at his own expense, and June couldn't help but picture him as a dopey overweight clown, shrugging and tripping over his feet as he skulked out of the spotlight.

She held the door open for him. "Off to the crime scene, Pagliacci."

It was early afternoon as they pulled up alongside the police cruisers flanked with yellow tape, and luckily, most of the cops were off getting lunch or sauced or both. The C-team was left in charge until the mayor or sheriff could return from Town Hall.

"Shitty!" some rookie cop called out as they approached, elated to see someone lower than him in the pecking order. There were two officers. The rookie cop getting into a squad car was obviously related to Sheriff Marrock, leaving Officer Azantian, the woman cop from the wreck late last night, directing nonexistent traffic around the yellow-taped area.

"Officer! The... uh... mayor sent me," Dad spoke carefully, remembering exactly what June had planned for him to say. "Wanted you to walk me through what we know so far to make sure the township is all on the same page." He folded his arms in forced nonchalance, and hopefully, only June noticed his tensed jaw, bulging vein on his temple, and profuse sweating. Mr. Szmydt was never good at telling lies or keeping secrets. He had to shop for Chanukkah gifts the day of, otherwise he'd reveal to June what they were beforehand.

"Okay. We got the victim, Vernon Carlisle, right here, hit with some crazy amount of... force." As the officer spoke, the rookie cop in the cruiser perked up to listen in. June could barely follow the officer's words. Her accent was so thick; she'd realized long ago that Miridical had its own squirrelly accent different from the rest of Rhode Island. Even after living here for over a year, she often found the locals hard to understand.

The officer pointed out the white taped silhouette in the brush uphill from the roadside. The body. Little yellow lettered notes stood around the body and the burn marks in the ditch and uphill. June sucked at her tooth, picturing something strong enough to knock a person off the road up five feet into the brush.

"Fire department from the car accident noticed the burn marks. They think something from the wreck slid down the hill." The officer pointed out several patches of blackened dirt on the hillside. "No murder weapon was found. We think from the blast marks in the hill here and here, and on this tree, it was some kind of…. gun."

But what kind of gun leaves burn marks? The Szmydts never owned firearms, and the little June knew about gunshots from tv and movies told her they didn't leave burn marks all over the place.

"It's going to be a pretty big bust for whoever solves this, huh?" Dad asked with schoolboy nervousness. June rolled her eyes at Dad's absence of game. Like a black hole of game.

Pulling away, the rookie cop in the cruiser barked, "Hey, get away from there, little girl! Shitty, is that your daughter?!"

June seethed. "Don't call him that."

"Szmydt, you gonna let her talk to me like that?"

"Now, Officer," Dad began to defuse the situation.

At the first word of her spineless dad's excuses and apologies, June rolled her eyes and wandered off. They were directly downhill of the car accident. Hopefully, Dad would get the exact time on both events; he'd talk about anything to avoid standing up for himself.

Staring up the steep hill that terraced once at the scene of the car accident and again at Prayer Point, she wondered if she acted just as gutless when Hailey and Chelsea and the rich girls bullied her.

Chelsea. As soon as June closed her eyes, she was back in Dabbitt's Forest, next to the squished cat carcass, holding Chelsea, kissing Chelsea, getting kissed by Chelsea. Her lips, her hair, the clean, honeysuckle smell of her skin. Then, finding out June's high school crush-slash-bully stalked her and worshiped her old bloody bandages. June had to put her attention somewhere other than confusing Chelsea feelings - butterflies in a gut full of disgust - and zoned back to reality, staring up at a cluster of yellow leaves just up the hill. And in the intersection of those branches of leaves, a shining, silvery object.

Wait, that shimmering silvery object! It was the cylinder she'd seen the night before, stuck about ten feet up in a tree. After confirming her dad was still self-deprecating with the officers, June ducked under the plastic yellow tape, shimmied up the big-branched Boston Oak, retrieved the cold metal object, and hopped back down. She thumbed dried orange clay off it to reveal a glinting metal cylinder, a little thinner than a lipstick case, as long as her middle finger, coming to a point at one end. A bullet. A big one. Like for big World War II machine guns.

Instinctively, she pocketed it.

Smoothing a stray hair behind her ear ever-so-casually, June wandered back down the road, called out to the officer, interrupting her dad. "What time did your shift start, Officer Azantian?"

The cop, her stern, beautiful face with big brown eyes, high cheek-bones, and full lips, was quite official in her baggy khaki uniform, but she had a body underneath that had Dad tongue-tied and gawking. And under different circumstances, maybe would have left June the same way, too.

"I've been up too long to get questioned by a kid."

"You were working the car accident last night, too. And all the other officers that were with you are now off at the diner, while you're still working."

"Don't you mean 'pigs'?" She leaned back, resting her hands on her bulky belt, legs spread wide. It was the kind of stance that looked more natural on a big fat guy. "That was the word you were using last night, wasn't it?"

"Why does the boy's club get the afternoon off while you're still on the clock?"

Dad wasn't sure what was going on, but he clearly didn't like it, standing between them with his big arms out to keep the peace. "Hold up now, ladies. June, I don't think I like your tone."

"I was only about to ask if she could account for the where-abouts of herself and her cohorts at the time of the murder."

"June!" Dad chided.

"I was just about to ask you and your father the same thing, Ms. Szmydt," the officer said.

"What kind of gun was it?" June pressed, changing the line of questioning, keeping the cop off her guard.

"Excuse me?" Officer Azantian took a step toward June, head cocked - either confused or pissed.

Unsure about an impending ass-whipping scenario, June instinctively took a step back. But she kept talking. "The murder weapon? It was something heavy-duty, wasn't it?"

But the officer had had enough. She swiveled on her heels and lay into Dad, obviously relishing her place above the Mayor's errand boy. "Look, sir, if you have any more questions, you can take it up with your boss or Sheriff Marrock. In the meantime, please take your daughter and her asinine interrogation away from my crime scene!"

June jumped at the opportunity, yelling, "Okay, come on Dad!" and hopped into the front seat of the Mini Cooper.

June could see Dad was taken aback by her obedience, but he played nice and bid the officer goodbye while smiling and gawking a little too long before getting into the car. "What's all that about, Junebug? We didn't learn anything from Officer Ani," he said, fitting snugly in the driver's seat.

"'Officer Ani?' Gimme a break. You've got a bit of drool..." She wiped the side of her mouth and pointed at him. As he did the same, she laughed and Dad caught on, laughing with her. She assured him, "I only wanted to make sure she and the other cops had nothing to do with the murder."

"Well, she didn't have anything to do with it."

"Okay!" June put her hands up. Dad was being awful sensitive about this Officer Ani, and June didn't want to think about why. "We should go talk to Mrs. Carlisle."

"Absolutely not."

"Okay," she said. "I think you should go talk to Mrs. Carlisle."

"Me? Why?"

"Because...you know...you can relate." June thought saying it slowly would lessen any effect bringing up Mom's death would have. They hadn't exactly opened up about it in the past two years.

"Your mother wasn't murdered, June," He said sternly. Good. At least he wasn't freaking out.

"I know!" June yelled in that aggressively apologetic way only teens can achieve.

"And not last night." He was getting angry.

"Okay!"

"I can't imagine what the poor woman must be going through."

After detecting what may have been his voice cracking, June

changed tacts. "Okay! Forget I said anything. We'll work with what we have, then."

But Dad was already fired up. "What do we have, June?"

"I snagged a clue." June pulled the bullet from her pocket and opened her palm to reveal it to her dad.

Instead of the reaction June expected, he furrowed his brow and tilted his head, looking at the bullet, confused. "What is it?"

"It's a bullet, Dad. A big one. And it hasn't been fired. Are you blind?"

Her words roused Dad from his tired level of energy. His eyes grew suddenly clear, and he shot an angry look accusingly at his daughter. "What did you just say?"

June was taken aback. "I said, it's an unfired bullet, Dad, jeez. And it's not from any handgun or rifle, I don't think."

"After that, what did you say?"

Ugh. She was getting exasperated, huffing and rolling her eyes. "Dad. We need to find out what kind of gun was used to kill Mr. Carlisle."

"You asked me if I was blind."

"Yeah, so what?"

"Why would you ask that?"

June had had enough. She pocketed the bullet and sat back in her seat, buckling up. "Can we just go?"

Face still angry, he softened slightly, eyes confused. Starting the car and putting into gear, he paused. "I'm not blind, June."

"Okay." June couldn't help but think of the blind man Town Hall rumor Dad mentioned earlier.

He drove off, muttering under his breath, "I'm not a blind man."

Chapter Five: October 29th afternoon

The little roller-skate-of-a-car zipped along the main drag toward town, half-filled retail plazas and Halloween-orange oak leaves whizzing by. Despite the crispy chill in the air, Dad was sweating. He sighed theatrically, waiting for June to say something. "This is already going a bit far, don't you think?"

"What?" June played innocent, eyelash bat, and all that.

"We interfered with a crime scene, for Cripe's sakes! And your little phone call? Impersonating a police officer and an elected official? Aren't these, like, felonies?"

"You're a government official, Dad. Own it. Act like one."

"I'm a mayor's assistant."

"Deputy Mayor," June corrected.

"To be honest, I'm not positive what that title means beyond assistant."

"And that gives everyone an excuse to walk all over you?"

"Why do you care so much about what people say about me? It doesn't bother me."

"It should."

"Do I embarrass you?"

"This whole town embarrasses me," she roared, staring him down. But he couldn't hold a serious face, breaking and grinning. He always broke first, but they both used to laugh when they play-argued; June hardened since then. But this time, despite herself, June smiled, which got Dad laughing even more. So she rolled her eyes and looked away.

"Fuck," she said.

"Language!"

"They gave you a ticket? How long was that there?"

A yellow paper fluttered under the windshield wiper.

When Dad's eyes returned to the road, they shot wide open, and he slammed on the brakes. The Mini Cooper screeched to a halt. June jolted against her seatbelt, knocking the air from her lungs. Her head pinballed back against the headrest.

"You okay, Bug?"

June was fine. Out of breath, suddenly cold yet sweaty, dry-mouthed, but fine.

Slowly crossing the street from the big stone church, Reverend LaChance helped old Mrs. Gunderson. Neither could see more than a foot ahead.

Dad put on a fake smile and waved while June called them assholes. Miley Cyrus started singing - Dad's ringtone. He searched for the phone, not in the console, not on his floorboard, and he grunted and squirmed to look around his tight space. A car behind them honked, and Dad hit his head on the rearview mirror.

"Damnit!"

"Got it." June held up the phone to show him. "Mayor Orbison calling."

"Give it to me," Dad reached. June pulled the phone back away from his thick, hairy hands. The car honked again.

Dad turned back toward the car and cursed warningly, "Damnit!"

"Dad. Drive." She commanded before putting a finger to her lips in a quieting gesture, then daintily lifted that finger oh so slowly toward the phone, while Dad was trying to watch where he's driving at the same time as he was staring her down. She touched a button, and the call went to speaker.

"Hi, Mr. Mayor!" Dad said with a bright, put-on voice.

"Shut up, Szmydt," the mayor's Rhode Island drawl grumbled hoarsely. "Fay says you haven't been by the house for the casserole."

"I'm sorry, sir, I'm on my way. I had to pick up my daughter."

"Well, hurry up and present it to Mrs. Carlisle. Piping hot. Stop and get flowers for her, too. Something big. And what about the dog?"

Dad stammered. He turned into an embarrassing invertebrate when speaking with his boss. "Are we getting Mrs. Carlisle's dog a gift, sir?"

"Goddamnit, Szmydt, pay attention! The dog from last night. The one you forgot to tell me about. It needs to disappear."

"To Mrs. Carlisle's?"

"No, Szmydt, to the bottom of a grave. Head over to the animal hospital, have it put down. We can't have wild dogs roaming the street of Miridical."

"It's a he," Dad muttered to himself dejectedly.

"What's that, Szmydt?"

"I'm on my way, sir."

"On your way to what, Szmydt?"

"To have the vet put down the stray dog."

"To Faye's, Szmydt, Faye's. Flower's. Carlisle's. Kill the dog. Orbison out."

June touched the screen to end the call as they slowed and took a U-turn.

"Dad, what are you going to do?"

"Bug, if I don't get the vet to put down that stray dog, I'll lose my job." He had that damn soft explaining-a-tough-life-lesson tone of voice June found patronizing AF. Then he cleared his throat and continued, "But if that dog gets chipped, vaccinated, and adopted, then I guess he's not a stray."

"So all we need is a replacement dog the vet can put down."

"What?"

"I'm kidding. Let's go get him."

"Does this mean–"

"Yes," she interrupted him. "He's our dog now."

####

The Kermit green Mini Cooper, doors decorated with Miridical's town seal of a bear getting hit by lightning, waited at the curb as June, arms full of an over-sized wreath of white carnations complete with black sash and Mrs. Mayor's green bean casserole, approached the town's funeral home. Thunder crashed out of nowhere, stopping her mid-step. It was barely overcast. Was that really thunder? Thunder boomed again in answer.

Swallowing hard, June readjusted her hold under the still-pretty-hot casserole and accelerated her walk up the brick stoop to the brick castle of spires and three-story towers. Its big, round-topped wooden door housed an over-sized knocker and June banged out a thundering boom of her own. There was a queasy dread in anticipation of talking to a woman recently widowed, like a weight pulling at June's guts.

Muffled music came from within the weighty castle door, barely a bass line and a whimper of instruments. Probably something wallowing and classical; emo for old folks. After a clicking and sliding of metal like opening an olde timey vault, the thick wooden door pushed out, its creaking sounded like pained wails. Behind was the new Widow Carlisle's broad, curvy frame... and music. Emo, but not mournful or orchestral. New Wave. Synthesizers and questionable British accents. Defiant grief. And June's U.S. History teacher, always so complacent and droll, looked rose-cheeked and out of breath, like she'd just been... laughing? There was a lightness about her, a healthy blush. Mrs. Carlisle looked relieved and twenty years younger, her eyes lighting up as they fell on her former student. "Ju-niper!" she sang as she grabbed the girl by the wrist and yanked her inside. "You're so nice."

The big woman lifted the bulky wreath out of June's hands, placing it by a side table that was nothing more than an ornate marble pedestal. June had Mrs. Carlisle for history last year, so maybe she had a soft spot for the teacher, but despite the happy relief of the widow, June couldn't imagine Carlisle as a killer.

The Carlisle home, which doubled as the town funeral home, was extravagant: paneling, crown molding, and art everywhere - landscapes of French countrysides, unsmiling white people in portraiture, and all kinds of fruits in bowls. June didn't know anything about art, but she knew stuff that looked expensive. Either the Carlisles were flush, or they worked hard to look it. And the enormous, high-ceilinged, marbled, etcetera house was spotless. Underneath the music, the rhythmic whoosh of a vacuum cleaner rolled overhead upstairs. There's no Roomba that could clean a place this big, and with Mrs. Carlisle at school all day and Mr. Vernon in Boston, the Carlisles must have had hired help.

"This is very sweet of you to come by, Juniper. Was your dad afraid to?" Carlisle swiveled and headed down the fancy red carpet hallway, her long black hair down for the first time June had ever seen, her gait and hips bouncing along with the music. They passed an expensive-looking glass display case set into the walls. Antique pistols. June couldn't tell the time period. Three of them. Locks and a keypad, it all looked expensive and secure.... real secure for a funeral home. June made a mental note.

Following Carlisle through the swinging wooden door, June brought the casserole into the kitchen, all stainless steel and industrial to serve enough food for big funerals and viewings. It was difficult to tell whether the Carlisles were loaded or if these were all trappings of the former family business. "I volunteered to come. But the Mayor was afraid to."

"I don't blame him. He and Vernon never saw eye-to-eye."

"Why do you think that was?" June probed.

"Who knows? Known each other forever. Of course, they moved here together when they first built Miridical."

"Of course." June had had no idea.

The towering lady lifted the casserole from June's arms and swung it onto a steel countertop. Carlisle said off-handedly, "Still saw each other once a week for cards."

"Yeah, who all plays?"

The widow Carlisle squinted at June without answering.

June checked herself and pretended to look at the industrial stovetop, rambling like it was no big deal, "Because my dad likes to play, and he needs more friends."

"Oh yeah... your father," Carlisle's eyes glazed over for a

second and June thought she saw cartoon hearts appearing in them. Ew.

"Cards? Who else plays?" June desperately steered the conversation.

"Juniper Szmydt." The widow's bubbly demeanor faded and sadness crept up, a distant sadness. "You need to watch out not to ask too many questions. There are secrets that could turn little towns like Miridical upside down, more literally than you know. I will miss him, though." She cleared her throat and smoothed her blouse, withdrawing other casseroles from the fridge to make room. "It's all for the best, I guess?"

"It is?"

"Vernon..." From within the fridge, she chose her words carefully. "He ran with some heavy hitters. The wrong kind of people sometimes. And then there was..." Again the widow paused before speaking cautiously. "His condition."

Wishing she could see the widow's face to read it, June questioned Carlisle's outstretched backside. "What was his condition?"

"Complicated." Carlisle stood, fridge still open. "Can I get you anything to drink? I could make a coffee?"

She shook her head no, and the widow began leading June back out, through the family dining room, but June needed to get more info out of the widow without causing suspicion "My dad's got a couple conditions. Something about his sciatica makes his bunions worse."

"Oh, God, not like that. Vernon just had... a treatment regimen. A strict schedule taking him all over Federal Hill. My husband was in pain and unhappy."

It dawned on June how much younger the widow was than her late husband. The wedding photos on the walls showed a maybe college-aged Emma Whatever-Her-Maiden-Name-Was at the altar with a middle-aged Vernon, gray at the temples.

"Then his pain is over at least," June answered, truly earnest. She didn't know what to say in this situation and immediately felt she'd picked the wrong thing. But Mrs. Carlisle didn't seem to mind. Maybe her pain was over, too. "I should probably get going."

Carlisle led June back out along the plush trodden red carpet. June scanned the glass display case again and tried to memorize the types of pistols they were. She couldn't stand there and stare, so she resumed following Carlisle out of the house. But June did manage to look through a door to see a maid vacuuming, a mousy gray-haired woman who quickly looked away from June's gaze. Before she knew it, June was sucked into the widow Carlisle for a long, warm hug. The woman felt like she needed it, tension holding her back tightly. The big, boring, hunched over teacher was a new woman, red-faced and bright and dancing to Duran Duran. Why was she so tense, then?

June felt a rush of emotion that must have been a pang, guilty to suspect a woman in such a tough spot in life. "What will you do, Mrs. Carlisle?"

"Well, I'm going to leave Miridical. Obviously. But I'm not the one to worry about, June. You and your dad take care. The people of this town can be..." She struggled for a word, voice catching in her throat. It was the first time Emma Carlisle had been choked up for June's whole visit. "Manipulative. And you and your Dad are just so darned nice."

The big lady pulled June in for another, shorter, hug. "Good-bye, Juniper Szmydt. You're going to have the best time figuring out who you are someday."

And then June walked headed out of the opulent house with the worn red carpet through its heavy castle doors.

####

The front door back home had weight to it, as well. June wondered if all the doors in Miridical were so ancient and weighty? Before forming a theory, the little black dog, barking his head off, bounded toward her and hopped up, pinning her with an incredible, unforeseeable force against the Szmydt household castle door. With a good amount of her strength, she pushed the small dog's paws off. He wasn't exactly small, only short. He came up to June's knee but was barrel-chested with thick haunches. His muscly front legs bowed inward, so he sauntered when he walked like he was sticking out his chest. And now he was her adorable little tough guy.

He looked up at June expectantly with big brown eyes. Or maybe the eyes were apologetic because he smelled like he just cut one. Luckily, he was just about the cutest thing June had ever seen, so she could forgive the gas.

Dad's booming voice interrupted before he rolled through the swinging kitchen door, explaining with his hands in front of him like he'd already been talking for several minutes. "Until I say otherwise, he does not leave this house or backyard. And the second he starts barking, we need to put him in the laundry room."

But June was cuddling a dog and had no time to listen to stupid humans. "Oh, I love his stupid smooshy face!"

The dog's tailed wagged bouncily in response to her pressing his jowls against her smile-sharpened cheeks.

"And you can't let anyone at school know," Dad chided.

Dad and daughter's eyes met and at the same time both said, "Except Connor."

"But you do need to tell me when Connor's headed over." Dad relented with a chuckle and knelt to pet the heavy smelly dog. "He really zips around the place. I was thinking we could call him..."

"If you say Zippy, I'm going to faint from embarrassment."

"I was going to say Zippy."

"You're the worst." June got to her feet. "I spoke with Mrs. Casserole."

"Did she like the flowers?"

"She did. She said thanks. She seemed... content. Relieved. Said Vernon owed people things? 'The wrong kind of people.' And that he was undergoing treatment?"

"Young lady, you said you weren't going to interrogate her."

"I didn't interrogate her!" June groaned as she whipped the pea coat off and unraveled her scarf. Kicking off her boots, she hopped over to the couch before adding casually, "I don't think she did it, by the way."

"June."

"What? I'm just saying!"

"Come in the kitchen and eat a sub with me. There's an Italian and a meatball."

June was off her normal school schedule and hadn't eaten lunch yet. The smell practically dragged her to the tall chair. "They call them grinders."

"Who do?"

"Rhode Islanders."

"God, it's weird here." Dad got pickles out of the fridge.

"Yeah. At least they got coffee milk."

"True," he said as he sat.

June stood and headed for the cabinet. "Want one?"

"If you're mixing. Extra sweet." Then Dad's phone buzzed, holstered to his belt horizontally in the most dad of ways. It buzzed again. And then again. Texts. One after another. He checked his screen. "Crap."

"Is it the mayor?" Even though of course she knew; June was already putting one of the two glasses back in the cabinet.

"Yeah, he wants me to meet him later."

And yet again, the mayor beckoned and Dad would heel. June didn't mind getting left at home alone – he'd always take her if she pushed to join him – but it was just another example of treating Dad like some mindless errand boy. June steered back. "Did you know that the mayor and Vernon Carlisle moved to Miridical when the town first incorporated?"

Without looking up, Dad answered in a vague mumble, "I didn't know that."

"Did you ever find out why he was at LaChance's car wreck?"

But Dad just stared blankly at his phone screen.

"Dad?"

He lowered his phone, but kept his blank stare, "Huh?"

"Reverend LaChance's wreck?"

"Oh, sure."

"Why was the mayor there?"

"The mayor cares," he said so calmly, he seemed asleep. Was the late-night catching up to him, too?

"Um... okay? Well, when do you have to jump to his beckon?"

"Huh?"

"When are you leaving to meet the mayor?"

Dad's eyes went distant for a moment, scouring the front of the fake woodgrain fridge for an answer to June's question before snapping back suddenly. "After you mix me up an extra sweet coffee milk. Now get with the syrup."

The doorbell rang and Zippy launched into his jarring barks, jolting both Szmydts.

"You need to tell me when Connor's coming over," Dad shouted over the din of the dog.

"Connor doesn't ring the doorbell," June replied.

They locked eyes for a moment, then both made moves for the front door.

With a hand on Zippy's collar, Dad pulled the beast back as June cracked the door open enough to see out.

On the porch, in a tailored black suit with a crisp, white shirt and no tie stood a short, serious-looking man. His olive-skinned face displayed a disapproving frown under a nose that looked to have been broken a couple times. Deep brown eyes looked as though they didn't believe her before she even said anything.

"You must be Ms. Zmite," he said as his eyes studied and judged her.

"It's 'Szmydt.' Who are you?"

"Pardon me, I'm Mo Tilden, here from the Capital." He glared. "I believe you placed a phone call yesterday to the lieutenant governor's office, Ms. Szmydt?"

"Oh shit," June said, immediately stepping back and closing the door right in Mo Tilden's tough-guy face.

Dad, still wrestling Zippy by the collar, whisper yelled, "Who is it?"

June was panicking. "Someone from the lieutenant governor's office."

Dad's eyes popped as big as saucers. He whisper-screamed, "Oh, shit."

She whisper-yelled, "I know!"

"Take Zippy." Dad wrestled his weight, pulling at the little dog by the collar toward June.

"How? He'll drag me to kingdom come!"

"Give him a meatball!"

The dog seemed to understand this exchange clearly and bolted back to the kitchen to wait by the table, June following. She tossed some scraps into the laundry room, shut the dog in, and walked back to the living room, where Dad was offering this Mo Tilden guy a seat.

The short man in the suit took the room in with his eyes and a deep breath through his nose.

"I wish I had known you two were eating Italian tonight. I could have brought you some Manicotti from Federal Hill. I know a place; it's amazing." Somehow, Mo Tilden made the offer sound like a threat. "I couldn't help but notice on the drive down here, the foliage."

"The foliage?" Dad was caught off-guard.

"That's what I said."

"Well, yeah, I mean, it's a beautiful time of year."

"It is. And I know most small towns around here are usually plagued right about now with leaf-peepers. New Yorkers burning gas to get a glimpse of the beauty of nature."

"Yeah?"

"But once I crossed the bridge into Miridical, I didn't notice any New York plates. All local drivers. Nary one leaf-peeper."

June and her dad leaned in, waiting for some big point that Tilden seemed like he was leading up to. But the man simply glared back at them, accusingly, mouth clamped shut in a pursed grimace.

Finally, Dad spoke. "I'm sorry, Mr. Tilden, was it? This was about our request to the lieutenant governor for help with a murder investigation?"

"You know, Mr. Szmydt," Tilden nodded, agreeing with no one in particular as he spoke to June and her father, "impersonating an officer of the law and making false claims to government officials are very serious matters in the State of Rhode Island."

June swallowed hard, her chest tensing as she did her best to not stare at Dad, awaiting his reaction. She was afraid he'd be pouring sweat any minute now.

"And what does that have to do with me, Mr. Tilden?"

The man's eyes narrowed as he pursed his lips. He regarded Dad, Juniper, then Dad again. He sat forward and spoke quietly, "There's a lot of... corruption in this state, Mr. Szmydt. Good men have to work very hard to keep their consciences clean. They say the road to Hell is paved with good intentions. Sometimes to stray from a righteous path, a moral path, all it takes is something innocuous, a small favor, maybe the offer of a gift, a pay increase or a promotion, and then you could find yourself indebted. Forced to do something you don't want to do. Something against your moral compass. A man can lose sense of who he is. Suddenly the very nice people who offered the gift reveal themselves to be some very bad people."

Again the Szmydts found themselves at the edge of their seats, leaning in to hear Tilden's low timbre and to follow his words. But he'd made whatever point he was going to and said no more.

Dad spoke in a low, earnest voice to match the serious man's, "I'm afraid I don't follow you, Mr. Tilden."

"I think something's going on, Mr. Szmydt. In your town. I think the powers-that-be in Miridical are covering something up, something big, but I'm not positive what it is. So this is your chance, Mr. Szmydt."

"My chance? To do what?"

"To step up. To save the day. Be the hero. Blow the whistle."

"What whistle?"

Tilden laughed a bit, but it wasn't from anything funny. He seemed annoyed, at the end of his rope. Wiping his stubbled face with his thick hand, the man was straining to look calm. "That's cute- 'What whistle.' This is your chance to say something. Now. The both of you."

Dad just shrugged uncomfortably under Mo's focus.

When Mo looked to June, she asked, "Whose office are you with again, Mr. Tilden?"

"Smart girl. What if I told you I'm a Persian diplomat and I work closely with the UN, the FBI, and the CIA?"

Something about him felt so... dangerous. But, she held his threatening gaze, despite doing so sent her heart rate through the roof. "Then, Mr. Tilden, I'd say that Persia's not a country anymore."

"Smart girl," he repeated. "Nice family you got here, Mr. Szmydt. But if there's nothing you two would like to talk about, I suppose I'll be on my way. I'll leave you my card, but if you're suspicious of any goings-on, I need to know yesterday." He stood and handed Dad a card, then made for the door, before turning and adding, "I couldn't help but notice the Mezuza at your front door. Shalom."

Faking a chuckle, Dad asked, "The name didn't give it away? I'm afraid we're not practicing."

"That's too bad. Myself, I'm from a long line of Persian Jews."

"There are Persian Jews?" June blurted without meaning to.

Silently, Tilden looked at June for just a moment, but long

enough to chill her blood, before heading for the door again.

"Don't have a coat?" Dad asked as if he just noticed, "It's pretty cold out there."

"'How does one keep warm alone?' Ecclesiastes. Mr. Szmydt, Ms. Szmydt, Have a good night." And he let himself out in just his black suit, closing the door behind him, Dad following to lock it.

"What was that all about?" June asked.

Holding it in both hands, Dad read over Tilden's business card. "I don't think that guy worked for the governor at all."

June rolled her eyes. Of course Mo Tilden didn't work for the governor of Rhode Island.

As if suddenly alerted by something, Dad unlocked the door and looked outside, but Tilden was gone, with no car driving off in any direction.

"That was weird," Dad said, closing the door behind him.

"That was creepy." June couldn't help but pull her legs into the chair with her protectively. Something about the way Tilden spoke, it... wasn't a threat... but maybe a warning.

A sudden knock at the door made June and Dad jump. He calmed himself and swung it open with an accusatory announcement beginning with, "Mr. Tilden–"

Only it wasn't Mo Tilden. It was Connor Spellman.

It was such a relief that June and Dad let out a pathetic laugh.

"What's wrong with you two? You just see the murderer?"

"I think we just saw a cop," June said without certainty.

Connor shrugged it off, presenting June with the yellow paper from the Mini Cooper's windshield wiper. "Did you guys see someone left a note?"

"It's a note? I thought it was a ticket."

"I think," Dad said, standing aside to let Connor come in,

"that the mayor's gonna be wicked pissed if I'm not at his office five minutes ago. Bye guys, I'm ghosting."

"Bye, Mr. S," Connor said.

"That's not what ghosting is." June rolled her eyes and led Connor back to the office, opening the note.

####

As always, Connor played with, brushed, and failed at braiding June's hair as she worked, zoned out comparing photos of bullets and antique pistols on her dad's desktop, like thirty windows open at once. By the keyboard was the one-word note someone had put on Dad's car, most likely a warning to stay out of the investigation.

"Watchdog."

Well, Hell yeah, June was going to be a watchdog with a cartoonishly toxic and dumb Sheriff's department. June didn't care about empty threats. That's not true; June was pretty fired up from this empty threat. She'd investigate harder. She'd crack this case and make the Sheriff's patrol look like the doofuses they were and whoever wrote this note would be livid June was living her best life. It was like standing up to a bully without all the embarrassment.

"All these sites are scary AF," she murmured to herself.

Connor gasped dramatically with a realization. "I bet the widow Carlisle paid someone to kill dear Vernon, just to keep her name clear and not endanger the life insurance policy. Probably a lover she convinced to help her. She seduces the poor sap, shows him her awful life as a kept woman –I'm not ruling out abuse from old Vern - and leads him to come up with the idea of killing the old man off! You aren't listening. It's no fun if you aren't listening... I feel like I'm playing Clue by myself."

Almost cross-eyed from staring at her computer monitor, June blinked hard and diverted her focus. "What?"

"I'm trying to establish motive? Haven't you seen Law and Order? Ugh, L&O is my ish."

Holding the bullet she'd found in the tree up to a similar one on the screen, June ignored him. "It looks like an old fifty caliber, but that bullet would liquefy someone's head."

"Maybe Vern wasn't shot in the head. You have to find out the angle of the bullet and consider the suspect's height. That always works on L&O."

June sighed. As a high schooler, she was not going to get the access of television detective. "I'm not going to look at a dead body."

Connor stuck his tongue out in a disgusted face. "You sound let down. You won't have to. Just ask Papa Bear if Mr. Carlisle was turned into a bowl of pudding."

June pursed her lips to the side, considering the photo on the monitor carefully, rocking in her chair, running her tongue over her askew canine tooth. "Yeah, maybe..."

"And ask Mr. S to find out the angle the bullet was fired. But don't let a hip shot throw you off the trail!"

"And what does it mean if Vernon Carlisle wasn't shot by a fifty caliber bullet?"

"That the killer had his bullet collection on his person at the time of the shooting?"

"Or that I found some old bullet from who-knows-when and researched it while the trail went cold."

"That's why we should be establishing motive!"

June was relieved to hear her dad's keys at the front door

until Zippy barked, a bark like a guttural roar of a chorus of chainsaws yanked to life at once, striking her chest cavity like a drum, and June jumped. Connor flinched so hard he yanked a handful of her hair. She howled, and he screamed as Zippy just kept woofing, running to the foyer - or trying to, his paws sliding on the hardwood floor as his nails made clumsy, tap-dancing sounds. Once Zippy got going and made it down the hall, the barks ceased, followed by a crashing sound, screaming from Dad, and laughing from Connor. June and Connor bolted down the hall.

Dad sat, his back pinned to the front door, Zippy standing in his lap to lick his face, a face sullen and shadowed. The old wedding photo, the only picture on display with June's late mom, had fallen to the ground, the glass cracked in a spiderweb. The center of the shard edges converged over her veiled face, obscuring most of mom's features, changing her into some smiling monster.

"Zippy! Get off!" June pleaded as Dad shoved.

"How are you this heavy?!" Dad grunted with no irony in his voice. June and Connor both grabbed Zippy by the collar and leaned back, but the pup didn't budge.

"Get off me!" Dad finally roared, scaring Zippy and sending him cowering into the other room, tail literally tucked between his legs.

"Geez, Dad, take it easy," June said, genuinely taken aback by how aggro Dad's tone was.

"You okay, Mr. S?" Connor asked tentatively, offering a hand to help him up.

But Dad stayed there, seated on the mat at the front door, taking the broken picture frame in his hands. In a firm, tired tone, he said, "Connor, go home."

"Dad?!" June protested until he shot an angry look up at her.

They didn't talk much about her anymore. Mom. And June doubted he would now. For a guy that was usually joking, always taking everything so lightly, a dark concern cast a shadow on his face. What would he be like if he opened up about her? About losing her and suddenly taking on all the responsibility? June knew she felt abandoned sometimes, and then felt like an asshole for being selfish, but she didn't think Dad was one for deep thought. He was happy, tired, or hungry. He'd been mad before, of course, but it was rage at a broken lawnmower or bowling. This was silent, bubbling, and terrifying. Was this all from one broken picture frame?

With a put-on insulted air, Connor placed a hand on his chest and spoke dramatically in an attempt to defuse the situation. "I don't have to take this. I'm going home." Then he marched through the house grabbing his bag and coat, not stopping on his way out the back door.

"WTF, Dad?"

But Dad wasn't playing. As he got up off the floor, he didn't take his eyes from the broken picture frame. He kept staring at it as he walked through the kitchen to sit at the dining room table. June watched, holding her breath. Placing frame carefully in front of him, he gingerly pinched each shard of glass and placed it to the side with his thick fingers. "June, get me a cardboard box."

Too freaked out to know what to say, June quietly obeyed with wide eyes. The pinched triangles of glass went into the box as he spoke slowly, eyes still on his task. "There's something we need to talk about. Get a couple of spoons and the Ben and Jerry's, would you?"

This was serious.

Inflated veins on his temples pushed up the fluffy taperings-off of his bushy eyebrows, angled to a point like they always were when he was keeping his own feelings in check. Whether he was angry, tired, or sad, June couldn't tell, but the fact that he kept picking glass from the frame instead of grabbing a spoon wasn't a good sign.

"You've been asking," he said dryly, "since you started at Miridical Prep if you could transfer to public school instead."

All the big shards removed, Dad lifted the frame, tipped it over the open shoebox, and lightly tapped the sides of it, dust and chips of glass falling out. He then grabbed a napkin from the holder at the center of the table, flipped the photo, and blotted the picture with the folded napkin to collect the rest of the glass. Then with a heavy sigh, he held the frame at arm's length, looking at the scratches from the broken glass, leaving squiggles of white where his late wife's face should have been. He placed the frame face down on the table then dragged his weary eyes up to meet June's.

She wished he would lose his temper. That he would yell about the frame or the dog or her seeing Connor too much, or June's snooping getting out of hand. But instead, he spoke as if exhausted, his voice quiet and sad. "There's no bus that comes out all the way to Miridical, and I don't have time to drive there and back twice a day."

He considered the two spoons flanking the sweating carton of mint chocolate chip, then stood up and pushed the chair back under the table with a whining dragging noise that made Zippy whimper from the corner whimper. Keeping his hands on the back of the tall chair, Dad's bulking figure sagged, and he said dejectedly, "Once your birthday comes around this spring, as long as you pass your driver's test, we'll pull you out of Miridical Prep and you can go to New Salem. Until then, you stay."

And then without another word, he slunk off to bed, his hunched-over bulk shuffling as he groaned. Something was not right. Nothing about this was right. Possessed by the sudden urge to say something, to connect with the guy in a way that didn't deflate him more, June faked enthusiasm in a thin, fragile voice. "Hey, Dad? Mrs. Carlisle said Vern played poker and owed people money."

"I don't want to hear another word," his words filled the house like a shout, but he spoke with an unsettling calm, adding, "about the murder."

June sat dumbfounded, having gotten the news she had wished to hear for the past year and a couple months. But now, it just left a heavy emptiness in her stomach... which she filled with ice cream.

Chapter Six: October 30th, morning

The next day while Zippy did his morning business out in their backyard, June texted with Connor about the investigation. They listed their main suspects: Evens Bonhomme, Reverend LaChance, the Carlisle maid, and maybe, but most likely not, the widow Carlisle. Connor also suspected Sheriff Marrock, Mayor Orbison, Principal Donnelly and the Armenian sisters who ran the bookstore, but June figured Connor was using this as an enemies list. Anything not to take this seriously.

But that was Connor- too good to be bothered with caring. And June was usually above it all, too. But her investigation was making progress. And Connor was just making fun. He was infuriating. June was getting aggravated. And the damn dog had already sniffed this one patch of grass like ten times already.

"Just go! Poop! Anywhere, it doesn't matter! This backyard is a postage stamp!" The words echoed in her mind. Not her own voice, but her mother's. Complaining about their old house in Massachusetts. White vinyl siding. Black wrought iron. Little rectangle of grass. A postage stamp.

Dad's voice snapped her back to the present. "June, let's go!" he bellowed from within the house, in no better mood than last night. What happened when he went out to meet the Mayor?

After closing Zippy up in the laundry room that now permanently smelled like dog fart, June got ready for school. Throwing on her Miridical Prep button-up, she thought back to the nights pleading, crying with her Dad to go to a different school, but not bringing herself to admit to the disgusting things the girls were calling her. She wouldn't allow her thoughts to linger on Chelsea, but when June threw on the backpack and grabbed homework from the computer desk, she noticed something was missing.

"Where's the bullet?" she asked Dad as he was throwing on his big brown puffy coat with a fake fur hood.

"I'm taking it to the sheriff," he answered gruffly without looking her in the eyes.

"The sheriff couldn't solve a murder if he committed it."

"June, the sheriff is the sheriff. I can't believe I let you take evidence from a crime scene."

"And what's going to happen to you when you admit that to the cops?"

"I don't know, but it's the right thing to do."

"Letting a murder go unsolved is the right thing to do?"

"This is not up for debate." He walked past her, gathering up his things, headed for the front door.

"And what? You'll get fired, or demoted, or arrested?"

"That's between the sheriff and me."

"So you can be even more of a joke in this town?"

"I'm going to be mayor of this town!"

The words hit June's ears like a sentence in another language. The idea was so alien, so ridiculous, June let out a laugh. "In what universe would you be Mayor of Miridical?"

Red-faced, Dad said quietly, "Get in the car. End of discussion. You're grounded. No indoor soccer, Connor can't come over, and why aren't you ready yet? It's time to go."

"Back off! I still have to brush my hair."

"Then get going. Four minutes until I leave."

"Okay."

"Four minutes."

"Okay. I heard you."

After she took her time brushing her hair and grabbing her book bag, the Mini Cooper was buzzing out of the driveway.

Dad had threatened to leave without her tons of times, but she never thought he'd actually ever go.

She was mad, then hurt, then mad at being hurt. But more than anything, she was cold. She had to start walking. To keep warm, yes, but to get to school on time. And this late in the morning, there was only one way she could go.

She said the name to herself like it was the F word. "Dabitt's Forest."

####

The only thing in Dabitt's Forest thicker than the mist was the memory of yesterday's... intimacies. To be honest, it felt like a month ago. June's run for her life, the musk of the wild animal chasing her, even Chelsea's soft vanilla kiss seemed like years back, yet still so vivid.

June wanted to be angry, though. She wanted to curse at her dad under her breath and laugh out loud at the idea he could win an election in a town that hated the Szmydts. But the woods were too still, and her seizing breath curled up too slowly before here.

The trees appeared barer now, wading in the morning mist. Every noise, each rustling leaf, squawking animal or flapping wing sent her jumping. There was an angry heaviness in the pit of June's stomach that resisted being in those woods, that wanted to skip school, run back home, run away, anything but walk deeper into the misty brush.

She stopped often to hold her breath and listen for noises remotely feline. All she heard was the crunch of leaves under her own shoes and the pounding of her own pulse. When she did walk, she forced herself faster and faster, not just because she was late for homeroom, but to get out of the woods. Away from where the animal attacked. Away from Chelsea hoarding June's old Band-Aids.

June pushed away a branch thick with orange leaves and there she was again. The clearing with the stump, the site of the disgusting ritual. Only now, on the stump, sat a mason jar without a lid. June found herself holding her breath and tiptoeing toward the object. Within, a small green shoot of a plant sprout pushed out from a mess of roots. The little white noodles at the bottom of the jar weaved in and out of a white swatch of cloth stained deep red, and June's blotted brown Band-Aids.

She swallowed hard; there might have been a little vomit coming up. Then in an instant, she took off running, sprinting as fast as she could for school. Her lungs burned like they did on the second day in a row of serious use. Like sore trash bags that were easier to inflate now that they've been opened already. Pushing her legs without slowing, she left the woods and Chelsea and whatever was in that jar behind her.

Stopping at her locker, she was doubled over, hands on her

knees, gulping breaths, hoping not to vomit.

"Why are you running?" Connor gasped, "Is the murderer chasing you? Is this turning into one of those old slasher movies? Are you going to be the final girl? Am I going to be the final boy?"

"Fuck off, Connor."

"Calm your tits, it was a joke."

Hot and beet red, June caught her wind enough to head to class, Connor in tow. "Well, none of this is funny anymore. I'm grounded. Dad's pissed. No more investigation. He's pulling me from Miridical Prep."

"Wait. Just because the dog broke a picture frame? But Mr. S is such a pushover. I can't imagine Papa Bear getting angry."

"Yeah, I've never seen him like this."

"But we get to attend New Salem in the Spring?"

"Connor, you never needed my dad's permission. You could have been attending public school this whole time."

"Not without my little Nipslip!" He hugged her while giving a noogie. Feigning disgust, she pushed him away. Connor was the closest thing she had to a brother, which helped when she was fighting with the only other member of her actual family.

"I need to stop by the library on the way home. There has to be a better reference for fifty caliber guns, and I may need to start watching out what I leave on Dad's search history." June tamed her hair, a springy mane from her morning run, into a pom pom of a ponytail, hoping it was small enough not to notice and elicit trolling.

"You're still doing the L&O thing despite the fact that it led to the biggest fight ever with Papa Bear?"

"Of course. We're looking for a military cannon. Big guns mounted on humvees and boats and tanks."

"Like the kind The Rock shoots with his big muscly arms?"

"Exactly."

They stopped at what used to be Mrs. Carlisle's classroom, Connor's homeroom. He leaned against the doorframe and whispered with urgency, "While we're there, maybe we should also identify whatever attacked you in the woods? I mean, besides Chelsea's bi-curious phase."

"Shut your hole, Connor."

Back to being loud and dramatic, he said, "My hole is none of your business, young lady. Uh, speaking of which..." He looked down the hall past June.

June made a grossed-out face. "Speaking of your hole?" Then she felt a shove from behind her. It was Hailey's gaggle.

"Smells like shit over here," one of the girls laughed, "Oops, I mean Szmydt."

And per usual, Connor had slipped off, most likely into home-room, leaving June solo in the ambush. Quickly composing herself, June wheeled around, just to find herself face to face with Chelsea, her greenish eyes pleading, her usual haughty air melted away.

Of course, Hailey noticed June's googly eyes. "See anything you like, kike dyke?"

The embarrassment was too much for June to snap back at the intersectional pejorative. Pushing past a snickering Hailey and Chelsea, who June couldn't even look at, June headed to her own homeroom.

"Hailey, just fuck off, okay?" Chelsea raised her voice, and June stopped when she heard the distinct sound of books hitting the linoleum followed by a high pitched grunt. She peeked between students to see Chelsea had pushed Hailey onto her ass. Like, skinny little twig of a girl Chelsea Blackstone pushed a taller, meaner Hailey Daley onto her clique-leading booty.

The rich gaggle stood around them, blank-faced, looking from Hailey to Chelsea, uncertain of what to do. They'd never seen a power struggle before. They were wholly unequipped to take sides or think for themselves, like paralyzed prey in a nature video.

"Fuck off... Blackstone!" Hailey yelled from the floor, her words garbling like she wanted to call Chelsea something else.

The noise and circling up of teens was enough to warrant attention from teachers, and seeing the girls involved, they promptly sent the most probable parties involved to the office. The likely instigator, June, and her victim, Hailey.

June's big butt knew the wooden pew outside the principal's office intimately. Like the rest of the school, the administrative offices were beauteous and antique. Warm wood in paneled squares separated offices and made up the half-walls carving out reception. And set between the frosted glass door to the principal's office and the reception's bustling front desk (staffed with Spellman cousins who'd invariably graduated from Miridical Prep), the skinny hall with the pew had surprisingly little supervision, as evidenced by the amount of graffiti carved into the wooden arms. Nothing salacious was written, just squiggles and scribbles all over that June often found herself tracing with her finger while awaiting punishment.

Acting all in her feelings like she'd never been sent to the headmaster before, Hailey Daley, holding an icepack to the back of her head for effect, pouted and worked up the lamest fake cry June had ever witnessed. God, what a terrible actress.

So June there sat in a slump, going through in her head how she'd explain this to Dad, wondering what was one step worse than being grounded, scared it meant no more New Salem High. And of course it would be harder to continue looking into the murder (she still had to talk to the maid and LaChance). June nervously rubbed her finger on some abstract carved letter on the pew.

A voice from down the hall at reception rang out loudly, but with a nervous waver. Chelsea. "Can I talk to Principal Donnelly, please? It's urgent."

Trying to hide her surprise, June leaned out to see those blue-green eyes for the first time since in the woods a day ago. What was Chelsea doing here?

"The fuck are you doing, Chels?" Hailey whispered in cold anger through gnashed teeth at her former BFF.

The only answer Hailey got was a dagger-stare and clamped jaw. But that was answer enough.

Chelsea was flipping on Hailey.

Compared to her usual aesthetic, Chelsea looked a mess. Normally perfectly straight and bouncy hair was pulled back off-center with uncharacteristic fly-aways, her alabaster skin showed blotches, lacking her normal attention to makeup, and her turquoise eyes were puffy and pink from lack of sleep, tears, or both. When she approached June, anger and embarrassment bubbled up inside her while all the dirty thoughts of their kiss bubbled downward.

With a dragging, worn-out voice, Chelsea spoke flatly to June. "She doesn't hate Jews. Or lesbians, most likely. She's just happy to get the attention off her weird uber-catholic family."

"That's not true!" Hailey suddenly didn't require the cold

compress anymore, dropping it as she stood.

But no matter how hot Chelsea was, or how amazing their kiss had been, June had written Chelsea off as a scumbag. "I don't need to hear excuses for anti-Semites."

In a whispered scream, Hailey was about to lose it. "Don't talk about me like I'm not here!"

A clearing of someone's throat got all the girls' attention at once - Hailey sitting back down, Chelsea stepping away, and June doing a terrible job of acting relaxed. Miss Housler, the cross-eyed school counselor stood in the half-opened frosted glass door to the principal's office and called for Chelsea. Little Miss (formerly) Popular either couldn't or just didn't bring herself to look at June as she went in and the door to the lion's den closed behind. June's mouth hung open, her chest full of frothing emotions, her brain going a million different ways.

"She's lying," Hailey assured either June or herself.

But June felt a numbness when the door had shut - excitement over exoneration mixed with the dread of owing something to Chelsea Blackstone, the scumbag.

"I hate you because you're a bitch, a suck-up, a snitch, you're stupid, probably blind, gay-" Hailey went on and on.

But June barely heard, too busy telling herself she didn't owe Chelsea anything. This changed nothing. Chelsea Blackstone had a gross obsession with June she wanted no part of.

Then why couldn't she stop thinking about her?

When June snapped back to reality, Hailey was still complaining. "And if I get suspended because of some Jew girl, I'm going to whip your ass. I'm not antisimitic. I don't want another Holocaust or anything. I just know what to expect when you deal with a Jew."

June's teeth clenched harder each time she heard the word;

she imagined them cracking and breaking. But Chelsea was right. She'd wounded Hailey and now Hailey was lashing out using the word "Jew" as a weapon to protect herself. Like a child.

And Hailey had spent over a year dragging June on the daily. How insecure was this poor girl to go to so much trouble just to have a sliver of control of what other kids thought? With the sudden calm of figuring out why Hailey always acted this way, June leaned back in the pew, head resting against the ornate wood-paneled wall, and said, "Well, what do you expect from a Jew? Bad sex, self-deprecating jokes, and money-lending?"

Hailey's eyes narrowed. "Snitches and snakes, bitch. Jews killed Jesus."

June couldn't help but laugh, high on the relief she found above Hailey's childishness. "Believe it or not, Hailey, I wasn't there. You know, I'm not even really Jewish. We don't practice. I didn't even have a Bat Mitzvah."

About to go off, staring daggers at June, Hailey Daley spat, "It's in your blood. Like a curse."

Again June snickered, "'In our blood?' Like we're demonic snake people?"

Hailey was getting angrier. "If the shoe fits..."

There was no reasoning with her, and June doubted that Chelsea was right. This wasn't a defense mechanism because the Daleys were weird; this was ingrained hate. Ignorance. And June was going to waste her time with that and slumped back into the pew, before asking from a realization, "Wait, why'd you say I'm probably blind?"

The door creaked open and Housler, face twisted in a disappointed purse, said, "Juniper Szmydt, you can go back to class. Hailey Daley, come in please."

Hailey muttered under her breath before joining the counselor, the principal, and Chelsea in the office, leaving June to think about how fired up Dad had gotten the day before after being called blind. She walked back to class before she could worry about what trouble Chelsea just volunteered for.

Chapter Seven: October 30th, afternoon

Through the rest of her day, June stayed zoned out, sleep-walking through Algebra, Chemistry, and two hours of study hall. She fought to keep her mind on her suspect list, copying it over from a Connor text to a doc on her phone. But whenever she went to list each suspect's possible motives, she'd get distracted, picturing Dad holding that busted photo of Mom or losing the bullet which was her only clue or the firm squish of Chelsea's lips. June almost forgot to stop by the school library to grab a book on military weaponry. She had already made a paper cover to hide it from Dad.

What is his problem anyway? Thinking about Dad got her antsy. This was the longest he'd stayed mad at her since she could remember. Why did he suddenly want to be Mayor? Dad hated his job. And even if he wouldn't say so, he hated his boss and pretty much all town employees. He'd never talked about running for office before. As far as June knew, he'd simply fallen into the opportunity of Deputy Mayor, glad to get out of security work.

"Earth to Nipslip?" Connor broke her from her thoughtful stupor on their way after school to the library.

"What?" she snapped, angrier than she meant.

But Connor was looking elsewhere and whispered out the side of his mouth, "You've got a heart to heart coming your way."

"What?"

"Chelsea Blackstone, on your six," he said before crossing the street, most likely heading to Del's.

Sure enough, up jogged Little Miss Popular, inducing an eye roll and a sigh from June, who'd been out of fucks since about 10 am.

"Hey," Chelsea said, sidling up to match June's stride.

"Hey," June replied with a mutter, mad at herself for the rush of heat to her cheeks and flutter in her belly. Her hormonal teen body was betraying her.

"Any plans for Halloween?"

"I usually just hand out candy with my dad."

Chelsea cocked an eyebrow incredulously. "Do you guys get many trick-or-treaters?"

June wanted to give a smartass remark, but thought about it and answered honestly, "No, we didn't get any last year. But we figured it's because we were new to Miridical."

"Oh."

Reactions like that usually meant someone realized they were talking about June's Mom's death. Always awkward, but maybe June could use it to get out of this cringe-worthy conversation.

Yet, Chelsea persisted, "Well, you don't have to. Hand out candy. None of the kids in town are allowed to trick-or-treat. Because of all the religions? The kids that do go to Pawtucket or New Bedford."

"Great," June replied in unenthusiastic monotone, praying Chelsea would catch the hint. No such luck. They walked for a bit, June tight-lipped while Chelsea smiled too hard. Just all of the awkward. All of it.

Finally, Little Miss Popular burst like she'd been holding her breath, "Listen, I'm really sorry about Hailey. She's a real bitch. And I'm not even really friends with her; our parents are friends. And cheerleading. And we live close by."

But June wasn't having it. "So, like an arranged marriage."

"Listen, she wasn't always such a bitch, alright? And for the record, I never made fun of you for being Jewish, or being... being a... girl who... you know..."

"Is 'lesbian' the word you're searching for, Thesauro?"

"Look, you know... you wind up being friends with people and come up with inside jokes, and you don't notice when they stop being funny and suddenly you're picking on people, and then your friends are saying things that are, like, gross."

"I don't know, Chelsea. The guy I'm friends with only makes fun of me, and only about things I'm cool with."

"Who?"

"Connor."

"Connor? Who's Connor?"

June was getting pretty annoyed with Chelsea's following routine, but gave her the benefit of the doubt when she realized Chelsea and Connor probably just didn't have classes together. "I guess the great Chelsea Blackstone can't be bothered to learn the names of all the little people."

"Blackstone?"

"Yes?"

"Do you think that's my name?"

What was this girl's problem?

"It is your name, you wicked pervert."

"Do you not see things for what they are, June?"

"What does that mean?"

"Are you..." Chelsea ducked in closer to whisper, her proximity exciting June enough to tickle her knees a little, a reflex that flustered June further. But then Chelsea said it: "Blindfolded?"

The word hit June like a soccer ball to the face. "What?"

Chelsea nudged June along, but huddled in close to keep her voice down. Their arms touched and June's heart started a drum solo.

"Are you?" Chelsea spoke so close, June smelled strawberry. Gum or lip sparkle or something.

"Am I what?"

"I wonder if you'd even know it. I'm no good at remembering... laws," Chelsea mumbled.

"Laws?" June cocked her head and made a face.

"Laws?" Chelsea made a face right back.

"Why would you memorize laws?"

"Laws is the word you're hearing when I say... laws?" Again, the girl garbled her last word. The Miridical accent.

"WTF are you talking about, Chelsea? Why do you think I'm bli–"

Chelsea clamped her slender pale hand over June's mouth, which was completely gross because she was making an "l" sound and wound up licking Chelsea's palm. "Sh! It's a legend. I thought it was an urban myth. Every kid growing up in Miridical has heard the story."

"Then why are we whispering?"

"It's a secret, nobody talks about it in public. Nobody knows who the person is except a select few. I imagine the ones who," again, Chelsea mumbled, "wrote the laws. You didn't even know."

A toothy smile spread across Chelsea's face, and a low rumbling sound bounced in her throat. It was a laugh. A goofy, uncool laugh that June and probably the rest of Miridical Prep hadn't heard before. If June hadn't been hearing so many whispers about a blind person, she would have thought Chelsea was trolling her.

"What's funny?"

"I thought you were just trolling me this whole time. You really think my name is Blackstone, don't you?"

"Well, yeah. Isn't it?"

"No, not at all." Chelsea had a good, long laugh, a laugh so big and genuine, it was impossible to look cool. She was just an awkward goofy teen, laughing like a nerd.

It was difficult for June to keep up her level of anger and disgust, and she couldn't help but crack a smile. Whatever his blindfold meant, June couldn't ask just anyone about it, so she was stuck asking the last person she wanted to talk to right now about it. After Chelsea let out a big sigh and wiped a tear, June asked, as nonchalant as possible, "So what does it mean?"

"What, my name?"

"No, the..." June whispered, "Blindfold."

"I don't know." Chelsea shrugged as she stared at June. Well, not at her, but up around her face, like June had something stuck in her hair. The attention from the perfect blond girl did get June rather heated and antsy. Without looking away from the space around June's face, Chelsea said, "It means you can't see things. Hear things."

"What does that mean?" June checked her loose strands of hair for whatever Chelsea was looking at.

"It means things might be different from what you see."

"What things?"

"Everything."

Chelsea said it so softly, so earnestly, like June was supposed to know what the hell she meant. "What are you, a Sphinx?" June finally stood on tiptoes to lock eyes with Chelsea. "Tell me what a blindfold is and what it means."

"It's a...law." That garbled word again.

"Goddamnit, Chelsea!"

"I can't just come out and tell you!"

"Why not?"

"The blindfold!"

And that was about all June could handle. She ducked her head and sped up, turning off the main road onto hers, passing the rows of near-identical suburban houses. Trying to lose the Blackstone, or whatever her name was, on her tail.

But Chelsea caught up. "I'll figure out a way out of it."

Sure, let her think she's helping. Whatever ends this conversation. "You do that, Chelsea. You go away and figure it all out and leave me alone until you can be helpful."

Only Chelsea didn't budge. They walked in silence, Chelsea not looking away from June. Leaves rushed by in wind and Chelsea had the most beautiful strands of hair loose, flapping about her face, making the blond girl even more statuesque. June was hoping she wasn't blushing.

Finally, Chelsea stopped and broke the silence. "Can we talk about what happened yesterday?"

"You mean how you stalk me and hide in the woods, hoarding my fucking blood?" June had to put up a front now, pacing and raising her voice. "Then you get me attacked by a fucking cat?"

But Chelsea didn't take the bait to fight. She spoke evenly. "Juniper. I like you. I like, really like you. And I'm sorry you saw... whatever you think you saw in the woods. And I'm sorry our first kiss was after we were attacked..."

June interrupted, "Hold up. 'First kiss' implies there will be more, Chelsea. And there won't. I'm not going to be the gaycation for the bitch that's made my life Hell for two years. I'm leaving Miridical Prep soon enough, just leave me alone until then. Pretend like yesterday never happened and pretend you don't know me."

June rushed off, leaving Chelsea alone on the leaf-strewn sidewalk, calling after her. "Juniper, one day you're going to realize I'm the only fucking person in this town who's going to be nice to you. Who'll actually tell you the truth."

The Miridical Library was yet another enormous antique building, too nice for this podunk New England town. The steeple of a clock tower, seven stories high, loomed over the rest of the town square, dulled grey stone up to its wrought-iron spire. From each corner of the structure reached more points, and the clock face itself was roman numerals pointed out by two hands raised up from the brick and iron. The library towered over Miridical like some Gothic cathedral condescending to unworthy parishioners.

She texted Dad that she was headed to the library. Not volunteering the fact she was researching the murder felt more like a lie than a secret. Secrets growing up had been fun - parties, gifts, good surprises. But secrets always turned mean in school, turned sticky, implicating the people who heard it.

Keeping her research from Dad made her feel lonely. Connor was around, but not dependably. And June would rather never see Chelsea again in her life rather than ask for her input on the murder. Her loneliness hung like a weight in her chest as she entered the library. The whole cathedral aesthetic always gave June the creeps, and as she walked through the heavy glass-in-oak doors guarded with bars of more iron, her skin prickled.

Aside from one quick half-day field trip, June had never been to the town library, and it was more vast than she remembered. The foyer opened into an atrium displaying five floors of oak shelves, winding alabaster staircases curving from one level to the next. The air smelled like dust and mothballs with an undercurrent of mildew. The ceiling seemed impossibly high, and the ground must have been dug out for as many floors down it went.

Behind the front desk at the edge of the foyer was a sullen man with the Spellman complexion and face shape. Long, askew tufts of grey hair sprouted from his temples, flanking a spotted bald head. His gold reading glasses look like if they were removed, his comical hair would come off with them.

The wall behind the desk was a huge antique map of Miridical in browns and auburns and reds. The majority of the acreage, however, was verdant, occupying either side Fortune Hill, Dabbitt's Forest, and the Wolf Wood. The entire island was surrounded by the Providence River that split to encircle the town. The map itself was exquisite. All the words in a looping font like a hand-written fantasy novel.

Even though the map was beautifully well kept, many of the words were smudged, including the entire key in the map's corner. That little square greatly interested June, as she didn't understand what the color-coded dotted lines going all over the map represented - green dashes encircled the town, blue dashes made up a series of concentric blobs, almost like a topographic map, but instead of marking the height of Fortune Hill, they centered on June's neighborhood. But most disturbing of all was the series of black dotted lines coming in from other parts of Rhode Island and Massachusetts, about a dozen of them all converging on a single point, like a grotesque asterisk, centered precisely where the Szmydt house stood.

Squinting at the key, June could nearly make out the words in the key explaining the black dotted line. Something something linchpin?

"Miss, can I help you?" the sullen librarian Spellman said.

"Yeah. Yes, sorry. I'm sorry, but I've never noticed this map before, what is it of?"

"The township of Miridical."

"No, I know that. I mean, what are all the lines? Like, the dotted lines?"

The librarian's pronunciation changed, and soon he spoke with the thick Miridical accent, drawling unintelligibly. When he was finished speaking, June founding herself leaning in, brows furrowed, still trying to understand.

"I'm sorry, could you repeat that?"

He did. Still garbled nonsense.

"Say that one more time, only slower?"

It was like listening to Charlie Brown's teacher.

Suddenly a woman librarian interrupted, severe and direct, coming out of nowhere. "Ms. Szmydt, may I help you?"

Thrown by the new librarian's entrance, June put forth a little more effort to remain pleasant, "Yeah, I was just asking him about the map."

"Well, I'm sorry, my coworker is new to our town. Maybe I can be of service," the lady said, a polite veneer hiding annoyance or aggression. Her coworker was obviously a Spellman; June doubted he was new to town.

"I was just asking about what the dashes, the dotted lines on the map meant. I'm having trouble reading the key."

The severe woman nearly spread her cat-butt lips into a smirk but curled it back. "Perhaps you should get your eyes checked."

Was that an insult from an adult? "Excuse me?"

"Fault lines. The dashes are known fault lines," she said plainly then pursed her lips once more.

"Okay... all of them? The blue ones, too?"

"The water table."

"And what about the black lines?"

"Migratory patterns. Will that be all, Ms. Szmydt?"

The severe librarian's answer didn't make sense, but the way she said June's name was what rattled her. "How do you know my name?"

"I'm aware of who your father is. Now, was there anything else I could help you with?" She spoke like addressing June bored her and tasted bad. Beyond not winning any customer service awards, the severe woman obviously had a problem with the Szmydts. June had to wonder if she also had a problem with Jews.

"Yeah, I'm just looking for a reference book about guns."

"Guns?"

"Yea, pistols. And specifically, bullets." June was losing patience.

"Pistols and bullets?" The librarian's face remained blank as she asked her non-stop questions.

"Is there an echo in here? Yes. Bullets. Aka rounds."

"I'm afraid we don't have any books on rounds."

How annoying is this lady? Either June was going to blow up in this woman's face, or she'd cut her losses and take what she could get. "Okay, well anything on military weapons or vehicles should work."

"I'm afraid we don't have anything like that."

BS. The librarian didn't even check the computer. "Seriously?"

"Seriously."

"In the whole library?" June raised her voice.

"Is there anything else, Ms. Szmydt?"

"I guess not," June said as she stormed off from the reception desk, sure to clomp her Doc Martens, an echo following her out while the lady librarian let out piercing shush.

Having never been asked to leave a place before, June couldn't be sure about this feeling that she was kicked out of the library. Or maybe run out was more accurate.

She could hang out on the giant stone landing; it's not like she was escorted off the grounds. But June couldn't help but think that she'd been singled out, like the librarian was a part of one of those small town watchdog groups June had read about, getting in trouble with the law, or accidentally- Wait.

Watchdog.

The note on Dad's car. What if it wasn't a threat, but a warning that a watchdog group could be on to them? Did that make any sense or was June getting paranoid?

She walked to clear her mind or keep her body busy. TBH, the orange of autumn suited the quaint town with its hodgepodge of ancient buildings, but all June felt was cold, angry, and running out of options to identify the round. She defiantly stared down the enormous ripple of earth that was Fortune Hill, a wave of orange foliage except for the protrusion of granite that was the rocky bluff, Prayer Point.

As she walked, June placed the crime scene a quarter way up the hill. She could see the road where they found the body beside. The blacktop cutting through the Boston Oaks would have caught some of the light from the square the night of the murder. She pictured an old man like Vernon Carlisle heading uphill, walking in the middle of the street. A quarter mile drive away from any sidewalk.

Why was he even there? Was someone chasing him? Did he see his killer and run?

Past the iron and brick police station and the tall white-siding church, June remained focused on the hill. Her tongue worked against the back of her outstanding canine tooth. If Mr. Carlisle had been knocked from the road uphill, then the murderer could have been downhill at the edge of Dabbit's Forest.

Coming to the alley between the florist and dry cleaners, June gasped when she noticed the alignment. A straight path cut into the trees from down in the town square to a quarter way up Fortune Hill. Branches split and treetops had been trimmed – no, burned– as something or someone had cleared a line going straight up through the woods to the crime scene. How had she not seen it sooner?

Squinting, she traced an imaginary line from the spot up where Mr. Carlisle was murdered down to the square. Whatever left this mark - maybe heavy artillery got that hot - it came from farther than where she stood. It must have been back toward the library. Searching the trees in the center of the square for any sign of scorching, June stepped off the sidewalk to–

A car horn blared. June leaped back. The chrome bumper of an ancient car lurched to a halt. It was the mousy woman from the Carlisle house; was she a maid? June's heart raced, and she was instantly sweaty and out of breath. Despite all that, she managed to signal the woman to roll down the passenger window of the big crimson boat of a car. "Hi, I'm wicked sorry. Thank you for stopping."

"You need to watch where you're going."

June remained polite. Smiling, sweating, out of breath, almost just died, but sooo polite. "Totally. I totally do. I was actually looking for you, because my dad was asking about the poker game Mr. Carlisle attended? Do you know who hosted?"

Instead of answering, the mousy maid's eyes narrowed as her lips pursed.

June filled the silence. "My dad's never played poker, but he just paid for lessons and he wants to learn more?"

The woman let out a disgusted "feh," or maybe a "flech" then barked, "Stay out of the street!" and sped off.

Drivers honked, pedestrians stared, a couple of guys June didn't know approached and offered help, so then she was flustered and bolted in the direction of the bookstore. She no longer could figure this artillery angle thing out right now, and reminded herself to come back. Later. When life was less embarrassing.

Fat chance.

Which Book's For You was the locally owned bookstore just off the town square. Operating out of a cute house, stucco with exposed wood beams and shutters and a bright red door, the store was obviously a family heirloom. The old couple who used to run it passed down the retailer to their two daughters. Oddly enough, despite being a voracious reader, June had never been into the shop (definitely more of a "shoppe") nestled against a giant arching Boston Oak. Besides having tons of books around the house, whether the spy thrillers of her dad's or the cozy mysteries her mom had hoarded, June mostly read off their tablet or her phone.

The shoppe's front yard wasn't manicured, but the white picket fence, tufts of wildflowers, and unkempt bushes all looked super cute. Wooden hand-painted signs affixed to the Boston Oak proudly displayed they were open, as well as the name in goofy, faded blue lettering.

Small town bookstore run by a couple of eccentric sisters was an absolutely delightful idea, and June daydreamt of enlisting their help in solving Mr. Carlisle's murder, throwing around sharp, biting banter over over-sized espresso drinks.

June had tired of scary militia websites and had been conditioned in her Boston suburb middle and high schools to research in reference books. So if the school and town libraries had nothing that could help, maybe the bookstore did. Heck, maybe they had a bulletin board with a flyer for the town watchdog organization. But that was just wishful thinking.

Approaching the stone path delightfully winding to the red front door, June pushed against the white picket gate, but it didn't give. Locked. Slightly taken aback, she pushed again, then searched for some locking mechanism. There was none. Before she could think about how odd it was for a gate to be locked during business hours, she noticed the hand-painted wooden sign on the tree saying the bookstore was closed. It hadn't said that before. But now, there it was, above the reach of any person, permanently nailed to the tree, a sign declaring the shop closed.

Reminding herself to leave a nasty Yelp, June kicked rocks and headed home after convincing herself not to get a Del's. What was with this town and the buildings that held books? Was something or someone was trying to steer her away from the case? As a last resort, June would take her query to the school library tomorrow, where hopefully the weirdest occurrence would just be her existence, the freaky gay Jewish girl who scares everyone away.

Chapter Eight: October 30th, dusk

Connor was so embarrassing when he talked dirty. "I've always fantasized about getting freaky on some strong daddy with a big... dirty... truck." Thank goodness the cafeteria was loud enough to drown him out. "But I'm telling you, no one in town has a truck that could hold a giant, heavy machine gun."

Miridical Prep's lunch periods were taken in a converted ballroom, vast with dark wood. There were obvious outlines on the walls where portraiture must have hung, and whatever fancy floor they had was covered in taped- down strips of black rubber matting. The rows and rows of plastic, built-in bench tables populated with teenagers looked so out of place against the expensive handmade architecture, they looked like green-screen computer effects.

Connor and June sat in a far corner, the emptiest part of the room. "I'm not talking about some spoiled white guy's Jeep. I'm talking about a professional grade truck that can haul weight. Like the towing company, for one. And haven't I seen LaChance driving a rusty old yellow pickup?"

"The one the church uses for parade floats?"

"Maybe. Does that mean LaChance was working with the murderer?"

"But what I don't get is if the murderer fired from here," Connor pointed at the ketchup packet that represented the truck, in front of the pepper shaker representing the library, "how did the bullet you found wind up here?" He pointed to the middle of the water bottle representing the scene of the murder up Fortune Hill.

Nudging the ketchup packet along the cafeteria table past the smartphones, napkin dispenser, and salt shaker representing the rest of the town square, June spoke quietly when the truck metaphor got to the crime scene metaphor. "They went to make sure he was dead. Drove to check on the body, accidentally dropped a round."

June was working on the conundrum of the angle of the bullet not lining up. Super-annoying that the guy who took none of her investigations seriously had made the point about bullet angle so early. She noticed he'd gotten quiet, staring at the tabletop representation of Miridical. He swallowed hard, then winced as he said, "June, maybe your dad's right. Maybe we shouldn't do this."

"Do what? Use this accurate to-scale model?" she gestured to the town square sarcastically before picking up the school, or rather, her phone. "Fine, we can look at it through satellite maps."

"No, I mean, maybe your dad is right about letting this one go. Just put your head down. Pass your driver's test. We'll be at New Salem before you know it."

With a cold, dead stare, June addressed Connor. "And the murder?"

He flinched as he suggested, "Leave it to the police?"

"The Miridical police are all cousins who gave each other jobs, Connor. If I don't do this, if we don't do this, Mr. Carlisle's murder goes unsolved."

"Okay? He won't mind, and his wife didn't sound too broken up over the whole thing."

The bell rang. Lunch was over.

"Connor, the murderer's still out there. They shouldn't get away with it." June realized she'd raised her voice as she stood. She leaned in to Connor and said in low tones, "Someone killed Vernon Carlisle. It can't be swept under the rug. It's the truth. People deserve to know the truth."

"People deserve to believe what they want, June. Not everyone is obsessed with truth. Some people like their illusions." Connor shrugged and sulked off to class.

Great. Now June had alienated herself from her dad, her crush, and her BFF.

The school PA system crackled to life. "Juniper Szmydt, please report to the principal's office. Juniper Szmydt to the principal's office."

Of course, this was met with a chorus of "oooohs" from all the students near her in the halls, but June honestly didn't give a damn. The day couldn't get any worse.

Finding herself again outside the principal's office, June wasn't even nervous, just bored... ready to get this over with. Racking her brain about how Reverend LaChance, drunken bachelor man-of-God, would benefit from Vernon Carlisle's death, she absentmindedly thumbed the nonsense carved into the pew's arms.

She had to find out who was in this poker game. How high were the stakes? Would LaChance help kill a man over money? Her fingers traced the carved vandalism. And if LaChance was driving up the hill, whoever was driving the truck must have been the shooter. Did that exonerate LaChance?

She squinted while covering up the carving with her thumb, and the symbol seemed to change, like an optical illusion. But when she moved her hand, the carving went back to scrawled gibberish. The vandalism on the wooden pew is changing. But that's impossible.

With her blood rushing and a queasy curiosity egging her on, June covered the vandalism and closed one eye then slid her hand back, revealing the edge of a circle with points within, like a star of David, only skinnier...

"Ms. Szmydt?" Ms. Housler, the curt woman, said so suddenly, it made June jump. When she looked back down, the symbol scratched in the wood was just doodled loops. Funny. That was not the star within a circle she'd just been looking at.

"Ms. Szmydt?" Housler was losing her patience.

With a big sigh, June pouted all the way into the office, then froze when she saw who was inside. Dad... sitting in one of the chairs facing the desk. His leg bounced, and he flexed his jaw rhythmically, though he didn't turn to look at her. Whatever this was, it was serious. Her body went cold and clammy, her stomach clenched, ready to blow, and she swallowed back hard. Suddenly, June was on the verge of tears and she hated her reaction to the sight of him.

"Juniper," he said.

"Father," she replied coldly.

"Have a seat, Ms. Szmydt," the old Bernie Sanders-looking principal said, gesturing.

June slumped in the chair, feeling awfully small in the office, surrounded by disappointed adults.

Principal Donnelly sat on the corner of his cheap plastic desk, almost knocking over the V of the state and American flags, folding his arms and furrowing a brow. Everyone was scowling, but the principal was playing the part of the especially bad cop. Lowering his tone, he said, "Ms. Szmydt, I'm only going to ask this once. Where are they?"

"Who?" June peeped, burning under so much laser-focused attention.

"Stealing school property is serious business," the principal's voice dropped lower and lower each time he spoke.

Housler, standing behind June, joined in as the good cop, pleading softly, "If you return the stolen property, Principal Donnelly has agreed not to press charges."

June was taken aback. "Press charges?"

They were serious. Even Dad's face was unmoved, now glaring at her. Getting sent to the office again, June had anticipated getting in trouble, maybe even arrested for misleading the lieutenant governor's office. She didn't have a clue what this was about. But as always, there was a feeling that the more she talked, the deeper the trouble she was in. "I didn't do anything."

Principal Donnelly said, "The sooner you admit it, the sooner all of this will be over."

"Admit what?"

Though sitting in the wooden chair next to her, Dad seemed far away on the other side of some interrogation table. His big brick-like fist came down on the chair's arm. "Young lady, don't be a smartass. Just tell them whatever you did."

"I'm not being a smartass!" she pleaded to Dad.

"Language, Ms. Szmydt," chided Housler.

They were coming at June from all directions. She was trapped. "I don't know what you think I stole."

With a shrug of defeat, Principal Donnelly said, "Then I have no option but to bring the sheriff in."

June didn't know what to say. She looked down at the floor of the principal's office for what felt like forever.

"I mean it. I'll call Sheriff Marrock." Getting up and rounding his desk, Principal Donnelly picked up his phone.

"Okay," she squeaked, at a loss for words. She wasn't really calling his bluff since June had no idea what she'd done.

Dad bubbled over. "Juniper Laurel!"

Hearing him bark at her like that elicited a physical reaction June beyond her control. Her teeth set, her stomach clenched, and fighting her tears suddenly became a losing battle. Eyes burning holes into the office floor, her voice failed her, creaking out the words, "No matter what I say, I'm screwed."

"Young lady..." Dad got to his feet.

June flinched. She genuinely didn't know what he was going to do, and it terrified her.

"Please, Mr. Szmydt." Principal Donnelly stood to regain control of the situation. "Alright, June, you can go back to class. If Sheriff Marrock needs to see you, you'll be contacted."

On the way out of the room, June couldn't look at her father. Things had been rough; he was angry with her, frustrated with her, had disciplined her for the first time she remembered. But now he'd betrayed her. He'd turned his back on Team Szmydt. Despite constantly trolling Dad, ever since Mom died, it had been the Szmydts against the world. Against Miridical, at least. But not anymore. Now, he was just another adult who didn't believe her and assumed the worst. Now, she was alone, kicked off of Team Szmydt.

####

Sometimes when Connor spoke, June wished she were just alone.

"So New Salem's colors are yellow and black, and of course I look like shit in yellow, and definitely won't dye my hair that. And I don't want to dye by hair Basic AF Black-"

He hadn't shut up the whole walk home. She should be happy he was still talking to her after their blow-up in the cafeteria, but June was too numb to muster gratitude. Zoned out, hugging a stack of books to her chest, June hadn't said anything. She hadn't said anything about being called to the office, or the most recent skirmish with Dad, or even about their beef at lunch. June hadn't even looked up to the scene of the murder to check the artillery angle as they through the square.

"Like sheer white, like mother-of-dragons white, then dye the tips for events like homecoming, or, like, big games-"

"Connor, I really just can't right now."

"Can't what?"

"I'm just... exhausted, you know? I think I need to be alone for a sec."

"Well... you're grounded, you're alone all night. Can't I walk my BFF home from school?"

"Normally, yes, just... give me the night off today, if you don't mind."

"Okay. You're not about to go do something stupid investigating the murder, are you?"

"Connor..." She was about to let into him, but she was too tired. She shrugged and shook her head. "No. I just need a minute."

"Text me if you need anything, I guess?" Connor pulled her in for a hug, something the two rarely did. She felt his cold, bony embrace, comforted by the fact that he was there for her, even when she didn't want him to be.

As she walked alone through the town square, past the old brick post office and the stucco pharmacy, she couldn't help but think that Connor was the perfect friend. Not many kids were out at Miridical Prep. He had experience with bullies at school, and when the whole town laughed at Dad, and by association, her, he'd stuck by her. To this day, he was the only student at Miridical Prep who would sit next to her at lunch.

But, per usual, June pushed everyone away, probably when she needed them most.

"Psst! Juniper!" The hedges by the town hall rattled and whispered.

If she was about to get visited by a burning bush, June was going to take the rest of the week, maybe school year, off. Upon a closer look, someone was inside the bush, exposing the arm of an expensive red puffy coat. Chelsea.

"No way," June hissed and hurried her step away from the girl in the shrubbery.

"I promise I'll leave you alone forever if you just listen to me!"

Stopping in her tracks, June considered this. Chelsea had committed social suicide by ratting out Hailey to Principal Donnelly, now relegated to sitting by herself at lunch and study hall for the rest of the school year, if not until graduation. In fact, June had the honor of only being second-to-last place when picking volleyball teams in PE, thanks to Chelsea's fall from grace.

Reluctantly, June decided to hear the former mean girl out. Chelsea had thrown away her social standing to stand up for her, even though she got that social standing by being shitty. June amped up her not-feeling-it face.

"What do you want, pervert?" she snapped.

"I wanted to give you this." Her leather gloved hand emerged from the bush, holding a brown paper bag. "And to say I'm sorry. For everything. You never have to talk to me again."

June rolled her eyes and snatched the bag. "Guh. You're so dramatic," she said, reaching in for the tea-saucer sized content within.

"Don't open it here! Don't let anyone see you with it!"

Gasping, June clutched the bag; this must have been the stolen contraband from the school. Was Chelsea setting her up? Was this a plot to get Chelsea back in good standing with the rich girls while June took the fall for theft?

"If anyone sees you with this," Chelsea said slowly, "I don't know what'll happen, but it won't be good."

Whatever it was, June was certain it wasn't worth the trouble it's given her today. "God, I can't wait until I'm at New Salem."

"June, there is no New Salem. They wouldn't let you go to another school; they won't let you out of their sight." At this point, Chelsea sounded paranoid or delusional.

"Wait, what? Who won't let me out of their sight?"

"Just go home, shut your windows, and then unwrap it. You'll want to take it out of the house, but no one can see you with it."

June knew she should shove it right back at Chelsea, that this was some setup. Or even if it wasn't, June couldn't get into any more trouble at school right now. But she was too curious. She had to know what all the excitement (bringing her dad to the principal's office?) was.

She held the bag in her hands and examined it. There was a box within. Flat. Heavy. June's curiosity was going to win this one. She sighed and glared daggers at Chelsea. "I swear to God, if this is a friendship bracelet, Blackstone, I'm going to slap you."

"It's... Blackstone," Chelsea said to June, as if to correct her, but the sudden Miridical accent muddled her words.

"That's what I said."

"Just go, Juniper. And goodbye." The gloved hand receded back into the bush.

Bullshit. An entire life of being Jewish steeled June against pathetically lesser attempts at guilt. She didn't buy Chelsea's attempt at martyrdom for one second and wasn't going to let her blond bully have the last word. Peeling back stubborn branches and dense waxen leaves, June pushed open the bush.

But Chelsea wasn't there. June searched about the town hall landscaping, but there was no place Chelsea could have hidden or run off. Reality seemed to spin around June, or at least shift under feet a little with a dash of vertigo. Something was going and understanding was right in June's periphery, but she never quite saw what was going on.

Shaking off the dizzy feeling, June clutched the paper bag and speed-walked home, repeating under her breath to herself, "Fuck my life. Fuck my life. Fuck my life."

####

As the night got dark, the temperature really dropped for the first time that autumn. Her phone said forty degrees, but the sting on June's cheeks said below freezing. She hopped from one foot to the next as Zippy nosed about the backyard, searching for the perfect spot.

"I really don't see Mrs. Carlisle as the gunner type and that little maid isn't handling artillery that big. Then the question becomes, is there a connection between the maid and someone who might have been operating the gun for her? Like Evens! Come on, Zip, just pop a squat!"

So as not to feel completely friendless, June had taken to voicing Zippy's half of conversations with her, a voice somewhere between baby talk and Eric Cartman. "No, Mama, I have to find the perfect patch to sniff while I relieve myself. Like how you find the best article to read on your phone."

"I guess that makes sense. The more I think about it, the more I wonder if all of this is about owing someone money from a poker game. Money and love are the most common motives."

"Oh! This looks like a good spot! Oh man, shouldn't have eaten all that dog food... oooh, that feels better. Now pick it up my poop, Mama!"

Disposing of the waste in their trash can, June and her dog headed back inside. Her eyes lingered on the tall wooden kitchen table. In the pool of the little 1970s hanging chandelier, next to the napkin holder June had made at camp, was the package from Chelsea. Just thinking of the girl stopped June mid step. Once Chelsea had run with the pack that teased her mercilessly every day at school, but then June would go home and fantasize about her skin, hair, and touch during private time behind her locked bedroom door. But now the Blackstone girl was a desperate stalker showering her obsession with gifts... who somehow disappeared from bushes at will.

Dad texted to let her know he was working late, and a slight pang hit her in the feelings. Working late was something that used to guarantee June riding along as a sidekick. Of course, now that it was too late, she wished she'd appreciated her time with Dad instead of burying her nose in her phone and flinging smartass comments from the backseat.

After printing off the satellite view of Miridical, zoomed in on the space between the square and the spot of the murder, June cut and bent flashcards, estimating the heights of everything. But her memory wasn't perfect, and June couldn't think of the number of library steps or the height of the walkway on the roof of the police station.

There was satisfaction seeing the town so small. All of her problems, everything that made her life feel so out of control, existed within the parameters of this town. It all seemed so manageable at this scale. When the crude-if-not-accurate model of the town was finished, June examined it, lifting and turning, looking up at the hill, looking down from it, even removing the card tabs representing building facades to see from all angles.

When she removed the library to look over the center of the town square, her face dropped. It was too high for any truck. Unless she had the height of the burnt trajectory off, which she didn't think she did, but she wasn't sure. Sucking against her outstanding canine tooth, making a wet whistling noise, June could only surmise that the shots came from the front landing of the library. Surely that wasn't right...

Her phone vibrated and June realized she'd been staring at the paper model with her mouth open. How long had she been working on this? She still had homework to do. Her phone vibrated again. Dad texting. Don't wait up.

She left Paper Miridical in her closet and paced the house.

Ever since moving into this cramped house in this cramped town, June never felt at home. No matter the lengths Dad went to buy and build and paint it, June always felt trapped in the brown house with the vertical siding... caged. And she couldn't stop thinking of Dad, out and about, running errands for the mayor, maybe helping with the investigation, maybe even getting his own hands dirty, doing some dirty work. The mayor was still on the list of suspects. Was he the one who coerced the maid into murder?

But there was nothing for June to do. She couldn't go out, ask questions, double-check the height of the library stairs or the trajectory of the burns. Helpless. Cabin fever was striking, and June felt antsy. She dug into some salt and vinegar Utz chips. Connor wasn't heading over or he'd get grounded if Dad came home early and busted them, but she had to do something. The world around her was moving, and if she didn't make a move, too, she'd miss learning its secrets.

Almost as if afraid of what June was thinking of doing, Zippy regarded her with a whine and tilted his head. "Don't do it, Mama."

The stolen contraband in the paper bag called to her from the kitchen table, its sweet siren song of forbidden love. She wasn't supposed to have it. Dad had been called into school to help find it, and Chelsea had been adamant about keeping it a secret. What was it?

June couldn't help herself. "Don't give me that, Zips. You know, all I wanted to do was investigate a murder. But all I got was trouble. So let's give trouble a try."

Giving in to the urge, she rushed over to the kitchen table, Zippy chasing her, playfully hopping about and sliding on the hardwood floor. Gripping the parcel, June sat at the head of the table and tore into the brown paper. Within the bag was a flat square box, about five inches by five inches, not even an inch thick, stamped "Miridical Prep Academy", but the words underneath were smudged. Not smudged, just maybe printed over. "Science and Science Lab."

Science and Science lab? That's a pretty odd name. She knew where MPA's STEM labs were, but no classrooms on that hall were marked "Science and Science Lab." She opened it, and out slid a round mirror. That's it? A mirror? That's what everyone freaked out over? Holding it in her hand, she examined the plastic backing, which had a label stamped identically to the box. "Miridical Prep Academy Science and Science Lab."

Looking in the mirror, June could barely see herself. Either it was dusty or had some filter on it, obscuring her face with kind of a brownish mist.

Zippy whined at the front door. Leaning back in her kitchen chair, she saw straight to the foyer where the dog seemed a bit scared, cowering by the house entrance.

"Why are you nervous, Zip?"

She answered in his play-voice, "I don't know."

Turning her attention back to the mirror, she said, "Well, don't be a scaredy ca-" In the reflection of the mirror, June saw behind her. Taking up the bulk of the hallway, an enormous beast, glistening white fangs, stared back with six red eyes. A monster.

With a scream, June's heart skipped, her hands jerked, she fell back in the chair, tumbling to the floor. The mirror landed next to her with a high pitched tinkle and the quick slicing noise of cracked glass. Instinctively, June scrambled to all fours, body tense, chest frozen, eyes wild, and scouring the hallway for the giant monster she'd seen.

But the only thing in the house was Zippy, sitting at the front door, ears submissively slanted back.

"What the hell was that?" an out-of-breath June asked the dog, not in a talking-to-herself-with-silly-voices way, but more of an I-just-saw-a-giant-creature-so-what-are-you-going-to-do-to-protect-this-house-dog kind of way.

In answer, Zippy just tilted his head and whimpered. Whatever that beast was, the little dog must not have seen it.

Holding her breath, June listened for any noise in the house. Whatever that thing was, it was dead silent. But it had to still be here; nothing was fast enough to run out without her hearing. For a moment, she thought about the strange hopping wildcat, but the six-eyed... thing she had seen in the mirror was no cat.

Her hands shook as they reached for the overturned mirror. Lifting the plastic backing, triangle shards fell to the floor. Eyes pinned to the reflective surface, she swallowed hard against a throat suddenly desert-dry. Daintily, she pinched a fat triangle of mirror, careful of the edges, from the ground. In the reflection, June saw herself, again her face dustily obscured. Then she turned the reflective fang to see a slice of the kitchen floor, tilted it to the kitchen ceiling, and finally leveled it to the front door.

There was the beast.

June gasped, hot sweat forming on her forehead and armpits.

Sitting on its haunches, it was at least four feet tall, not counting the ridge running down its back of spines, four rows of blood-red eyes, dripping teeth so long, they showed through the beast's closed mouth. Nightmare incarnate in the Szmydt foyer.

Tears pulling at the corner of her eyes, June's mouth spread as she stifled a sob. She mentally prepared herself to die from an attack by whatever this thing was.

Then she heard the familiar whimper of Zippy, and the beast opened its cavernous maw, a thick black tongue unfurling and hanging out. It panted, its eyes (all of them) looking at her expectantly.

June gasped. "Zip?!"

Hearing the name, the beast's tall black-tufted ears came forward to hang at the sides of its enormous jaws, a serpentine black tail with a barb at the end wagging happily. Its head tilted. Just. Like. Zippy's.

June looked back at the front door, seeing the tiny black dog she'd known for the past few days. But then, through the mirror, it was a monstrous beast with fanged jaws, prehensile tail, and rows upon rows of red eyes. But they were both Zippy.

"What. The. Fuck."

Chapter Nine: October 30th, night

June: Hey, weird question, do you have Chelsea's number

Connor: Oh, hey June, I'm good.

And yes, I accept your heartfelt apology for pushing away my friendship.

J: Sorry, life is srsly fucked rn. Thnx for giving me space today

C: You're a jerk

But I love you

J: So...

J: Do you have her #?

C: Y wd I have that dilly bitch's #?

J: I don't know! Who would?

C: Kris maybe? They were friends over the summer.

J: Kris! Thnx!

June: Hey Kris, long time no talk

Kris: whadoyouwant

J: Was wondering if you had Chelsea's #?

K: ... why?

J: That bitch took my Chem notebook and I need it.

K: U take hers?

J: Her what?

K: Chem notebook

J: Yeah?

K: Write "I luv 2 bang my toothbrush" in the corner of every page

J: WHAT?!

K: Do it and I'll give you her #

J: WHY?!!!?

K: No reason

J: Um…

ok

K: 678.555.6906

J: Thnx

K: Write it on each and every page.

J: K Thnx, Kris.

June: WTF did you give me?!

Chelsea: Who is this?

Juniper?

J: WTF is this?

C: A stupid mirror

J: I know it's a mirror. What kind?

C: A stupid mirror

J: WHAT KIND OF STUPID MIRROR, Chelsea?!

C: Look thru the mirror at this text

Grabbing the fanged shard of mirror, June held her phone screen up to it and through the reflection, sure enough, Chelsea's message read clear as day, though backwards, A Scrying Mirror.

J: What's a scrying mirror?

C: A mirror that reveals sexual arousal, stupid.

J: WHAT?!

C: Look thru the mirror

And then again, in the reflection of the mirror that was revealing secrets to her for the very first time, she read something else, A mirror that reveals magic, stupid.

Magic? The thought distracted June, and she squeezed the shard in her hand, slicing a line across the heel of her hand. She cut shallow, and the line stayed thin and red for many moments before trickling blood. June wrapped her hand in a napkin from the homemade holder.

J: WTF is going on?

C: I can explain. Can I come over?

J: Is this some weird plan to bang me with your toothbrush?

C: What?

J: What?

C: Whyd you say that?

J: Fine, you can come over, but not for long, I'm grounded.

C: Cool. What's yr address?

J: 18 Oak

At the thought of being in her house alone with Chelsea Goddamn Blackstone, June's heart fluttered a little while other body parts fluttered a lot. And frankly, all this fluttering was pissing her off. Suddenly, Zippy's woof boomed, loud enough to make her jump. The little dog was going nuts, barking over and over while pacing in front of the dining room wall.

Barely visible, a line formed, dark like a shadow, running down the wall as if some invisible person were drawing it. No, not a shadow. Upon closer inspection, June realized it was water. A slow trickle. Several streams only a few inches wide dribbled down slowly, thicker than water, each stream widening into a pour, and the pouring streams connecting until June had a genuine water feature - a thick liquid waterfall from out of nowhere on their dining room wall. But for reasons unbeknownst to her, June didn't panic. Instead, studying the cascade, fascinated by it, sucking on her outstanding canine tooth before turning away from the wall entirely to retrieve the scrying mirror shard.

Through the scrying mirror, she saw something much different. As if the wall were injured, a horizontal slash a little higher than eye level bled, crimson running down the wall. Her stomach turned. Zippy continued barking. Cold jolts of dread coursed through her with each bark.

June stood behind the dog-beast, fear simultaneously making her antsy legs shift while weighing her feet down beyond any hope of running away. From within the wet red wall, something bulged, a protuberance pushing out from the sopping wet surface. It reached straight out, a toe leading a foot attached to a soaked red leg extending from the wall. The impossible beauty or beautiful impossibility of a slender nude leg stepping out of a bloodstained wall got June feeling light-headed.

As the room spun, the slick foot touched the floor. The rest of a body followed, a thin female figure, drenched from head to toe, climbing through the wet spot on the wall, until she stood in the Szmydt dining room. Still behind Zippy, June stood paralyzed in fear, her grip on the fang of mirror shaking.

The figure swayed and tipped over, landing on her hands and knees. From the viscera-laden face, pale green eyes opened. Chelsea's eyes. She looked up at June through the slash of mirror and asked weakly, "Do you have any OJ or maybe some milk?"

After she washed up and toweled off to reveal black yoga pants and sports bra, Chelsea still held a dark crust of dried blood in her pulled-back hair and settled around her eyes, nose, and mouth, exaggerating her features like dramatic lighting. It was tough for June to keep eye contact with such a striking version of Chelsea Blackstone. She smelled like rusty honeysuckles.

"My name's not Blackstone." Chelsea let out an annoyed growl as she finished off the gallon of juice. June found Chelsea's caloric consumption positively adorable but remained on high alert about the feelings she had for Chelsea, Whatever-her-name-was while alone unchaperoned in her house. Chelsea dipped her head to catch June's eyes while taking her hand. June's breath caught, but Chelsea only took the mirror slice from her, asking, "Do you have something to write with?"

Putting aside her annoying bodily flutters, June grabbed her Civics notebook and handed a pen to Chelsea, who wrote, "Chelsea Blackstone gets places by walking." And even though she had perfect, bubbly-bouncy penmanship, certain phrases had the same smudged, blurred look of the Library's Miridical map.

Chelsea said, "Now read it through the mirror."

Carefully picking up the big shard, June read the reflected words that appeared backwards. Once she wrapped her brain around the reversed letters and the odd blurry beige tone the reflection had, June could make out the message in the nice looping handwriting. "Chelsea Bloodstone travels through blood portals by cutting herself."

"Holy shit, Chelsea," June blurted out, as much to the girl as she to herself. Through the dizzying jumble of her thoughts, she managed to ask, "WTF?"

Chelsea wrote on the line below, "Miridical is a safe community, everyone in it is a citizen, and all of them are lying to you."

Translated through the mirror: Miridical is a safe haven for magic, everyone in it is magical, and all of them are lying to you.

Chelsea continued. You are cursed. Blindfolded. Some call it "The Blind Man," but that's ableist + sexist. Blindfold keeps you ignorant so the Elders can use your powers. According to Miridical legend, you're the most powerful person in town.

Reality began tilting once again beneath June. It was all too much, all too weird. Her breath quickened, and the room got hot. She took off her sweater, stripping to a tank top. With a sudden flood of restlessness, she paced about the room, running her hands over her face and forehead, sucking on her teeth as she made sense of it all.

Magic was real? That she could believe after seeing Zippy for whatever he really was. But she was the most powerful person in town? What did that even mean? And there was that word again - blindfolded. Did that mean people Dad overheard in the town hall thought she was somehow involved in the murder of Vernon Carlisle?

June felt like she was going to be sick.

"Most powerful?"

They say your magic powers the entire town.

She didn't feel powerful. She felt stupid. Embarrassed. Like the butt of some big joke that the entire town was in on, thousands of people laughing behind her back while pretending to be something else to her face. TBH, they all laughed in her face, too. Was it possible that literally everyone in town was in on this?

"My dad?"

Chelsea shrugged.

But that didn't make sense. Dad didn't have the garbled Miridical accent. Based on his recent behavior, he was probably also under some sort of enchantment, similar to June. "If I'm blindfolded, he definitely is."

Everyone knows the Elders cursed someone with the blindfold. Maybe to keep their secret, they cursed you both?

"Who are the Elders?"

Whoever runs Miridical.

Someone ran the town? Like a magical mafia? This wasn't happening. The room was spinning, and June breathed deliberately through her nose.

"And why didn't they just tell us they needed us to power the town?"

Chelsea shrugged.

"And why wouldn't Connor say anything to me about this?" Despite deep breaths, June was losing control.

Chelsea cringed and shrugged. June had been steadily raising her voice as she stamped about the room losing attempts to hold back tears. But Chelsea wouldn't let her hold back, pulling June's head into her chest, rubbing her back and petting her hair while June sobbed and sobbed, reality no longer tilting or spinning, but crumbling. Even with her nose starting to run with her ugly crying, June smelled rust.

Through the scrying mirror, June saw the cloth clearly, sepia-colored lace that hung over her head like a 19th-century bride. When she turned her face to either direction, the veil followed, swinging here and there. But when she brought her hands to her face, her touch would not disturb it.

"What is it, exactly?"

"It's a," across the tall kitchen table, Chelsea pointed to the word 'Magic' in the notebook before finishing, "veil. Leaving you unable to..." Chelsea wrote and pointed to the words see or hear, then again the word Magic.

It was a slow form of communication but was better than Chelsea writing every single word out and June reading backwards.

"Why hasn't anyone mentioned this before?"

Chelsea shrugged. "People have all kinds of wards and protective spells over them. Chad Johnson has the ghost of a hawk following after him, everywhere he goes."

"Who put it there?" June asked.

"The hawk?"

June almost got mad, but appreciated the little laugh. "No, the veil."

"I don't know," Chelsea said with earnest sadness.

"And," June chewed her lip and looked away before asking, "what you were doing in the woods, with my band-aids? That was blood magic?"

"Yes," Chelsea answered, "Kind of like..." She wrote, Summoning spell.

"Summoning? I guess it worked then."

"My family's like super-powerful in..." Blood magic.

"Why were you summoning me?"

Shrugging, Chelsea's face went to an adorable pursed smirk. Her voice caught as she spoke, "To apologize?"

"For what?"

The tears shook in the fair girl's eyes. "For dragging you all the time."

Again, June couldn't look across the dining room table at her. "Because you liked me?"

Chelsea looked down at the pieces of the scrying mirror and nodded yes with a sniff. A sudden rush hit June, like she wanted to scream or jump all over Chelsea, but instead June tensed, clenched her teeth, and held so tight to those feeling all that came out were barely a tear and a high pitched squealing sigh. Immediately clearing her throat, June swerved back to the original line of questioning. "So, instead of all the magic everywhere, Dad and I only hear and see stuff that's easier for muggle brains to process, right?"

"Right."

"And everyone in town knows?"

"I don't think anybody but the Elders know. Every kid growing up in Miridical has heard rumors about the blindfolded man who isn't allowed in the library, but it's just rumors. Legend. I didn't know how it worked until tonight."

"Even Connor?"

"Why have I never seen you with this Connor?" Chelsea asked, maybe a tinge of jealousy creeping into her voice. June thought about it and had never seen Connor and Chelsea talk before. They may not have had any classes together either.

But she and Connor were so tight, how did he not notice she didn't see magic? That she didn't know Chelsea was a blood witch and Zippy was a Hell beast and whoever else was actually whatever else they were. He had to've known. He had to have been in on the big joke at June's expense.

With a sharp exhalation out her nose, June moved him from her mind and focused on getting more info. "Do you know how to lift it?"

"The veil?"

"Yeah, the spell."

"No."

"I thought you said your family was powerful." June teased.

"We are." Then Chelsea's eyes lit up. "My mom is! Do you have a sharp kitchen knife?"

June grabbed a thin-bladed filet knife, then was horrified by what came next. Starting at the inside of her thumbnail, Chelsea sliced along the webbing of her hand up to the edge of her pointer fingernail. Keeping her hand in an L shape, she touched her thumb to her lips, and finger to her ear.

"Lauren Westminster... Blackstone," she whispered, then changed back to her normal bubbly tone to speak into her hand like a phone, "Hey, Mom!"

June was confused at the sight. But through the scrying mirror, Chelsea's blood-gloved hand, shaped like an L against her face like a phone, emitted a strange ray of light straight to...no through the south wall of the Szmydt home, like the ghost of the bat signal. A blood magic phone call, international, no roaming.

"I'm good, how are you? How's... Mexico City? Yeah, I'm looking for a... recipe," The words were garbled through June's cursed veil. "To lift a... lasagna... okay. Okay. And where can we find one of those? Still in Miridical. Wow, thanks Mom, that's perfect."

Chelsea sighed and rolled her eyes, a normal teen chatting with a parent. "Yes ma'am. Yes, ma'am. All A's and a B in Chemistry. Yes ma'am, I'll work on it. Okay, love you too, bai!"

"Your mom's in Mexico City? I thought she drove you to school every day?"

Chelsea wrote some more in the notebook, taking a moment

to think of the right word, her pale green eyes lost off to the side long enough for June to catch herself staring slack-jawed with just a touch of drool. Then Bloodstone said and gestured to her written word. "No, she's in the..." Realm of the Dead. "The lady that drives me to school every day is..." Chelsea pointed to the words she'd spent so long searching for: Hologram Version. "Kinda. If that makes sense?"

"Holograms are blood magic?"

"They're any kind of..." Magic.

"So what'd she say?"

Grabbing the pen with her bloody hand, she scrawled on the paper, Witchdoctor, then said, "We need to see him."

"Where can we find him?" June asked.

"The north side of the hill. At the Bonhomme's."

"Shit, my dad's there now. Can you blood magic travel us there or whatever?"

"Tonight?"

"Yes?"

"I guess, but that's a lot of blood." Chelsea looked away, sucking at her lower lip.

June caught herself staring at Chelsea's mouth, swiveling to rest her legs on Chelsea's chair.

"Oh. Is it too much? I don't really know how it works. Do you, like, need a minute?"

"A minute? Are you kidding me?"

"What? I don't know how it works!"

"June, does it have to be tonight? I mean, I just got here." With a flash of a smile, Chelsea leaned in. Below the table, her calf rested on June's. Even through two pairs of jeans, June felt the heat off Chels's leg.

June felt that rush again, that burst of energy she could barely contain. She didn't want to ruin the moment, but June had her priorities. In a low whisper, she leaned in, closing much of the distance between them and said, "The first forty-eight ends in six hours. If we don't have a lead, a clue, or a suspect in the first forty-eight hours, we won't solve the murder." June was not good at talking sexy and immediately felt awkward, considering retreating from being so close to Chelsea's sweet-smelling face.

"The murder? Vernon Carlisle's murder? June, how can you even think about that when you can't even..." Chelsea raised her voice, but it all came out garbled to June, except when Chelsea repeated the phrases, "your veil" and "your life."

June froze up, immediately got to her feet and pacing. She was so sick of things hidden from her! She was finally starting to see what was actually going on in the world around her, and through a stupid freaking mirror! June wanted to punch something.

"It's too much, okay! I don't want to think about it. And this may sound dumb or paranoid, and I don't know how, but I know it's all connected. The murder, the bullet, the curse on Dad and me, LaChance's car accident. Hell, maybe even Zippy and the watchdog note."

The dog tilted his head as the girls looked down at him. His true self was still a bit shocking; June preferred looking at him through the veil.

"Humblebrag, but I'm the only one in this town that can figure it out. And for reasons I have yet to figure out, I'm the only one who wants to find out the truth."

"What if the truth gets you killed?"

Flinching at the thought June squawked, "Jesus, Chelsea. Take it down a notch, okay? If there's a secret that got Vernon

Carlisle killed, then that secret could take another life. If someone else has to die, we might as well get the truth out of it."

"That's hot."

Immediately, June burned with embarrassment. But a fantastic, invigorating embarrassment. "Shut up."

"Okay, give me like twenty minutes? Is there any meat in the house I can eat?"

"I can make roast beef sandwiches?"

"Yes. Do that."

####

After they ate, or rather, after Chelsea finished eating everything in the fridge as June silently debated whether it was a fetish to consider Chelsea's appetite attractive, Chelsea figured out a plan to use the scrying mirror in public without drawing attention. "I need a hot-glue gun and a watch you don't mind ruining."

June wasn't sure exactly how well-off the Black-Bloodstones were, but they were far better off than the Szmydts. "I don't have a watch I can ruin, Crazy Rich Caucasian."

"Well, anything that fits on your wrist that looks like a watch."

After she thought about it for a sec, a giggle bubbled up from within June, growing louder and louder, shaking her shoulders. She laughed until tears came out the sides of her eyes and June turned bright red while she clamped both hands over her mouth.

"What is it?"

Giggling so hard, June could barely say, "From camp. An old

friendship bracelet."

They laughed together for a while, then set to work, gluing a round shard piece to the old beaded piece of jewelry so the scrying mirror, or at least the salvaged triangular pieces, could pass for the face of a watch.

Masking her pain, Chelsea sliced her palm with the thin blade. Deep. As blood wept from the wound, her hand went out to the drying stain on the Szmydt dining room wall. Whispering sacred words under her breath, she wet the circle on the wall and took June's hand, then they stepped through the stargate portal of blood.

Immediately, June was frozen to the bone. They were outside and June was in a light sweater and a tank top wet with blood. But at least not covered like Chelsea was. In the pitch dark, June couldn't see anything, holding a hand out in front of her like some kind of mummy or zombie to make sure she didn't walk into anything. All she felt, besides Chelsea's clasped hand, was drifting freezing rain.

"I can't see anything," she whispered to Chelsea.

A gruff, low voice with an odd accent answered them, "You're trespassing on private property, and y'all picked the wrong clan to fuck with."

Any hairs on June that weren't already standing from the cold suddenly prickled, and June tensed her hold on Chelsea.

Finally, June's eyes did adjust, and she saw the hooded man pointing a machete at them.

Chapter Ten: October 30th, still night

A blade the size of her arm pointed at her throat really put a damper on June's first outing with Chelsea, which while technically a date, had already involved alone time unchaperoned, about three meals worth of food, and hand-holding. But instead of playing it cool, June was digging her fingers into Chelsea's arm.

The hooded black guy's brandished blade didn't have the same effect on the Bloodstone girl. "We're very sorry to bother you, sir," Chelsea's perky polite voice gushed, "we were just looking to speak with the doctor."

"What you want with the... doctor?" His accent shifted on the last word as the machete pointed at the girls, eliciting a whimper from June.

"This young lady would like to take off her... hat."

"You the Szmydt girl, eh?" He waved the blade again, which was when June noticed it was no blade at all; he'd threatened them with a flashlight. A big one that wouldn't stab her but could easily bludgeon her to death. Somehow, she was freezing in the icy grip of fear while burning up in the heat of his angry attention. She stammered, "Y-yes, sir."

"And you don't anything about... chicken?"

The sentence took her aback, June had forgotten about misunderstanding magic without the aid of the scrying watch, as the situation had taken her mind off the blindfold and the Miridical accent. "Chicken, sir?"

"Not chicken... chicken."

Chelsea said flatly, "She can't hear that word, my guy."

"So that's how it works." The young man scratched his chin with the tip of his flashlight. June flinched at the sandpaper-grinding sound. "Come this way. She will want to see this."

As they followed their guide in the dark clutching to each other as they stepped carefully, June snuck a peek of the mirror on her wrist. The man walking ahead was illuminated by green and yellow geometric symbols floating over his head. As his dreadlocks swayed with his gait, another symbol, this one bright white, peaked through from the center of his back. A living tattoo, a heart filled with diverging ocean waves flowing in time to his heartbeat, all of it topped and footed with filigree. It looked like some intricate centerpiece to a wrought-iron gate. Soon, June found herself bringing the mirror close to her face to glimpse the details of all the symbols.

Her breath caught when she saw the sky, a beautiful, swirling, orbiting galaxy of stars, like an intricately choreographed dance of multi-colored fireflies. Only it wasn't up in the sky; it was within the woods, barely taller than eye level, right where their broad-shouldered guide was taking them. As they approached, she realized the pinpoints of light were icons circling a plain handmade woodshed within the evergreen trees. A chandelier of symbols, smaller than the ones hovering over the man in front of them, shone much brighter, so bright that once too close, June had to look away from her scrying watch.

"Beautiful, isn't it?" Chelsea asked.

"It's something," June kept her voice down, uncertain.

The inside of the shed smelled of boozey breath and rot. An electric camping lantern sat in the corner casting a hazy blue light over everything. The contents of the room sat frozen in still life, saws dangling from rusty nails, a dusty countertop flanked with clamps set far enough to restrain either of them, a half-empty bottle of Smirnoff. The only movement was the constant buzzing of flies through the air, from the countertop up to a trash can and onto the body in the rocking chair.

Noticing the body in the rocking chair, June gasped, her intake of air drowned out by the creaking of the rusty door hinges as they swung to close them in. For a moment, June thought the broad-shouldered man brought them there to kill them, to add to the body already here. The corpse was laid back, head lolled to the right, snow-white hair twisted into beaded braids and dreadlocks. It wore ripped jeans and torn long johns, and June spied skinny ribs in the holes of the shirt.

"You bring that evil glass onto holy land, cracker," the corpse, or the woman who was practically a corpse, wheezed.

She spoke with the weight of importance, and June felt the air of the room bearing down on her, mouth running dry as she licked her quivering lips, stuttering to string together words. She needed to say something respectful but firm, a way to gain trust and state her right to be there, but most of all, something that wouldn't get her killed.

Before June spoke, Chelsea said to the ancient woman, "Hey, she's actually Jewish, so I don't think cracker's the right term."

"Silence," the broad-shouldered man bellowed behind them.

"Calm yourself, Blaise," the old woman's voice creaked. "Why risk yourselves coming here, cracker girls, playing...

dress-up and flirting with danger?"

The scrying mirror didn't make the people of Miridical any easier for June to hear.

"You got something wrong with your eyes, too? We're here," Chelsea spoke defiantly, "to remove her... ingrown hair."

"Chels!" June whispered, but whatever trouble Chelsea's mouth was going to get them into was inevitable. And June knew that the blindfold had garbled the word Bloodstone meant: curse.

The old woman grunted as she sat up, scooting forward in her chair, one arm on her thigh, the other lying limply at her side. The broad-shouldered man went to her and grabbed beneath an armpit to help her up, but the old woman swatted him away then addressed the girls. "Now tell me why would I remove an... ingrown hair... when I don't know why it was put there in the first place?"

June recognized her melodic accent as French, but the dancing quality of her words made them no less scary. Swallowing back fear, June spoke, her voice cracking, "I don't know why it's there, ma'am. But someone in this town put it there. And on my Dad, too."

"Ah yes, Papa Bear. He's at my ex-wife's house now, warding me off with salt and fire. But I am more afraid of the bear." She displayed few teeth in a smile.Or maybe she was baring her teeth in some animalistic ward-off-predators way. With a swift clawed hand, the old woman pinched June's chin, pushing her face this way and that, discerning eyes picking her apart. June's hairs had been on end since she walked in the shack, but being studied and looked over by that grin made her queasy.

"Rush job," the old woman said, shoving June's chin away. "It is an... ugly headpiece placed by an ignorant and conceited white... man. You, cracker, tell your friend through that evil glass."

Chelsea pulled out her smartphone, brightening the room considerably, and typed. Through her scrying watch, June read, It's a ghost veil placed by a crappy white wizard.

"Can you remove it?" June asked.

"Can? Can't? What does it matter if I don't want to?"

"Please," Chelsea said softly. "We'll do anything. Give you anything you want."

At her words, their guide crossed his arms and gave a sinister smile of his own.

"What could you have that we want?" the young man laughed.

June's eyes darted from him to the old woman. She didn't laugh with him.

"Enough, Blaise. Go get me a LeCroix."

Chelsea stifled a giggle.

"But, Sister Anne-"

"Go!"

Sulking, the broad-shouldered man exited the shack, staring down the girls on his way out. Averting her eyes, June looked down to her scrying watch to see the old woman as she truly was - bigger, heavier, luminous dread-locked hair floating about as if she were underwater, a black goddess in white halo. Her eyes glowed a solid white, and every trace of skin was covered in luminescent tattoos, some of the same symbols orbiting the shed. But her arms. Matching the one skinny flesh one, her left arm was made of grey smoke, like an arm-shaped glass vessel full of billowing clouds. When June looked up from the watch, she noticed the old woman's left arm wasn't feeble or weak; it was missing, leaving the one sleeve of her long johns dangling flacidly.

"If I help you, you must help us," she said in a sing-song tone that sounded like a warning - a creepy AF warning.

"Anything," Chelsea asserted. June nudged her, afraid of what the old woman would ask.

"You must free my boy," she said.

"Who's your boy?" Chelsea asked.

"My boy, the... doctor," her words garbled.

"The... doctor? We thought you were the... doctor?"

"No. I am but his hands."

"So who's the... doctor?"

"Jean Evens Bonhomme. Evens," the old woman stated.

Evens Bonhomme, law clerk for the township, was a Haitian witch doctor?

The information didn't faze Chelsea. "Free him from what?"

"Don't you know? They arrested Evens. For killing Vernon Carlisle."

Chelsea recited the plan. "We blood-travel into the jail cell, stay under the veil, throw it over Mr. Bonhomme-"

"Doctor," old woman Sister Anne corrected, then sipped her LeCroix.

"Throw the veil over Doctor Bonhomme and blood-travel back. Easy, breezey, beautiful."

"Only a fool would make a plan for the impossible and call it easy," the broad-shouldered Blaise said.

"Well, we've got a wild card," Chelsea said with a Cheshire smile. "If anything goes wrong, June calls in the Deputy Mayor and explains the whole thing is just a big misunderstanding."

But June was barely following the conversation. Once Sister Anne had removed her veil with the ghost of her arms, June saw a whole new world. It was like Dorothy walking into color, or Neo leaving the matrix. Or maybe it was just like doing a shit-ton of acid; June hadn't ever done hard drugs and was pretty sure she'd never need to if this was what the world was going to look like from now on.

Her skin, smudged with Chelsea's dried blood, glowed and crackled with light, and when she waved her hand about, light and starbursts trailed behind. Crusted, dried blood covered Chelsea, but she was still so beautiful, like a supermodel playing the part of Stephen King's Carrie. The inside of the woodshed was now bright, lit by the glowing auras of Blaise and Sister Anne. *How could Connor have kept this from me?*

"Juniper!" Chelsea barked, snapping her fingers in front of June's face. June blinked with a drunken euphoric look, seeing Chelsea's eyes sparkle now. Like, literally sparkle. Anime style.

"It's the magic," Sister Anne said gruffly. "She never seen it before."

"It's fucking annoying is what it is, Sister. You got another LeCroix?"

"We have pamplemousse and cola."

"Yuck, nevermind." Chels made a face.

"Dad," June said as the realization suddenly struck her. She blinked hard to focus her thoughts. "Can you take the blindfold-"

"Ghost veil."

"Ghost veil off my father's head?" June didn't understand why the same spells had different names depending on who she spoke to.

"The curses on your father are not so easily lifted."

"Curses? Plural? More than one?" This was getting over-whelming.

"More than I've ever seen. His blindfold is a chained veil, locked into place with the Papa Bear's own humanity. There is a trickster spell on him so that someone's whispers fill his mind. My boy cursed him with the evil eye."

"And what does that mean?" Chelsea asked.

"Unless you found the four to twelve wizards and witches who cursed him and convince them to undo their work, he shall not know of or control magic until the moment his life is extinguished."

Chelsea seemed annoyed by the answer. "Well, can't you use voodoo?"

"Evens is the witch doctor. I don't touch voodoo."

Chelsea's tone immediately shifted to conversational, a polite question asked by rote, "Oh, and what discipline do you practice?"

"I'm a level three Gardnerian cosmic witch." Sister Anne finished with a nod then added reassuringly, "Means I'm magic as all Hell, sweetie."

Blaise folded his thick, muscular arms, puffed out his broad chest, and said in swelling baritone, "I'm a level two Alexand–"

Sister Anne interrupted, "You ain't shit, Blaise."

Of course, Chelsea laughed, but June was still reeling, face somewhere between slack-jawed and blank. Not just all of the different magics and levels, but all the people involved, all of them had their hands on Dad. Cursed. Cursed like she'd been, with this gorgeous, unbelievable enchanted world all around, and instead to see and hear only lies. But cursed until he died? This was too much. She had to stop this. She had to stop them.

But none of it even made sense to June. It was like trying to solve a crime using only clues written in a different language. She needed help. "So, no one else is powerful enough to remove all the curses?"

"I don't think anyone is smart enough. At least, not with Carlisle gone. Why would anybody want to kill such a nice white man who made such good lemons squares?" Sister Anne shook her head as though the loss was a shame.

"I don't know who killed him, but I know why," said June in sudden realization.

"Why?"

Her voice shook with the truth coming at her, "To make sure Dad stays cursed. If someone is controlling Dad, using him, that means he's the blind-folded man, not me. People at town hall weren't talking about the blind-folded man doing the killing. The blindfold is the motive. Carlisle must have realized how to lift Dad's. The killer is still out there and will do anything to keep Dad cursed."

Instead of being stunned by the idea, June was relieved. Magic and curses she couldn't handle. But this was a suspect and she could get in a suspect's mind. Breaking the curses wasn't about defeating them, the mysterious Miridical Elders, it was about outsmarting the murderer. Which admittedly, June'd never done.

"So I guess I just don't understand," Chelsea said, working it out as she spoke, "why we don't just... leave him alone? We can take your veil off. If the veils are linked to the murder, whatever Evens knows will help you solve it, right?"

"I can't leave my dad like this for another minute I don't have to. You don't understand; your entire life's not a lie." The words just poured from June and mattered more than she meant for them to, causing her voice to crack and trail off a little.

"Okay," Chelsea said with solid resolve before asking sister Anne, "Will Evens know the other wizards or witches who put the curses on Mr. Szmydt?"

"Most likely."

June nodded seriously. "Then we should know what to do once we break your boy out of jail."

"I'm going to need to make some more blood," Chelsea said, mostly to herself.

"Ew." June couldn't suppress a grossed out face, then caught herself. "Sorry."

Sister Anne laughed, then spoke in her gravelly French accent, "Thank you, silly crackers. Your blood magic is blocked here, you'll have to go to the farmhouse if you wish to open a portal; Blaise will take you back."

"Well, thank you for inviting us into your murder shack," Chelsea said in a surprisingly earnest tone.

"It's my she-shed to hide from the wife. Know what I mean?"

Both girls nodded and shrugged, tight-lipped

Sister Anne's smoky magical arm raised to wave them good-bye. "Feel free to stop and get a LeCroix for your journey."

Because it felt like the thing to do, June bowed her head in thanks and reverence. Chelsea made a gagging noise. "Pamplemousse, gross. No, thank you."

One arm holding a Birkenstock shoebox containing the ghost veil, her other holding Chelsea's clammy hand, June gasped as they walked out of the shack into the swirling, light-filled night outside. Now on another planet, June only had Chelsea as her guide. Chelsea, whom she had to trust now they were both implicated in the theft of the scrying mirror... Chelsea, the only person who'd tell June what was going on.

Enamored by seeing the magical world for the first time in her life, she rubbernecked at all the beauty of the woods, every so often stumbling on root systems, especially the undulating ones from the pulsing and moving trees.

But then June got a good look at the house. If the shed was orbited by a galaxy of illuminated symbols, then the farmhouse was the universe. And honestly, it appeared less to June like a farmhouse, and more like a church. Simple, earnest, clean, and pure. Only it was guarded by a giant beast. It was monstrous, walking about on all fours yet taller than a horse. Each of the furry beast's paws was chained and shackled, and swirling about the animal was an aura pulsing like fast-forward footage of a thunderstorm. That's one hell of a guard dog.

With her next step, a twig broke beneath June's foot, drawing the beast's attention. Bristling, the hair on its shoulder standing on end, its stormy aura crackled with energy and light. Its electric blue eyes shone through the night, searching for the source of the sound, though it didn't move any closer. Loud wheezing snorts sniffed in the air, as the girls froze mid step.

June's heartbeat pounded in her ears. Her knees locked and her butt clenched. The terror of it. The same frozen terror she'd felt with the wild cat bearing down on her. Chelsea pulled at June's clasped hand, urging her to continue onward, but June couldn't move. Were the bear's eyes on them, or simply glancing into the black night?

Suddenly a low voice called out. "Hello, cracker lawman, here for some more LeCroix." Blaise. As the broad-shouldered man kept the bear's attention, the girls snuck by the nearest wall, where Chelsea sliced her palm and flung her blood while repeating spells. June couldn't help but peer around the side of the house at the monster. Why had Blaise called that animal a cracker lawman?

But before she could think about it too much, Chelsea's blood-slick hand closed around her wrist, and they stumbled through the portal. Stepping back into the warm Szmydt house, June's head was reeling, but in the comfort of home, she felt somewhat grounded. By contrast, Chelsea took one step onto the hardwood dining room floor and collapsed.

Instinctively, June slid to her knees, cradling Chelsea's head in her lap as if it were as delicate as a hurt bird. Please let her be okay, I only just now got to her. June whispered the girl's name over and over, fingering the hair out of her face. After a moment, Chelsea's eyes focused and met June's, and their faces softened into that hardened, smiling at the edge of panic, the edge of hysteria sort of smile. NBD.

"Are you okay?" June's voice quaked in sappy relief.

"Yeah, just a little anemic." Chelsea heaved herself up to her knees, then, with June's shaky like a baby deer help, to standing.

June collapsed into the tall kitchen chair. "There's no way you're going to be able to do this tomorrow. We'll find another way to get Evens out. I'll think of something."

"I'll be fine." Bloodstone pushed off from the table and shambled away. "I just need my iron supplements, fourteen hours of sleep, and a big rare steak." Chelsea spoke as she made her way to the front door, but her weight gave and she leaned on the wall.

"Chelsea, no." June rushed to get under Chelsea's shoulder, to hold up her weight, but the skinny blond girl pushed her away, surprising June with the strength she could muster.

"Juniper. STFU. I've been using magic longer than you. And I have ways of recovering. I just need to get home first."

"How? You can't travel anymore tonight."

"Oh, hell no, I'm not traveling," Chelsea grabbed one of June's coats from the open closet and threw her arm into a sleeve. "I can walk. I'm just on the other side of the Enchanted Forest."

June's wonder betrayed her, and she squealed, "There's an enchanted forest?!"

"You're going to be so annoying now, aren't you?" Chelsea's tired mouth curled into a sly grin.

"Wait, is the Enchanted Forest the real name of Dabbit's Forest?"

"What's Dabbit's Forest?" Chelsea asked as shuffled slowly away.

"Let me walk you home," June said as the girls got to the front door.

"No way. There's too much you have to get used to with experiencing magic. And you have to make sure you don't give away that you're seeing it for the first time. You'll have to wear something over your head like you usually do."

"Like I usually do?"

"The blindfold - it looked like a veil. That's why no one in Miridical knew it was you."

"The ghost veil. No one thought it was weird I was wearing a veil?"

"June, you haven't seen what Miridical really looks like. A girl in a veil doesn't stand out. Do you have anything you could use for tomorrow to cover-up? Like a doily or a lace napkin or something you can wear to fool people at school tomorrow?"

When June realized that she did, in fact, have the perfect

thing for that, sadness swelled in her throat. It didn't last, though, as Chelsea nudged her chin to look in her eyes. "We can pull this off, Juniper. We can save Evens and your Dad and this whole nightmare will be over, and all the bullshit you've had to put up with from school and this fucking town will. be. over."

June couldn't stop the tears welling in her eyes, couldn't still her quivering lip. As an ugly crier, this just pissed June off, preferring to show her hot crush her prettiest self.

"I guess I never even knew it was a nightmare. It was just..." June searched for the word and shrugged. "Life."

"I am so sorry, Juniper. For everything."

They hugged. A real hug - warm, consoling, surrendering in each other's arms, pressing wet eyes into shoulders, feeling comfort from rubbing backs and rocking in unison. June let out a sigh, let out all the tension from their night seeking voodoo in a toolshed in the woods, let go of all the pain of her fight with Dad and suspicion of Connor and pressure for solving the murder, let go of all the anger and hatred she'd kept for nineteen months for Chelsea Blac... Bloodstone. Even as she whispered, June's voice cracked, "I know. I guess I forgive you or whatever."

Letting go felt cold, and both girls tried hard to smile as they backed away from one another, sniffling and wiping their eyes. They were in the foyer, at the front door, Chelsea opening it and backing out into the night, stepping down onto the slab. Before the hot chick, aka, June's former bully and crush since June ever lied eyes on her, turned walked out into the night, June said under her breath, "Yolo," and threw her lips onto Chelsea's.

Fireworks. The world stopped spinning, then spun even

faster. They embraced for what felt like forever. Lips on lips. Magic and electricity more powerful than the scrying mirror passed between them, connected them, pulled them together. June wished they could kiss forever, and they might have for all she could tell. They could spin like this forever.

At some point, the kiss did end, one of them pulled away, or maybe the universe simply created distance between them. And June could have sworn she would float off into space.

Chelsea, all big eyes and dopey smile, walked into the night heading for the woods, the goddamned Enchanted Forest, exhausted and caked in blood. June was content to check out her ass as she left.

Even though she knew Dad couldn't see it, June couldn't leave the bloodstain, especially when Zippy, the hundred-plus pound, spike-spined, bull-horned, six-eyed hellhound wouldn't stop licking one of Chelsea's footprints.

Eventually, once the house smelled more like Lysol than rust, June collapsed in the recliner to see a text from Chelsea.

WE. CAN. DO. THIS. Goodnight, beautiful (kiss emoji)

June sent a kiss emoji back at her and rested her eyes for a moment.

####

The sound of Dad's keys woke her, and June still didn't have her wits about her when he walked into the house. Lightning flashed and June saw spots but heard footsteps and... chains? The world became visible again and June saw him - normal, tubby, scruffy six foot two inch Dad, only he was surrounded in golden light, a shining, pulsing aura in the shape of the giant furry monster she saw outside the Bonhomme farmhouse.

The look of the thing startled her, and she had to remind herself she wasn't in imminent danger. Dad was in there, like he was walking within the ghost of a giant beast, or inside some sort of hologram. The monstrous aura's eyes shone blue, as did Dad's behind his ghost veil. He lumbered to the closet, each step punctuated with the clanking of heavy metal, chains manacled to paws. The beast made of light moved in tandem with Dad, its bright shining eyes sharing his focus. And the animal mouth, displaying big canine teeth, moved along with his words. "What are you still doing up?" he growled sternly at June while removing his coat and kicking off muddy boots.

"I wasn't up, I was just... waiting to make sure you got home okay." She realized she wasn't lying. Until he walked in that door, June was afraid that the giant bear at the Bonhomme's might have attacked her father.

"Well, you need to be in bed," he said without looking at her as he shuffled down the dark hall.

"Okay, Dad. Goodnight. I love you."

"Goodnight," he said before closing the bathroom door behind him.

It was almost too much for her, being so distant from Dad, especially now that there was magic in the world. And Chelsea! So many amazing things going on in her life that she couldn't talk to him about. Her eyes were hot and tired from crying so much today, her face numb, her throat swollen and sore, her body begging for bed, to forfeit the fight for Dad until morning.

But she had to try.

She knocked on the bathroom door, rapping the beat of "shave and a haircut," something she and Dad did ever since they watched Who Framed Roger Rabbit together forever ago.

"What?!" he roared from the other side of the door.

"Dad?" Her voice scratched out of her raw throat. "Can I show you something?"

He swung the door open, his bear face snarling, his furry spirit taking up the entirety of the little bathroom, his human bulk in an old dirty tank, the belt to his wet khakis undone. "What is it, Juniper?"

Without saying a word, she handed him the scrying watch, the beads tapping against one another in her hand. Looking at the bracelet, then at her, Dad said in protest, "I'm tired, Juniper."

Pushing the scrying watch closer to him, she said, "Just look at it. Tell me what you see."

His jaws flexed as he clenched his teeth twice before snatching it from her with his big right paw. He threw a dead stare down at the thing, working the beads in his fingers. Then he took a deep breath and his thick eyebrows lifted for a second. Without looking up at her, he spoke gravelly. "I see a very tired man who's very worried about his daughter."

"Is that all?"

"Damnit, Juniper, are you on drugs?" He stepped out into the darkened hall as he spoke, his mass, which always dwarfed June, now came at her menacingly, exaggerated by his beastly, ethereal body. "Is that what this is? All the defiance? Acting up in school? Stealing from the labs? Disobeying me? Treating your father like shit?!"

He'd never cussed at her before, she realized. Her eyes grew hot with emotion, but were just out of tears. She couldn't even answer him and instead retreated into her room, slamming the door behind her.

Whatever they were, these curses, they were affecting Dad - changing him, brainwashing him. They must have been because that was not Dad. Something was wrong, and it was getting worse. June wasn't going to let someone else she loved was taken away from her. No matter what it took, she would fight to lift these curses, all of them. Even if it killed her.

Chapter Eleven: October 31st, morning

Walking silently to the Mini Cooper, June saw their ugly brown home with the vertical siding for what it was: a wooden dome, an ornate two-story cage. A dull, cramped, birdcage. But the streets, normally busy with the stop and go of cars headed to schools or commuting out of town, was in reality populated with flying brooms, carpets, and pegasi, around which was more traffic of twinkling clouds, glimmering energy, billowing light beams, floating force fields, and flocks of explosions. Not to mention non-flying magical transport like unicorn, centaur, satyr. June caught herself with her mouth hanging open.

Luckily, pissed-off Dad let her stare out the window silently, their town new to her again, brilliant, effulgent, splendiferous. Alive. If she tried to take it all in all at once, she felt a headache developing behind her eyes - or maybe that was some kind of second-hand magic brain tumor, so June silently flitted her eyes about, like a baby in a stroller getting pushed down the Las Vegas strip.

As overwhelming as the sight of Miridical was, it was no match for the teeming super-humanity of the Miridical Prep student body, an imagination menagerie, a mass of evolution-bucking phantasmagoria, the highlight reel of a late-night sugar-binge nightmare.

Even with the forethought to wear the dust-ridden lacey bridal veil of her late mother, June was not prepared. Putting the thing on made her sick to her stomach, and clipping it into her up-done dark hair was just wrong. The picture of her mother in the veil at her wedding was in one of the boxes in the attic now, but the image dominated June's memory. Nicky Wolfsbane Szmydt, successful chemist and MIT Ph.D., reduced in her own daughter's mind to an old film camera photo of a bride. The latent misogyny wasn't lost on June, who took the opportunity to reclaim the patriarchal ritual artifact of a veil and wear it for defense against magic - one girl's battle against evil. A little melodramatic, but where's the lie?

The matching maroon-plaid-clad pubescent teenage society of Miridical Prep was actually a spectrum of shapes, colors, races, religions, magics, and what must have been species. All types of auras -fiery, electric, animal-shaped, smoking wispy tendrils - surrounded fairies, witches, wizards, trolls, giants, slendermen and slenderwomen (slenderpeople? slenderfolk?), centaurs, a zoo of anthropomorphism, and too many others unrecognizable to June's reeling mind. Plus all the little flying what-not buzzing everywhere in busy clusters.

Topped with lacy gray, June's red plaid uniform looked like a crappy attempt at a ghost Halloween costume surrounded by Miridical Prep students in the best costumes of monstrous special effects with unlimited budgets. Taking it all in through her dead mother's wedding veil, June stood, slack-jawed, in the middle of the hallway, beginning to understand the magnitude of the magical truth kept from her. It took a couple of minutes for June to convince her Doc Martens to move.

As June pushed through a throng of letter-jacketed lizard people, one student, who appeared to be a hive-minded pile of insects shaped like a person, threw a football that barely missed her head over to a horned Sasquatch, pissing off a nearby tentacled teacher. June caught herself staring, put her head down, and plowed through the eclectically populated hallways, refusing to rubberneck at the spectacle of it all. It would have been overwhelming enough, if it wasn't all moving with the frantic energy of a high school before first bell.

Obscuring her locker, a couple was making out, hands and feathered wings wrapped around each other's maroon suit jackets. After she cleared her throat, they rolled their eyes and moved, revealing the scratched graffiti on June's locker in its entirety.

"Juniper Szmydt can't even use magic."

The words hit her like a shock-wave and brought her back to some sense of reality. In all of this beauty and madness and magic, all these kids were still bullies and nerds and jocks and rich bitches. And June was still on the bottom of the food chain. She tossed her backpack in her locker and retrieved her books.

"Hey, Nipslip. You and Chelsea make up? Or should I say out?" Connor laughed from behind her.

His voice grated on her, instinctively tensing her shoulders. She was ready to let Connor have it - for keeping Miridical from her, for pretending to be her best friend. To crash a dramatic cacophony, June slammed her locker...or tried to, but her backpack straps were hanging out and catching the locker door. She tried to push them back in quickly, but it didn't work and she was super embarrassed, like everyone in the hall was watching until finally, she scooped the straps in while slamming it loudly, which got even more attention. She wheeled around to stare daggers into Connor.

"Holy shit, Juniper." Connor's eyes blew up wide before he whispered, "That's not your veil."

"You look exactly the same," June said, angry that her own voice was shaking. "I half-expected you to have devil horns or be a ghost or something."

"What are you talking about?"

"Like you said, Connor, it's not my veil." She leaned over and whispered, no spat, the words, "I can see."

He gasped.

June hugged books to her chest and pushed through the hallway in her school that was now Hogwarts for Muppets. "You know what? I don't even care what you are, Connor. When were you going to tell me?"

"Tell you what?"

"About Miridical? The veil? Everything, Connor." Angrily marching to homeroom, she wasn't sure where to direct her angry whispers while tucking her chin against the books she hugged to her chest, brushing past a couple of Elviras and a teen wolf.

"I thought you knew!"

"Then why would I wear this fucking thing?!"

"I don't know, I figured it was something you and Mr. S. decided on, Nipslip."

"No. Stop it. No pet names. No 'Mr. S.' You don't get to do that anymore. You don't get to play dumb when I lived a lie for so long." The words came faster than the thoughts, and angry tears burned behind her eyes, threatening to pour. She stood firm in the middle of the hall, no longer caring who in the bustling crowd of mythical beings heard her. "Pretending like you were my only friend, like you were standing up for me. I can't believe I was so fucking stupid, Connor!"

And then the bell rang, and the students scattered. Connor didn't answer. Despite getting all of that off her chest, June didn't feel any better. In fact, she was more alone than ever.

####

June: Why aren't you in Geometry? Everything OK?

June didn't want to admit how much she wanted - needed - to see Chelsea after her blow up with Connor. Not to talk about it. June absolutely did not want to talk about it. Rather, she wished to throw herself into the jailbreak plans. But without an answer from Chels, June found herself spending her morning classes filling the back pages of her notebooks with what she remembered as the layout of the Miridical jail. She'd been three times, tagging along on official Miridical business with Dad.

Dad. Yet another person she couldn't think about for too long or else a lump would develop in her throat. She couldn't imagine how puffy and red her eyes were from the constant crying and lack of sleep over the past two days. And she had yet to process the idea that her dad was under a series of spells that had somehow transformed him into a giant, chained-up bear.

So June continued her lonely day, over-worrying about the plan to break into the town jail, suppressing depressing thoughts of Connor and Dad, trying not to freak out about Chelsea missing school. But what if Bloodstone pushed herself too hard, making so many blood portals in one night? Honestly, June didn't know the first thing about blood magic and clung to the few tidbits Chelsea had said; she had to take iron supplements and sleep. Hopefully, only sleep kept her out of Geometry.

Sitting by herself at lunch, June wasn't hungry and was rather paranoid that Connor, somehow invisible due to whatever his magical prowess entailed, was stalking her. It was near impossible not to stare at the myriad of students, kids she'd attended high school with for over a year, in their natural forms. And weaving through the lunch tables was a clique of mismatched beings, look down their noses and beaks and what-have-you at the rest of the students, all following the lead of a bejeweled skeleton in clothes. After a moment, June recognized the clique as the rich girls and the skull dotted with colorful crystals belonged to Hailey Daley.

June practically jumped when her phone buzzed with a text.

Chelsea: Srry, slept in. Can u meet me in the woods?

June: I'm at school.

C: So? Leave.

J: How? I can't get busted again.

C: SE door. Next 2 softball field. Fire alarm broke

J: How do you know this stuff?

C: (shrug emoji) teachers tell popular girls stuff. C U soon! (kiss blowing emoji)

A girl's in trouble when her heart flutters at the sight of an emoji.

Trying to keep as low a profile as possible, June packed up her lunch, shouldered her backpack, and headed for the halls... and running right into the bedazzled sternum of Hailey Daley. Her eyes were flowers with petals that closed like lashes. Her red plaid jumper hung loose on her bony hips entwined with flowery vines. Ruby lips obscured her teeth clacked as she spoke. "Going somewhere, Lezburg?" Hailey sneered, some chick with deer antlers behind her chuckling.

"I was just leaving."

"Is it Gay Channukah already?"

That was it. Today was the wrong day. And maybe Hailey was the least annoying thing in June's life right now, but, fuck it, she was the closest.

"You know what, Hailey?!" June raised her voice louder than she figured, and before she knew it, she was the center of attention of the cafeteria full of fantastical students.

"What, Jew Szmydt?"

"I'm sorry that you're such a boring fucking person that you have to pick on somebody else to make yourself look good. Now get out of my way before I get Chelsea to beat your bony ass. And your acting sucks, you fercockt bitch." She pushed past her as Hailey laughed.

It wasn't the best insult. It hadn't turned the school against Hailey; it probably didn't even hurt Hailey's feelings. But June felt great for standing in front of the whole school of weirdos and at least saying something. Hailey would have to google the Yiddish insult later.

####

Of course, Chelsea was right, and June escaped school easily, heading to meet her crush-turned-whatever Chelsea and June were turning into. An item? Smash buddies? Life would have to settle down before June could name these feelings and this connection. But she practically skipped on the way to her make-out partner, knowing exactly where in the Enchanted Forest she'd be.

So New England in the autumn was, of course, beautiful.

But the Enchanted Forest was motherfucking whimsical. The wind smelled like pumpkin spice, petrichor, and fancy vanilla candles, and when it blew, it pushed formations of bright warm-colored leaves in meandering curly-cues. The Boston Oaks danced. Not swayed in the wind, or even demonstrated basic locomotion beyond the capabilities of plants as scientists understood, but danced to some bouncing, aggressive beat that only the oaks could hear. And the forest animals gathered round, watching her, peering from branches and behind trunks, brightly colored wildlife, all with unnaturally large, humanoid eyes displaying curious emotion. Among the chittering, whistling, and singing, June thought she heard some of the woodland creatures whispering in English. As she walked deeper into the bright, inviting woods, branches parted, vines lifted, and shrubs ambled deliberately out of the way.

Where the stump in the clearing had been now stood a tree. Towering and willowy with a gleaming white trunk and diaphanous red ribbon leaves, all of it swaying and dancing in the cold October breeze. And at its base sat Chelsea, fresh-faced, apple-cheeked, and smiling like the cat who caught the rat.

Mouth pursing against a grin and without saying a word, June approached the girl, pulled the veil off, and met her lips-first - pressing, exploring, and even bumping teeth once. By the time they separated, they were both blushing, Chelsea with more color in her face than June had ever seen, and June may be sweating a little, but it happens.

Immediately, June's focus went back to the stark ribbony willow. "Was this tree always here?"

Smiling and shaking her head 'no,' Chelsea pulled June in

closer, touched her forehead to forehead, and whispered in a quiet, sexy tone that made June expect some naughty secret, "Wanna get a burger?"

With a giggle, June agreed, but even as they left, she couldn't take her eyes off the enormous magical tree, at least fifteen feet high with dozens of branches arching overhead, waving shiny red leaves like handkerchiefs as if to say bon voyage.

"You are a powerful witch, Chelsea Bloodstone."

"Witch? Please. Do I look like a girl who would marry Satan? We're blood mages, thank you. And besides, that's not my magic that made that physicalization grow. It's ours together."

The ribbons fluttered in the pumpkin spice breeze and June couldn't imagine controlling the kind of magic that could grow a tree that size in two days.

####

Chelsea ordered two double bacon double cheeseburgers with cheesy bacon fries. For herself. June tamped down the bubbling jealousy of Chelsea's tight figure, focusing on the amount of blood Chels had lost to fuel such a binge. Still, there was something hot about a beautiful girl like her destroying plates of fatty, meaty food. Pausing in her gawking, June pulled out her notebook, laying out her recalled floor plan of the jail. The two girls set to planning.

"If you can get us into this cell through this wall," June pointed, "then, in theory, it's going to be in and out."

"If you still have the veil, we should be able to," Chelsea let out a belch that somehow turned June on, then continued, "turn it inside out, making ourselves invisible to anyone watching or listening."

"Are you sure?" June asked, tapping a pen nervously on her notebook. "Won't it just stop them from seeing our magical selves?"

"Honestly, I have no idea. But I'm all rested, got a full belly, and plan on traveling in and out of there before anyone notices." Chelsea shoved a pile of fries glued together with nacho cheese and bacon bits into her beautiful mouth. With it full, she said, "Which is why I think you should be the distraction."

"The distraction?"

"Totally. You wander in, ask about finding your dad or something like that, acting like the basic Szmydt who can't see magic. Chances are, the cops will take the opportunity to bag on you and your dad and won't notice Evens disappearing from his cell."

"No, that's way too dangerous for you."

"The cops in this town are a joke. Bitch, I'm a blood mage." Chelsea took a honking bite out of her burger, then pointed with it. "My family was created out of the mud of the battlefield of the Crusades. If I can't handle Andy Griffith and frickin Deputy Dog, I deserve to get caught."

"No. I won't let you. Your parents aren't even here to bail you out if you need them to."

"I won't need them to."

"Chelsea. This is on me. I promised to get Evens out of there. He's going to save my dad. I know the jail best. I'm going with you. End of story."

"God, you're cute when you assert yourself."

June's ears burned from the compliment. Something about Chelsea's attention made June squirm in a way she didn't mind at all. "Thanks."

Sucking on her soda straw until it gurgled, Chelsea let out

another belch and wiped her hands on a napkin. "Okay, let's finish up. We should do this before noon."

"What?! Before noon? It's eleven-forty-five!"

"Yeah, and you said shift change is at one, which means twice as many cops in the building."

"Fuck." June closed the notebook, put down the pen, then grabbed the ghost veil from her book bag. She then dropped the ghost veil and ripped the map out of the notebook. She kept looking around with her hands out, uncertain of what to grab next, until she made herself pause and breathe. "Okay. Let me wash up. I'll be right back."

"Oh, hey, do you have any money?"

"Well...yeah?"

"Good. I'm not paying until we go on a proper date."

June didn't have any blush in her for the thought of a proper date with Chelsea Bloodstone when they were planning to commit a felony. Worrying her cuticles off her fingernails with her teeth, June went to the restroom and washed up, forcing her game face on as she stared into the mirror. "We can do this, June. She's right. The cops in this town are morons. Let's go save Dad."

But when she went back out to the diner floor, their table was empty. Chelsea was gone. Under a tented twenty-dollar bill was a folded triangle of lined notebook paper. Unfolding to the flourishing loops of Chelsea's cursive handwriting, June read, "Don't worry, I got this, Juniper. In and out. You walk in the front door for a distraction in case I need one. Meet you and Evens in the woods by 12:15." Then Chelsea left a lipstick kiss underneath.

June dropped another twenty and sprinted for the police station.

#$##

With the ghost veil lifted, the town square was breath-taking. All the old stone buildings remained old stone building, but with ornate touches: larger-than-life gargoyles, two-story-tall wooden doors...and then there was the library clock tower. What had been white sandstone reaching up seven stories was now something altogether more sinister. A helixical twisting tower. Asymmetrical. Not just bone-white, but composed of actual bones. Bleached out skeletal bricks, clusters of tibias and fibulas stacked up to impossible heights, the blanched drillbit of a tower tapering up to a point. The whole building looked like a fang jutting up from the ground. The clockface was still there, about 2/3s of the way up the bony spire, only instead of two rectangular black hands pivoting to point at the time, the clock hands were hovering magic wands.

June ran past. She ran by a literal hole in the ground, a barrel with a door sticking up from a mound of dirt that must have been the Miridical Pub, and past the Presbyterian church that was on fire (a fact which didn't seem to concern anyone) to the brick castle that was the Miridical Sheriff's Patrol Offices.

A bunch of police officers beat her to it, though. A magical symbol above the station (as June had come to find that all buildings had runes or icons floating about them) was flashing red, which probably wasn't good. Something was definitely up, as Officer Azantian from the crime scene a couple days ago was now guarding the front door of the station. Albeit now her skin was green, and she had on a classic witch's hat. The witch officer's large, expressive eyes focused immediately on June as she jogged up the sidewalk.

"Hey, little Szmydt!" the officer cackled in a high pitch.

"Why aren't you in school?"

Instead of panicking, June just continued her pace past the station, calling out, "Cross country practice."

But June was panicking inside. Chelsea was trapped in the Sheriff's Patrol Station which was swarming with cops, and there was no way to get to her out.

Chapter Twelve: October 31st, jailbreak time

At some point in her life, June had learned how to lie to strangers. It was the easiest thing; when she met another person and they expected to take their first step in getting to know who she was, she simply decided what to tell them. The truth? A half-truth? Or something more deliberate? Whether it was a genius lie or a simple coincidence, Officer Azantian thinking that June was training for cross country allowed June to jog by the fortified gothic stone castle that was the Miridical Sheriff's Patrol Offices again and again.

As inconspicuously as possible, squinting against the midday sun which brightened, but didn't heat the October afternoon, June trotted by, trying to see into the windows into the station. All she could spy was the back of the cop's heads. One or two white dudes, plus guys with black wolf heads sticking out of their khaki sheriff's patrol uniforms. Maybe three or four of them. Maybe she was seeing the same two over and over again. Officer Azantian stared daggers back at June each time she passed by, but after one lap, it was obvious the green-skinned witch cop wasn't going to do anything, maybe even invisibly tethered to her post with some kind of spell.

The witch cop stepped to the side as more cruisers pulled up, dogs or wolves or whatever in uniforms jogging up and into the station. Officer Azantian wasn't like the other cops. It wasn't just the fact that she was new, but more that she was a green witch and the rest of them were either balding white dudes or six-foot tall canines walking on hind legs. Not being a Marrock, Officer Azantian lacked the family resemblance that most of the officers related to the sheriff had. And that resemblance, as June now saw it, was not light brown hair and a strong jaw, but rather that they were dogs, or were-wolves, or shifters, or some other kind of dog-people...magically speaking.

By her fourth pass through the square, she was tired and hadn't learned squat about Chelsea's situation. Helplessness had June in checkmate. If she walked into the station now and they had Chelsea caught, then what? June feared she couldn't keep a poker face if she saw Chelsea in peril. June would almost def give away the fact that she too was in on the jailbreak. And she couldn't call Dad, not with how he'd been acting.

Simultaneously tired from and brimful of restless energy wanting - no, needing - to do something to help Chelsea, June caught her breath between the edge of the Enchanted Forest and the square. With no other options, June headed back to the woods, to the blood-enchanted tree, the magical symbol of hers and Chelsea's relationship that had grown immensely in a couple days.

Rounding a corner past a bumping and grinding brightly colored oak, June's feet stopped and her heart sank. Something was wrong with their tree. Its bright white bark had darkened to a gray, the lipstick-red ribbon leaves all turned dull garnet. Even the droop of its willowy branches fell too limply; instead of an exaggerated shrug, they hung like shoulders of the beaten down and defeated. Part of her had expected, or at least hoped, to see Chelsea and Evens hanging out under the tree like NBD, but June knew better. So she sat with her back on the fading magical summoning tree and waited. She didn't have to wait long.

Like the ripping a part of wood, a tearing, cracking sound whispered right into June's ear. The grey mottled bark of the tree opened up in a slash tearing horizontally across the trunk. Then the wound began to bleed. A trickle, followed by a crimson pour. This was Chelsea's work, it had to be. But the tree trunk was about as big around as Chelsea's waist. There's no way she'd be able to travel through a portal like this, at least not according to the little June knew about blood magic (magery?).

Soon enough, the wound on the tree stopped its flow, and the blood began drying up. June didn't know what to do. Did Chelsea's spell fail? Was there something June was supposed to do from her end? In a panic, June pushed at the tree's cut, picked at the bark, unable to peel it back. Gripping the torn bark of the tree, she put a foot against the trunk and leaned back with all of her weight, then fell. She'd slipped, sending her on her ass, scraping her palm on a rock jutting out from the leafy forest floor. Sitting there, she cussed and screamed and threw the rock and sucked on the bleeding scrape on her palm.

The bleeding scrape on her palm. Maybe that was the key.

June bit into the tweat on the heel of her hand, opening the scrape into a cut. Not a lot of blood, but maybe enough? She placed her wounded hand against the slash in the tree bark and sure enough, the wetness against the bark changed, morphed, until it was less of a patch of blood on the tree, and more of a small window, a clear pane through which June could see some bars, the American flag, and the lightning bear seal of Miridical. She was looking into the Miridical Sheriff's Patrol Offices. Chelsea's veiled face peaked into the window.

"Juniper, you did it! Thank fucking God!" Chelsea exclaimed, not a quarter of her face visible within the tree.

"Chelsea, are you okay?!"

"I'm fine. I'm pissed, but I'm fine. Of course, the police would have wards set up against blood magic in their jail. Duh!"

"So you're caught?"

"Kinda. The wards redirected my portal so I couldn't enter the cell, but it triggered some kind of alarm and now the whole station's locked down and crawling with cops. They can't see me through the veil, but they know something's up."

"Well, be careful! And quiet; can't they hear you?"

Chelsea's lips pursed to the side. "I dunno. They woulda caught me by now if they could."

"So, how are you going to get out of there?"

"Not super certain, but we have to figure something out quick. They just called the mayor, and he's going to send your dad over."

"So?"

"So I don't know what happens when you double up a blindfold. Will he see or hear less, or...?"

June completed the thought. "We need to figure this out quick."

"Yeah. Do you think you can stop your dad?"

"Chelsea, I'm supposed to be in school right now. The principal's already on my ass, and the sheriff...Dad'll kill me."

"Cool. Well, June, it's been nice knowing you. Sorry we never got a chance to bone," Chelsea said flippantly.

"Wait! I think I know someone who may be able to help."

"I hope so. I'd still like to bone someday."

"Be serious."

"I'm sorry, my humor is a defense mechanism! Who can help?"

Out of breath, lungs burning, pumping her legs as fast as possible, June sprinted back to her birdcage home, just in time to see Dad through the bars, answering his phone. Sweating and wheezing, her heart pounded as she snuck into the car once he was in the house. Ugh, she was not built for all of this running. She whispered, "Please let it be here, please let it be here..." as she dug into the center console until she found it–Dad's wallet. Opening it up, beside the credit cards, was the last business card Dad had receive., Mo Tilden's.

Of course, now that she could see magic, she saw that it wasn't a business card at all, but a gold Tarot card, glimmering in the midday sun. Crawling out of the car and regarding the card with no name, number, or email, she whispered to herself, "Great, now how do I call him?"

A voice chided from behind her. "It's too late to call anybody, sweetheart." The short Persian man stood in his signature black suit, white shirt, and no coat.

"Shh!" June chided him, peeking past her home's thick bars to see where Dad was in the cage. Once the coast was clear, she motioned him to join her safely behind a dancing tree on the side of the house.

"I'm sorry to, uh...call you up like this, but you were right. There are bigger forces at work in this town, and I need your help. We need your help."

"I offered you my help. Two days ago. When the curses on you, your home, and your father were much weaker."

What, did this guy want her to beg? "Listen, I'm sorry; we should have listened to you. But I've learned a Hell of a lot since then, and I think this is my only chance to save the girl who can save the guy who can save my dad from all of these curses! Plus, if I don't, there's this one-armed voodoo lady who might turn me into a can of LeCroix or something."

"Well, see what sorry gets you, but my hands are tied now. The truth is, you and your Dad were so content being blindfolded you wouldn't listen to me, and now when you're really in the shit, you think you can summon me out of thin air and I'm supposed to fix it like your fairy godfather?"

She didn't get it. This was the guy that came to them to try to help. "What? No." Then the idea sunk in for a moment and she asked in a low voice, "Wait, you're not my fairy godfather, are you?"

"No!" Tilden yelled.

Zippy barked as Dad led him out and into the Mini Cooper, then backed out the driveway and onto the road.

Normally, she'd say fuck this guy, but Mo Tilden had more information on the forces at work. "I'm running out of time!"

"Yeah, you are! It's Samhain, which means at midnight, your dad's at his most powerful and the bindings are at their most powerful, too! So whoever's taking advantage of him has pretty much already won!"

"Well, what can I do?"

Tilden bubbled over with rage. "There's nothing to do, Szmydt! You blew it! You blew it! I came to your door when you could have made a difference and the two of you –"

"Then go back to Providence, fucker!" June was done with it, flicking the tarot card back at the Persian before darting back toward the Enchanted Forest.

First Sister Anne, now him— no one was actually willing to help June as she was trying to save her dad and free the town of tyranny. Sure, everybody knew the problems and could tell her all about it, but when time came to actually do something about it, all June got was a "good luck" and a pat on the back.

So June had to do all this on her own. Without magic. Or Chelsea.

Wait.

She could just help Chelsea use magic. Help Chelsea find something in the Sheriff's office to use to get out. June knew of something magical, but admittedly, she wasn't sure what exactly that something was. As she ran toward the lover's tree, she pulled out her phone and searched her photos. All the selfies with Connor were now just selfies June thumbed through. Then she got to the right pic.

June gasped when she saw it.

The thought had flitted through her head at some point during the day. So much of the town was different. From the people to the buildings, all of it had been transformed once she could see the magic in it. So obviously, what had been an antique bullet she found at a murder scene must have been something else.

She'd snapped a photo so she didn't have to carry the round to school when searching for a reference book to identify the thing. Between the books and the internet, she'd found about seven conflicting types of rounds the bullet could be. But looking at the photo on her phone with fresh eyes, all while still hauling her ass through the woods at a brisk pace, she saw it for what it truly was. A classic black with white tip magician's wand.

Once at the tree, she clawed at the scrape on her hand, drawing it back to bleeding. But when she wiped her bloody palm against the dried wound on the gray tree, nothing happened. The window had scabbed over, and what had been a dripping red wound was now dried and brown.

She needed Chelsea's blood. At least, she hoped that was all she needed. June fell to her knees and pawed at the ground. She'd left a patch of dirt free of leaves the last time she dug here, back when the giant magical love tree was but a sapling, and soon she uncovered it again, cradled between the two thickest roots - the jar of June's bandaids floating in a couple ounces of Chelsea's blood.

Man, it can't be easy being a blood mage.

June unscrewed the cap and splashed the red, life-giving fluid from the jar onto the tree's gaping wound. Again, she pressed her palm against the red on the tree, and when she removed it, another window was there in the trunk, this one in the perfect shape of June's handprint. In the sheriff's office jail, the veiled Chelsea chewed on her lip and constantly checked over her shoulder. Her eyes were tired and frantic, and Chelsea's fatigued panic brought out anger and despair in the pit of June's stomach.

"Tell me you're sending whoever you're sending to help," Chelsea blurted.

"No, but I do have another idea. Do you have any idea how to use a magic wand?"

"A magic wand? Fuck no!" she said.

Another voice, deep and syrupy, interrupted in an accent liquid like French but with a thick drawl. "I do."

####

Something had to give. Either June was finally going to get into shape, run a couple miles a day, and get this mother-fucking cardio in check, or she was never going to run again as long as she lived. She wheezed like her lung had a small leak. A stitch in her side, calves cramping, feet pulsing in pain, June made it to the town square just in time to see chaos erupt from the Miridical jail-slash-sheriff's office.

The officers along the brick rooftop parapets had changed into chickens, bawking, squawking, and flapping wildly about. The windows, doors, and black metal bars quickly melted into liquid, slowly pouring off the building. From the empty spaces the little black waterfalls left, goats and donkeys escaped, a few of them still wearing the khaki shirts of the Sheriff's Patrol uniform, most with belt holsters jiggling as they ran off.

The bright red flashing symbol above the building fell apart. The lines, squiggles, and dots making up the magical icon broke and tumbled to the ground, heavy chunks chipping away bits of brick from the building like falling construction beams. Some long leggy bird, like a stork or a heron, sprinted out a window, hopping to dodge the falling detritus.

And from the chaos, dressed in a classic tuxedo with red carnation, top hat, and tails, gripping and flicking the black and white magical wand like a conductor, strolled Evens.

BAMF.

June had never seen him cleaned up or sober; the old Haitian guy looked good. With an air of theatricality, he hopped to stand in front of June, and with a big bright smile, took a bow.

"Sweet Jesus, Mr. Bonhomme, what did you do?"

"Had some fun. White magic is hilarious! How do you ever

get anything done?"

"Where's Chelsea?"

"Who?"

"Chelsea? The girl who got you that magic wand and broke you out of jail?"

"Oh, T. Swift. Where'd she go?" He looked around as casually as if he'd misplaced his keys, then pointed the wand at the graceful white stork. He shot a beam of sparkles, and the bird's feet swelled, then the legs, color changing to pale white, the entire bird puffing out until Chelsea Bloodstone stood, very human and very nude.

Evens crossed his arms in self-pride as reality settled in on Chelsea, eyes popping open in shock before clamoring to cover her boobs and vagina with her hands. Her alabaster skin flushed crimson on her face, chest, and arms. She opened her mouth to scream but instead let out a high-pitched quack.

"I'm starving," Evens said, traipsing off. "Let's go get some food, shall we?"

"Um, no," June said, also burning in embarrassment because of Chelsea's nudity.

"Why not? Aren't you hungry?"

"Well, first off, Chelsea's naked!"

"Oh," he said matter-of-factly. With a flick of the little magician's wand, light and embers burst around Chelsea like a flower blooming. Once the bright light subsided, she was suddenly in a sparkly frilly romper with her hair and makeup done up.

"Is that..." June squinted. "Is she dressed like –"

"Taylor Swift's iconic 1989 tour look!" Chelsea exclaimed, checking out herself as she shimmied and posed.

"All right, Taytay, let's get out of here before..."

"Before what?"

"I don't know, it just feels like someone's going to get in trouble for all of this."

And they walked away from the police station overrun with animals.

Evens let out a huge belch after his second plate of pancakes. "That's better."

"Gassy?"

"Gas is the body thanking you for food. So tell me again what's wrong with your father."

"Well, he's cursed."

"I know that. I cursed him."

"You did?"

"Of course! I put a protective spell on him."

"So you didn't curse him?"

"It's still a curse. Some protective spells got downsides. He can't see his enemies or any harm coming his way. And it made him lactose intolerant."

"Ugh, that was you?"

"Sorry."

Chelsea shoveled more bacon into her mouth. "But he has more curses than that."

"Well, my protective spell is the strongest there is, and it is the knot that binds the blindfold. Thank you," he said to the winged waitress flitting a few feet above the checkered linoleum who dropped off more [pancakes. "You girls want anything?" he asked the June. June smiled politely and shook her head. When Chelsea smiled and nodded, June kicked her under the table.

Evens went on, "So, the blindfolded man. Think of the blind man. The blind man cannot see, so his nose grows stronger. And his hearing is sharper. And his skin can feel changes in temperature or the wind. And he can taste maple syrup from ten paces."

Evens swallowed a mouthful and belched again.

"Also, his sixth sense grows. His magic. He's like one of those exploding cellphones. Too much power, he may get too hot, and boom."

June dropped her glass of water on the diner table. "Dad's going to explode?!"

"Maybe."

"Can you lift the protective spell?

"I could..."

"Thank God."

"...If it weren't layered. If they weren't knotted."

"But those curses are all tied to his life, right?"

"Could be. He is very cursed. I do not know all of the rules that govern each of them. Different magics, different rules."

"Are there curses that would stay with him even after he died?" June asked, afraid of the answer.

"Of course. White magic is some scary shit. Like this thing." He pulled the squat magic wand from his pocket and placed it on the table. "This is powerful as all Hell, and it's only half a wand."

"Half a wand?"

"That's why it's so small, even for white magic. You know what they say about size?" That got Evens laughing, throwing back his head and letting out a big bellowing guffaw. "But it's still powerful. Did you see me turn that witch cop into a goat?!"

"How long will that last? Turning those cops into goats and chickens?"

"Hopefully long enough to cook them! Ha! I am fucking with you. Since I don't know squat about white magic, I don't know? Maybe it should wear off quick? But just in case..." Taking each end of the wand in his hands, he slammed it down over his knee, cracking it in two in a display of fizzing red sparks. He handed each of the sophomore girls half, then went back to his beer.

June felt it in her hands, the stick weightier than it seemed it'd be. A tiny thing, like a magic wand included in any children's magic kit. Somehow, the wand had regenerated, white tipped on both ends, and in proper proportions, making two smaller wands, about the size of mini-golf pencils. Holding it with a reverence, June examined the thing, turning it over in her cupped hands. Chelsea, however, pinched it and pointed it at everything on the table making 'pew pew' noises.

"Evens, how will this help my Dad?"

"It won't. You ask a lot of questions. Are you a bit dumb?"

"Hey," Chelsea cut in sharply. "She's just new to all of this."

"Haha! I didn't mean anything by it. Girl," He pointed with his beer hand at June. "I think you are the canary."

Chelsea pointed a finger at Evens. "Don't pick on her because she's a pixie!"

"I'm not." He belched. "Don't you ever shut up? You are the canary in this magical coalmine. You've managed to stay aloof your whole time here. And when the evil begins to settles over, or right before the magic dies, or just at the beginning of whatever the fuck, you're going to die. It will be a sign."

June had never knowingly been the subject of a legend before. Suddenly her death meant more than just the end of her time on Earth. It was frightening to feel so important and all at once infuriating that something else was taking ownership of something as personal as her own demise.

"Leave her alone." Chels's voice was all rage and gravel. "How do we help Deputy Mayor Szmydt?"

"You need to research the other curses. All of them." Evens counted the curses on his fingers as he listed them. "The Blindfold, the Loof, the Linchpin, the Chains of Epimetheus, Presto Hide-o, the Shaman's Bone Finger, and the Suck-ulator Three-Thousand. Find out in what order they were placed on him and how to lift them one at a time, or maybe find a way to do them all at once. Seven curses in total; that number is strong with puny white magic. Look up the seven and find the order they were placed."

"I don't think I can," June replied, looking down. "They're definitely guarded against the Szmydts at the library."

"Then go to the Miridical bookstore. Anywhere but that big book retailer online."

####

Since she'd moved to Miridical, June had noticed the bookstore, Which Books For You, as the tiny house surrounded by Boston Oaks at the far edge of the town square where the commercial buildings taper off into the woods at the base of Fortune Hill. But now that she saw Miridical for what it was, Witch Books for You was a spectacle to behold. It wasn't surrounded by the magical dancing trees June once knew as Boston Oaks, it was inside the trunk of the biggest of the swaying trees.

The enormous dancing oak towered over most buildings in the town square, only shorter than the regal-as-ever Hell-on-Earth called Miridical Preparatory Academy and the bone-stacked library clock tower. At the cartoon tree's base, nestled between two roots that came up to June's shoulders, was a round wooden red door that could almost be described as quaint or friendly except for its lack of a doorknob. She stood next to Chelsea, with a swaying Evens behind them.

"How do we get in?" June asked.

"Well," Evens belched then continued, "Do you want to get in?"

"Don't you?" June retorted.

"No. They'll probably call the cops on me. Too many cops for today. I got to get my ass back to the farm before Ma gets mad."

Chelsea said, "If you want to score some brownie points, pick up some more LaCroix on your way."

"Thank you, Taylor Swift. Good luck, little canary," he said before stumbling off down the road.

"Wait," June protested. "He still didn't say how we get inside."

"Do we want to get inside?" Chelsea asked.

June considered it then shrugged. "Well, yeah."

And then they were inside.

Chapter Thirteen: October 31, afternoon

The warm, wooden, cozy interior smelled of dust, cinnamon, and tobacco (but really expensive tobacco that says it's cherry flavored even though it only smells like expensive tobacco). Outside of sparse posters and worn carpet, the store was wooden and cluttered, to put it simply.

Walls of shelves were everywhere. Lining the snaking maze, ceiling-high columns of deep shelving housed neat rows of heavy books, but then piles of prone books on each shelf obscured those books, and piles of dust-laden books on small reading tables obscured the shelves, all cramping the converted home's warm wood and low ceilings. Like if a Hobbit were a hardback hoarder.

The light was warm and alive, as if candlelight, although June could trace no light source nor smell fire. And all the books were heavy leather hardbacks that looked like the types of books that carried hand-copied wisdom from cities and countries which fell centuries before. This was no two-bit lawyer's bookshelf. This ish was old. This was Ancient Knowledge, capital "A" capital "K," and June's murder investigation had officially taken her in way over her head.

"Witch Books, how can I help?" a nasal, high-pitched voice squawked from somewhere deeper within the store, a Rhode Island accent heavier than the dust smell. June followed the source of the sound, rounding a corner of book-lined shelves to a corridor of book-lined shelves. She checked around one more corner before she cleared her throat and called out, "Yes, we're looking for a book on curses?"

"Yes, please hold," the voice from nowhere answered, then yelled out in a louder, more annoyed tone, "Can I help you?"

"Um...yes, we're looking for a book on curses?"

"Well, that's the customer service you get when you order online. Call direct next time. Amazon can bite my butt!" Then her tone changed yet again. "Sorry about that, what is it I can do for you?"

"A book on curse-"

Chelsea took over. "Can I talk to a manager?"

From behind a shelf that June hadn't noticed before strode one pissed-off lady with an air that said she'd been having a bad day and was just begging whatever higher power she worshipped for someone onto whom she could release her scorn. "May I help you?" the book store clerk intoned nasally through teeth bared in a passable smile.

June was about to begin her curse-book question once more when Chelsea took the lead again. "Oh, are you addressing us this time, or are you on a bluetooth? Perhaps you're talking to Alexa?"

The short, tawny-skinned woman, black hair in a perfect bun, eyebrows sculpted well enough to fight Adonis Creed, held her predatory smile. "I'm sorry, young ladies, but I have a business to single-handedly run." She flashed angry chestnut eyes framed in fire-engine red reading glasses that matched the lipstick surrounding her threatening grin. Her make-up was bold but flawless. "If you're interested in customer service, might I suggest taking your query to the library?"

"Might I suggest you take your business to the-" Chelsea's tone reminded June what a bratty little rich child Chelsea must have been.

"Chelsea!" June chided before putting on her polite face. "We're in a bit of a bind and are looking for a book or two on curses."

Suddenly, the three women were in a different part of the store entirely, this one dustier but less cluttered, with high-backed leather chairs surrounding a coffee table covered in scrolls.

"Here's the curse section. I'll leave you two to peruse," she said before heading behind another shelf.

"I'm sorry, Miss?" June called out. "We really need help lifting some curses, and we have to do it before tonight."

"Last-minute shoppers, eh?" The woman's voice circled them from nowhere in particular. "Let me guess. You both need dates for Samhain but will just die if your prospective boyfriends see you like this?"

"'Like this?' The fuck does that mean?" Chelsea just wasn't having it with this shopkeeper.

"Chelsea, will you chill?"

But Chelsea wouldn't let it go that easy. "And we don't need boyfriends."

"Chelsea! Please, Miss, I need to save my Dad."

The shopkeeper, who had just walked ahead deeper into the store, appeared behind them suddenly, eliciting jumps and shivers. She whispered in both girls' ears, "And how will you be paying today?" Her breath carried a concentration of cinnamon, spicy and dry.

"Cash?" June took mental stock of the twenty or so dollars she had in her wallet.

Chelsea chimed in, "I got my Mom's visa."

"Muggle money? Gross. Can I interest you in a SPARKNOTES GUIDE TO MAGICAL CURSES, or maybe something in the Chris Angel canon?"

"I could give you this." June fished out the small wand from her pocket and presented it to the woman.

"A bit diminutive, isn't it? Does it work?"

"It worked on the police station this morning," Chelsea said to herself before holding her hands up to show June she was backing off.

"That was you two? Delicious. A quarter wand like that will get you some basic Anglo-Pagan curse relief textbooks."

"Listen, my father has a series of curses on him that we need to remove in a certain order."

"Ah, layering. I'm afraid that's a bit more involved. And can get pricey."

"I also have this," June reached into her backpack and produced the scrying watch. As she held it out to the bookstore owner, she noticed the woman's reflection — green skin, warts, crookedly pointy nose.

The woman immediately put a hand over the mirror fragment. "Sneaking a peek of a lady not made up, that's just rude, darling. But I must tell you, I have plenty of scry. That won't buy you a bookmark. Let me show you some pages within your budget."

Just then a door slammed and someone somewhere in the

labyrinth of shelves tossed a bag, or perhaps just collapsed, onto a chair.

"Fuck me, Vik, you'll never believe the fucking day I've had."

"One moment, I'm with customers!" Vik the shopkeeper said in a put-on sing-song cadence.

"Sorry!"

"Here." Vik dropped a stack of old leather-bound hardback books on the suddenly clear coffee table, stirring up clouds of dust. "You can look through these. The quarter-wand will buy any one of them."

June sneezed.

"Salud."

But before June could say thank you, Vik the witch was gone. Chelsea noticed, too. "Like Batman."

####

Being a social pariah lends itself to developing a taste for reading, which proved valuable as June leafed through the first of the spell books while Chelsea couldn't be bothered to concentrate. Instead, she listened in on the conversation the other two women were having somewhere within the tree-housed bookstore and insisted on periodically updating June.

"One of them has a crush on a guy from work, but is afraid she made herself look stupid today."

"This book says the order of the curses shouldn't affect reversing them as long as none of them were placed by Jesus Christ or his disciples. Or is this just Christian curses?"

"She feels underappreciated at work, loves her job, hates her boss and coworkers."

"I wonder if this only counts for Pagan or Anglican curses."

"She doesn't want to quit; she'd have to work here at the bookstore."

"Is there any way of telling?"

"I think they're sisters! And the guy doesn't work with her, but brought his dog to their office today."

"Chelsea, will you pay attention?"

"Juniper, I think you need to pay attention. I'm pretty sure the lady talking got turned into a goat today."

"So she's a cop?" June sucked at her tooth, then said, "Officer Ani."

"Yeah, and I think the guy at work she has a crush on is your dad."

"Ew. So?"

"So if you wanted to bone some dude–"

"That's my dad; you're sick."

"But no matter who it was. Say you wanted to bone me and you found out I was cursed. You might help out."

June felt she was blushing hard enough to boil the sweat she was certain her face was pouring. "Well, even if she did, we can't talk to her."

"Why not?"

"Because all the cops in this town know I'm the deputy mayor's daughter and everyone at the sheriff's office today saw your naked body!"

"Yeah, but she saw it through goat eyes, so I doubt she remembers. I'm going to call her over."

"Chelsea, no, don't. I'm serious."

"It's either that or read books all night and maybe find a solution."

"Yeah, that sounds great. Better than talking to some cop and maybe going to jail. Again."

"I'm calling her over. Uh, Miss?!"

"Chelsea, I'm serious."

"I know. That's what's so sexy about you!" She scrunched up her nose at June before calling out again with fake politeness, "Miss Witch?"

Leaning against the end of a bookshelf, Vik barked, "What?!"

"Hi, sorry to bother you, but I was wondering if you had any books about how owning a Hellhound would affect the victim of a curse?"

"Nobody owns Hellhounds. They are task-based creatures. One word commands. Proximity doesn't infer ownership."

"Oh, really? Because my friend is the deputy mayor's daughter, and they kind of thought that they adopted a Hellhound."

Vic looked at June. "You're the deputy mayor's daughter." It was not a question.

"Yeah, I thought everyone knew that."

"I thought she was veiled?"

Oh, shit.

June had removed it to read. Was this Vik one of the Elders? Did she know about the blindfolds? Was she a part of the plot to kill Miridicaliens to keep their power over Dad?

Flustered, June hurriedly gathered her backpack, took Chelsea by the hand, and walked through the maze of shelves, searching for a way out. "I think we've taken up enough of your time. Come on Chelsea, let's head to the library."

Turning a corner, the girls ran into Vik, leaned against an antique globe. "If you're smart enough to remove your own veil, then you probably already know nobody at the library is going to help you."

"Oh, I'm not smart, just interested in lifting a curse." June shrugged as she slid by the globe. She continued facing the witch, Chelsea in tow.

"Dear sister!" Vik called out as the girls made turns through endless shelves.

"What, Viktoria?" the cop's voice, devoid of its official on-the-job weight, whined.

"What did Sheriff Marrock tell you to do if you caught the Szmydt girl snooping around the murder investigation again?!"

The other witch, Officer Azantian, the cop who'd been guarding the crime scene two days ago and the sheriff's office just this afternoon, turned a corner, openly displaying her green warty skin, and blocked what may have been June's only way out. "Let me think, dear sister... 'Turn the little shit into a frog' were his exact words."

Chapter Fourteen: October 31, still afternoon

Jaws clenched, palms sweaty, June and Chelsea backed into each other, each facing one of the witch sisters. June had never been turned into a frog before (obviously), but was slightly heartened knowing that Chelsea had been a stork and Officer Ani had been a goat only a couple hours earlier. If June was going to get turned into a frog, she trusted Chelsea to get her back to normal. And if they both got turned, then they were just plain fucked. June closed her eyes and prayed it wouldn't hurt.

"There's not any snooping going on around here like the sheriff said, is there?" The witch cop had regained her air of authority.

"I...I'm just trying to help out my dad."

Officer Ani's green face softened. Vik didn't buy it, barking, "Poking around asking about lifting a curse, right, ladies?"

"And what makes you think lifting a curse would help your dad?"

"Alright, witches!" Chelsea proclaimed, drawing and aiming the little quarter-wand like a loaded gun, "Back off! I don't want to have to use this!"

"And I doubt you know how, darling," the tawny-skinned Vik replied, brandishing her own knotty willow wand. The sisters now stood at opposite ends of the book-shelved room pointing wands at the girls.

"Come on now," June said, attempting to diffuse the situation, "I'd make a terrible frog. With these thick calves?"

"So, someone lifted your veil and now you want to share all the magic in the world with Daddy, is that it?" Officer Ani took a menacing step closer.

June finally blurted in a voice much higher than she intended, making her sound real real scared, "I think the mayor shot Vernon Carlisle, cursed my father, and had Evens Bonhomme arrested to cover it all up, but I don't know why!"

"Stay back, bro, I'll use this thing!" exclaimed Chelsea, still pointing her wand.

The green-faced sister was confused. "Vernon Carlisle wasn't shot."

"He wasn't?"

"No, he died from self-inflicted wand wounds."

"But that could have been faked!"

"Maybe."

"By someone who wanted to absorb my father's powers at the height of Samhain!"

"Likely story darling," Vik drawled.

"Where'd you hear all this?" asked Officer Ani.

"The Persian guy!"

"Persian?" the witch sisters asked at the same time.

"Who?" asked Chelsea, genuinely thrown.

"Mo. Mo Tilden."

"You don't know Mo Tilden." Vik scoffed, dismissing June

making a face, and shaking her head.

"He came to our house, two nights ago. Left his card. But then after the veil was lifted, it wasn't a business card. And then he was at my house, and told me that someone was going to kill Dad and steal his power on midnight of Samhain."

"You? Had Mo Tilden's summoning card? Not likely, dear."

"It's true! I asked him to help us, to lift Dad's curse, but he just yelled at me."

"I don't believe you. It's froggy time for you two darlings." Vik swirled her gnarled wand in the air, sparks flying from the end, growing bigger and brighter.

"What did Mo Tilden say?" Officer Ani asked accusingly.

June clamped her eyes shut, bracing for the impact of the wands force while frowning and yelling in her best impression of the Persian Jewish man, "You blew it! You blew it!"

Both witch sisters gasped. "You do know Mo Tilden!"

Then Officer Ani got serious and asked, "Who's trying to usurp Dobiel?"

The question caught June off guard. Who's Dobiel?

Vik rolled her eyes. "Ugh, get over it, dear sister. I want to know about the summoning card. Do you still have it? Does Mo still have his moustache? Nobody could sport a push broom mustache like Mo Tilden."

"No, I guess I lost the card. Or left it in my yard. Who's Dobiel?"

But Officer Ani was lost in thought. "Maybe the Mayor was in on this, then. I figured it was Sheriff Marrock until we brought in Evens."

June asserted herself, she had to get an answer before the conversation steam-rolled her, "Who's Dobiel?"

The sisters looked at each other, eyebrows arching with

familial similarity. Officer Ani spoke delicately, "The ghost veil was recently lifted, right? Like just now?"

June felt like she was being talked down to. She took a breath to calm herself and humored the policewoman. "No, not just now. Last night."

"Okay, then do me a favor and tell me your father's name."

"What?"

"Just say your father's name."

"Uh, okay...Dobiel." The word hit June's mouth funny. She hadn't meant to say Dobiel, she'd meant to say Daryl, which was obviously Dad's name. She went to say Daryl again. "Dobiel. Wait. what am I saying? His name's not Dobiel, it's Dobiel. Why can't I say Dobiel? It's Dobiel! Dobiel, Dobiel, Dobiel!" June was near hysterics shouting it.

Dropping her wand, Chelsea grabbed June by the hands and shushed her in an attempt to calm her down.

"That's veil magic, sweetheart," Officer Ani said in soothing tones. "You are okay. You just never heard your father's true name before, never spoken it. It's Dobiel."

With the other women in the room distracted, Vik snatched the quarter wand from the floor, held her own in her other hand, and wielded them together. They flashed bright, blinding everyone in the room for a moment. The acrid smell of burnt flesh filled the air, and when everything cleared, black smoke marks accented Vik's hands and face like after a cartoon explosion.

"A necromancer's wand!" Vik howled. "You paid me with a filthy fucking necromancer wand?!"

"Vik, calm yourself," Ani warned.

"I will not, I could have been killed! What fucking use to me is a necromancer wand? Get out of my shop!"

"Vik! It's my shop, too, and they're staying until we figure this out."

"What's to figure out? This is Carlisle's wand, he died, and now it's fucking useless!"

"Maybe you just don't know how to use it," Chelsea snapped with attitude.

"This thing is useless unless you can control the dead."

"Why do you think Carlisle was killed?" Officer Ani was interested and pulled up a chair from the coffee table.

"Why are they still in my shop?"

"Vik, this is serious."

"Ani, she let me fire a necromancer wand!"

"I heard you the first time, Vik! There's nothing wrong with necromancers. And you're fine. You survived. Probably wouldn't have happened if you practiced your wand skills at all." Officer Ani continued talking to the girls. "What's the mayor's motive?"

"To protect all the curses on Dobiel until Samhain."

"Because the only way to lift his curses-" Vik began.

"Is to kill him?" Ani finished the idea. "So Carlisle was going to release the lynchpin."

"Evens mentioned that. What's the linchpin?"

"Some folks know about the blindfold. Holds the town together, full of powerful magic he can't see. The linchpin is another legend. 'From the simplest wheel to the most complex conspiracy, every machine has a linchpin, an innocuous part that can bring it all down, tear the whole thing apart, but stays pinned to the wheel, ignorantly spinning.' It's an obscure sorcerer spell. I've thought that the blindfold was the linchpin in Miridical for a while."

"He's also the Loof, and the..." June pulled out the diner

receipt she'd scribbled Even's list on. "Yep, the Linchpin. The Chains of Epimetheus, Presto Hide-o, the shaman's bone finger, and the Suck-ulator Three-Thousand."

Officer Ani froze. "Wait a second. If you think that killing your father is the only way to shed his curses, were you two planning to kill the deputy mayor?"

June looked away and shrugged. "Unless we find a way to undo all seven spells in the right order, we may have to." She turned and added urgently, "We'd bring him back!"

"How?"

"We'd also need to find that out from a book."

"Fuck me," Officer Ani said, slumping into the leatherback chair. "This is why the moon vanished. Why the beasts have shown up. Miridical is on a cusp. Vik, we're going to have to call in some help."

"Who?" Vik asked.

"Well, I'm not going to read every book in here to figure out how to undo all the curses, or, if we have to, raise him from the dead. You know the only ones who can help." The sisters looked at each other knowingly.

"We don't," Chelsea pointed out.

"Oh, no we're not. This is my shop, I'll not have it destroyed or eaten, or whatever they do! You want to run around town playing police officer, that's your business, but I'm the one who kept this place open, answered the phones, dusted the tomes, and even made a deal with the devil himself and sold through Amazon."

"And if the linchpin dies, the magic protecting Miridical will fail and there won't be a store anymore. We need help."

June was about to burst. "Will someone please tell us what's going on?!"

"If someone is planning on killing your dear old Dad, the linchpin, tonight, midnight of Samhain at the peak of his powers..." Vik reluctantly began.

Officer Ani picked up where her sister left off, "The murderer could extract his power to personally keep Miridical safely hidden forever without a linchpin or a blind man."

Vik finished, "And become the most powerful wielder of magic in Miridical, on Earth, maybe even on all the Earths."

"All the Earths?" June repeated.

"One thing at a time, darling. If we want to stop the murderer, whoever he is –"

"Or her," Chelsea interjected defiantly.

"Oh, please, dear, you know it's a man behind this."

"If we want to stop him," Officer Ani continued, "we'll have to figure out how to kill and resurrect Dobiel and free him of all curses while keeping the power structure in Miridical intact."

"What power structure?"

"Oh, I know this one!" Chelsea was excited, like there was a question in geometry she knew the answer to. She closed one eye squinting while reciting the answer, "The framework of the magical power in Miridical keeps the town hidden from the rest of the world. Only the magically touched can enter the town limits, and everyone's magic is more powerful the closer they are to the town square."

"Great, so how do we lift the curses and save the framework?" June asked.

Nodding, Chelsea threw in, "Yeah, which book is that in?"

The sister answered in unison, "We don't know."

"There are like thousands of books in here." Chelsea's eyes went to the book-lined labyrinth walls.

Vik let out a chuckle. "Thousands? Don't insult an Armenian

woman in her own home. We have millions of books and double that in storage."

June's heart sank. It was too much. This wasn't some mystery, figuring out who committed an act. This wasn't clues and witnesses and studying photos. This was taking apart a cloth thread by thread. This was untangling insects from spiderwebs.

Mysteries Juniper Szmydt could handle. Magical town secrets were just too big.

"Which is why..." Officer Ani set her green face, eyebrows slanted in determination, "I'm calling in the book wyrms."

Vik visibly shuddered.

June tried to hold on to hope that whatever could get under the skin of a powerful witch like Viktoria Azantian could also help them solve the mystery of how to save her dad and the town.

Chapter Fifteen: October 31, still afternoon, there may be some time-fuckery going on

While the girls, faces white as sheets, sat with their mouths agape, desperately trying not to stare when the bookwyrms arrived, the witch sisters couldn't stop arguing as they set up tea service.

"No, it wasn't that long ago. Mom and Dad were still alive. The sugar goes to your left, Ani."

"It's not facing me, it's facing you. The sugar goes to your left. Yeah, Dad never did get to summon any armies through books."

"He did always go on about it. Do take the chipped cup, Ani." Vik gestured to the girls sitting eyes wide and mouths agape at the ever-expanding number of book wyrms. "The boney one can have your old cup and the brunette can have Mom's."

"Don't be rude, Vik, we can't all disguise ourselves in spells. I can see why Dad obsessed over the book wyrms. I was expecting an onslaught of mystics; I was not prepared for this. They're so..." Officer Ani searched for a word.

Vik had one. "Attractive."

"Really, Vik?" Ani asked with a sour look. Aware of the sheer number of the skittering human-insect hybrids, she straightened her posture and began pouring from a ceramic teapot. Keeping her side-eye on the throngs of the chiseled masculine bugs, she asked, "Can they understand us?"

"I don't believe so, dear. They seem to have their own language."

"Well, I find them deeply disturbing. As is your attraction to them. I think this current dry streak may be affecting your perception." Officer Ani proceeded to serve tea.

From out of the book of spells that originally summoned them, more of the bald-save-for-antennae book wyrms crawled one by one, scurried out to the nearest shelves, opening each book and flipping furiously through pages using all of their appendages, speed-reading at a break-neck pace. And from the opened spell book, now a door to some other place, more and more of the little bug men kept coming. In very little time, the book store was literally crawling with them.

The sight gave June the willies, and she noticed the goose-bumps on Chelsea's arms, too. They split one of the high-backed leather chairs, the contact of their legs touching a comfort June clung to. Taking a lid off a dainty sugar jar, Officer Ani asked the girls sweetly, "How do you take it?"

With a smile hiding a grimace, June asked, "How do I take what?"

Chelsea matched the witch's even tone, answering politely, "Rough and all night long, thank you very much."

Unsuccessfully, June suppressed a laugh.

Without taking her eyes off the book wyrm's work, Vik said, "I like her."

Officer Ani looked dedicated to being a stick-in-the-mud and wasn't having it. "Ladies, please. How do you take your tea?"

"I don't know." June shrugged. "I've never had tea."

Both sisters snapped their heads at June, gasping. Ani almost dropped her cup, and Vik's spoon clattered onto her saucer. June's cheeks grew as steamy as her drink under their attention.

"Hello?" Chelsea interjected to rescue June, "This is Rhode Island? Don't you have any coffee milk?"

Vik's eyebrows lowered as she scowled and shook her head.

"What about coffee? Any Dunkin up in this piece? Starfucks?" Chelsea was just messing with them now, June knew, putting on a voice to make fun of the witches.

Vik rolled her eyes. Her green sister didn't let it get to her, answering, "How about one sugar and a lemon? Unless you'd prefer cream?"

The noise of the bookwyrms grew cacophonous. On top of the rushing of quickly flipping pages, the sound of so many scuttling legs filled the room with a loud white noise. They also communicated in short exchanges of surprisingly deep voices speaking in a foreign language that sounded like variations of, "Geegle gargle heegle google."

The tea was delicate and warming, and soothed June immediately, bringing her notice to how tense her shoulders and back were.

"So when did you remove the ghost veil?" Officer Ani asked off-handedly.

"Last night."

"And the two of you did the procedure?" the sheriff's Patrol Officer probed further, her khaki uniform untucked and her brown hair with blond highlights was let down, a much more approachable look than when she was on duty. June took mental note. This lady is good at interviewing witnesses. "Do it yourselves or with the aid of a spellbook?"

"We went to little Haiti."

"Oh, good people, the Bonhommes."

Vik smiled over a sip of tea. "Strapping, handsome lads."

"Vik, please, this is polite conversation. And what brought the veil to your attention?"

The girls looked at each other, then quickly away.

"Oh," Officer Ani said before diverting her eyes back to her own teacup.

Vik uncrossed and recrossed her legs, leaning into the girls. "I, too, dabbled in the love that dare not speak its name."

"Vik," Ani warned.

"I'm not shaming them. Stressful situations lead to strange bedfellows." Her eyes wandered to the nearest muscly little book wyrm.

Officer Ani dropped a teaspoon with a clatter. "I say good for you two. Young love is a powerful and magical force."

At the word 'love,' June felt panic rise in her, shoulders tensing once again. She spied Chelsea out of the corner of her eye, and the girl wouldn't back look at her.

"Don't embarrass them, dear sister," Vik said as she poured the contents of a flask to top off her tea.

The constant scurrying of millions of legs and flipping of thousands of pages halted immediately. One book wyrm, halfway out of the portal of the book, reversed back in from whence it came, followed by a rush of the other little creatures dropping their books wherever they were and heading back.

Approaching them, a book wyrm holding a book over its head,

skittered up the side of Officer Ani's chair to stand on the arm and presented her with a specific page.

"I believe they've found it."

As the room was still crawling with book wyrms heading back to wherever they came from after a hard half-hour's work, Vik paced around the two chairs, reading through the glasses perched at the end of her nose, "Blessed are you, king of the universe, onto your ball you sent your only bear, who will lose his immortality in forgetfulness, lose his path with blindness, and lose his family by his own hand. Only in death shall the bear again claim immortality, dying as a leaf on your ball, and a true believer's grief shall spring a spring leaf's green once more."

"I hate spells," Chelsea said dejectedly. "Tougher to understand than mumble rap."

But June was already breaking down the spell's wording. "So God's ball is obviously the earth. Who's the true believer? True believer in what?"

Vik shrugged. "In Dobiel."

"In Dad?"

Ani took over, speaking very carefully and avoiding a leer from her sister, "Your father is...this may be difficult to hear about your dad, but he..."

"Ugh. Gross. I know you're crushing on Dad, NBD. Don't want to hear it."

"That's not it."

"Isn't it, dear sister?" Vik smiled wryly.

"Damn it, Vik! June, your Dad's an ancient bear god."

Wait.

Doubting she heard that right, June started to chuckle at the absurdity of the idea that her big goofus dad could be a deity.

But the laugh caught in her throat. She knew it was true. She saw his bright beastly form, felt the power off of him. But...an ancient bear god? "What?" the word escaped her lips in a dry exhale.

Chelsea exclaimed, "That's sick!"

June's analytical mind fought against the idea, despite all the magic she'd witnessed in the past day. She clung to logic. "What do you mean? He can't be. We're Jewish, there's only one God."

Chelsea piped in to add, "Yaweh."

Desperation had shortened June's temper. "Chelsea, cool it!"

"Here, I can find this book myself." Vik perused a nearby shelf, running silver-ringed fingers along until they clawed onto a hardback spine. She laid it down on the coffee table before the girls. The words were all in Yiddish, and Vik fingered through pages, past illustrations of bearded men in tunics in the desert, in caves, or on mountain tops. She stopped on the illustration of the gates of a walled desert city guarded by a man in a loincloth who stood within the outline of a bear.

June's breath seized at the sight — beyond regal, godlike. "I thought the bear, his aura or whatever, was just one of his curses."

"That's him, darling. That's who he is. Dobiel, the Jewish bear god of Persia."

"And that's him in Ancient Persia? How old is he?"

"A rude question, dear."

"Vik," Officer Ani chided before looking sternly to June. "I don't know how old he is. And I don't think he knows either, I don't think he remembers who he is."

"But...but we can fix this. We can lift the curses."

"He'll have to die like a leaf on God's ball." Everyone looked expectantly at Vik. "Natural causes," she explained.

That made sense.

Vik lit up when the thought came to her. "Poison."

Her sister the cop didn't sound as enthusiastic. "Maybe don't sound so excited when thinking of a murder weapon."

"Why? You're not going to arrest me, officer dear, are you?"

Officer Ani laughed it off, but June wouldn't drop the subject. "But for real, if we do this, I have to know if you're going to turn on us if we do something illegal."

"Wait." Chelsea shook her head, like she was fending off nonsense thoughts to try to understand. "What exactly are you talking about here?"

The women and girls looked at each other for a moment, barely breathing, tense as a drum.

Ani answered June. "There is some seriously big time bad shit going down in this town. And a lot of people are lying about it. I'm here to protect the town. To save your dad. With you guys."

June was relieved, but Chelsea kept pressing for an answer. "Save her dad by doing what? We aren't really considering this, are we?"

But June was focused on her new allies, the Azantians. "Breaking this case could mean bringing down the mayor."

Ani frowned. "Why the Mayor?"

"He's been the one keeping Dad in his place. Turned Dad against me. I know he's the one behind all of this."

Slumped in her chair, the untucked officer asked herself with a soft sense of awe, "Can we kill an ancient god with poison?"

Vik pointed. "He's locked into a human form, so yes."

"And then we resurrect him?"

"The faith of a true believer, darling."

Chelsea stood and waved off the idea. "We can not be serious about this. We are not talking about murdering to solve a murder."

But June was stuck in deep thought, sucking hard at the gap behind her tooth. "Like...a Jew?"

"Oh, that's perfect." Vik splayed her hands. "Juniper, dear, you're Jewish, you believe in your Dad; your faith should resurrect him."

"And then we'll have a bear god on our side to take down the mayor," Officer Ani growled in her authority voice.

"And finally get the damn moon back!" Vik took a swig straight from her flask.

Vik and Ani stood, grabbing hands in excitement and jump-ing.

Chelsea leaned in to whisper to June, her words terse and chiding, like when she'd bark at Hailey. "This is ridiculous, June. You can't do this." This wasn't how Chelsea had been speaking to her since that day in the woods.

"You're right," June said, still sucking on her tooth making that whistling, squirrelly noise. She stood and confessed to the sisters, "I'm not really Jewish."

"You're not?"

"Well, ethnically, yes, but I never even had a Bat Mitzvah." Ani and Vik deflated, collapsed back in their chairs. A lump bubbled up in June's throat. "And we're the only Jews in Miridical."

The idea knocked the breath out of the room, everyone in a stunned silence. Except Vik; she hopped over to a shelf of scrolls June hadn't noticed before.

"Easy," Vik pronounced with determination, pulling out a

massive scroll, like two oversized rolling pins bigger than her torso. She plopped it down on top of the book illustration of Dobiel. "Let's have our own Bat Mitzvah! La heim."

June cocked her head at the familiar-looking scroll. "Is that a Torah?"

"It's the Torah, darling." Vik's bright white smile flashed behind her dark complexion and sinfully red lipstick. She winked at June. "It's a first edition."

"Don't we need a rabbi?" asked June.

"And a congregation?" asked Ani.

"And a synagogue?" asked June.

"Ladies, we have all of that and more." A sly smile crept across Vik's face. "We have the internet."

####

"Thank you again, Rabbi, for this opportunity." June's voice was quaking. Before her, on one monitor, was a live video feed of the Temple Beth-El congregation in Providence, rows and rows of dour-faced Jews, mostly elderly, flanked by two rabbis in full yarmulkas and scarves or other holy gear June couldn't identify. One rabbi was a handsome young man in his thirties, pale with tufts of thick curly black hair. The other was a confused old man wearing an expression that was half-smile, half confused.

On another monitor was a pronunciation guide to the Hebrew June was expected to sing. June herself had on a similar scarf, a personal microphone, and more make-up than she'd ever worn in her life. Vik had done it, complaining about the Jewish girl's complexion the entire time ("It's just too light for any of my colors!"). The rabbis squinted and looked through the computer expectantly.

"This is the absent mind?" Officer Ani whispered to her sister off-camera.

Vik nodded.

"What does that mean?" Chelsea whispered back.

"They think they agreed to this already, but forgot about it."

Chelsea's jaw dropped. "You incepted them!"

"Exactly, darling. They think this is her father's dying wish."

"That's cold."

"It's not that far off, darling."

The earbuds June had in gave June the melody she was expected to recited the foreign words to, as the monitor displaying those words lit up to the tune, like Hebrew karaoke. But she could barely hear herself think over Vik and Chelsea going back and forth.

With June's horrendous singing to accompany, the girls off-camera set to work at the coffee table.

"Okay, enough admiring your handiwork, let's pestle some poison." Ani opened the jars they'd pulled, dumping contents into a stone bowl.

Vik spoke to herself in a mocking tone, "'Thanks, Vik, for saving our asses,' 'What a perfect solution, Vik,' 'Vik, you're so much smarter and prettier than your older sister.'"

####

By the time the confused yet polite old rabbi pronounced June as a woman and an official member of the congregation, the other three had filled a vial with the fruits of their labor. It had a sharp evergreen smell that replaced the tobacco and wood scent of the bookstore.

June politely thanked everyone in what was now her congregation with a series of thank-yous and shaloms. Chelsea called from out of the camera shot, "Ms. Szmydt, it's time to visit your father!"

And June smiled pathetically and waved goodbye.

Vik turned off the monitors and asked "Do you think the Rabbi was single? Did you see a ring?"

"Oh, Vik, lay off." Officer Ani rolled her eyes.

"What? Oh for you, not me. You think things could work out between you and a thousand year old bear deity?"

With the relief of having a plan, June packed her bookbag with her veil and the poison, laughed, and said to Chels, "Well, now that I've gone full Jew, I guess Hailey's really going to hate me."

Chelsea shrugged it off. "Oh, Hailey was just happy not to be made fun of from being from such an uber-Catholic family." But rather than the buzzing excitement the other women had as the plan gained steam, Chelsea hesitated. "I don't think this is such a hot idea, Juniper."

June smiled, touched by the care of her former bully. This was the first time any of these feelings had been reciprocated to June. Someone who cared for her, that wasn't family or Connor, someone into her. "Thank you," June said and brushed a strand of hair out of Chelsea's face and behind her ear. They both smiled, but June's was hopeful and Chelsea's was shallow and scared.

Vik helped June into her coat. "Charming. Now darling, I hexed the contents of the vial to be painless, so with his veil still on, your father shouldn't be able to smell or taste the poison."

"Are you sure you don't want a ride back home in my squad car?"

"No, I don't want Dad to think anything's up. Besides, don't you guys have plans for Samhain?"

"Of course, darling, but we can get ready in a snap." Vik snapped her fingers, and both sisters were suddenly in beautiful lacey black gowns with high white ruffled collars, like couture Puritans.

Officer Ani glared at her sister and snapped, changing herself into a red pantsuit, seething, "I don't require any help, dear sister."

The sisters turned their attention back to the girls, all of them taking turns hugging one another.

"You'll be wonderful, darling. You've been so brave, walking into a witch's shop. It takes...what's the word? Chutzpah."

"If anything goes down, I want you to have your phone on and ready to dial 911. You can ask dispatch to send me."

June nodded and pocketed the poison.

"Do you want to get going, darlings?" Vik smiled.

And suddenly, June was back outside. It was dark by now, and much colder. She zipped up her coat and gloved up, careful of the vial in her pocket. "So I guess I can introduce you to my dad?" June asked Chelsea.

Only Chelsea wasn't there.

June looked around the front of the book store. She was standing outside the short white picket fence in the dusky grey, barely any light coming off the wards and runes protecting the buildings of Miridical. June had always heard this known as "the witching hour" but enchantments seemed to be waning.

Where'd Chelsea go?

And as soon as June thought it, Chelsea was right there in front of her. Even with unkept hair and a sad tired face, Chelsea looked clean and fresh and beautiful. But so sad. She had tears in her eyes. The moments Chelsea stayed back in the bookstore were spent crying.

They stood a few feet away from one another, a whistling wind tugging their coats and hair. It felt like they were a soccer field apart.

"I can't go with you," Chelsea said, her voice breaking higher and higher, as if she were afraid to say something so sad.

June let out a meaningless laugh. Hot tears pushed up under her eyes. "Well, I can't do this alone."

Chelsea took a step forward, like she wanted to run, but only for a split second. "Then don't. What if we confronted the mayor, or called the sheriff?"

June could only shake her head. They both knew there was nothing else to be done.

But Chelsea kept trying. "Or went back to the Bonhommes? Or took the evidence to the Governor's office or the RIBI? Or..."

Chelsea searched for more wrong ideas, but said nothing. She was crying now, tears streaming down her cheeks, eyes locked with June's. Not that June was keeping it together. She honestly didn't know if she could do it alone, even if she did know that Chelsea had been against killing Dad since they brought it up.

"How did your mom die?"

Chelsea's change of subject made June bristle. Then she swallowed hard and answered, her mouth mucusy with emotion. "She was killed in a car accident."

"Were things different before she died? Were you different?"

June shrugged. "Everything was different."

"Then don't risk your dad."

The thought of him, of both of them, being helpless against the curses controlling Dad lit a fire in June, and her answer rumbled low. "That's not my dad. I have to get him back."

"Blood mages can't do anything to physically hurt other creatures."

The idea almost made June laugh. She felt pretty hurt being left by Chelsea. "So you won't help me?"

"I can't."

And then there was a moment, a lull in the conversation when June was so full of emotions that if she didn't say something, she'd burst. "No one's ever liked me like this. Like you. I thought you hated me." The word hate was insufficient, but June filled it with bile and contempt. "And I tried to hate you back. And now I have to do this thing, this thing I've been moving towards ever since I found out about this murder. And even if it means losing you, I have to do it, because there's nothing else to do, and fighting this thing is who I am and..." Then the words failed.

But then Chelsea was on her, hugging her, cradling her head against her chest.

"You're not losing me, Juniper. But I can't do this with you. I can't support you doing this. There has to be another way."

"There is no other way," June whispered into Chelsea's tear-dampened hair.

"Then you're going somewhere I can't follow. And I hope to the Demon you can come back."

June looked up at Chelsea, her eyes darkened by the oncoming night. And June kissed her. Deeply.

"I'll come back for you."

"I'm so sorry, Juniper. I feel like I got you into all of this with that stupid summoning spell, and the manticore, and the jailbreak. And now when it gets really tough, I'm just abandoning you."

"Hey, hey." June took Chelsea's china-white chin in her

hands, thumbing away streaking mascara. "I never would have known the truth without you. Never would have seen this. All of this, this magical place I've lived in for years but was blind to...you gave me all this." June's lower lip quivered and her voice shook as she spoke. "You've saved my life in so many ways, and getting to know you, really getting to know you, is what my people call a Mitzvah."

June got on her tippy-toes and kissed her former bully and crush on the forehead.

And then Chelsea walked off back toward her house on the other side of Miridical. June checked her out as she sauntered away and managed a smile.

"Now." June cleared her throat and collected herself. Her voice was coarse and low, fatigue pushed by determination. "Time to go kill my dad."

Chapter Sixteen: Dusk

The town was eerily quiet and dark in the moonless night. Not sleeping, but coiled, ready to strike. Even the houses, which had been emitting light and symbols, now only faintly glowed, as if conserving energy. June felt eyes on her peeping from every window.

As houses were full of Miridicaliens preparing for Samhain, not a single trick-or-treater was out to make light of such a holy day. The streets betrayed no shimmering reflection, as if the inky black sky could somehow reflect a lack of light. The gentle shushing of the swaying Boston Oaks reminded June of partygoers waiting to spring a surprise on a birthday girl. Only this surprise would be much more grim than some sparsely attended party.

June had never been popular, even when they lived in Massachusetts back when Mom was still alive. But now...now it was her against everyone, against the mayor and most likely his stooge sheriff, against whoever all these elders were, against everyone. Alone. Her most trusted allies were at best neutral—witches not actively against her, her hot blood mage crush too busy to help, and her father sidelined by curses. To say she was in over her head made too light of the situation - drowning people weren't being pushed down my magical forces. Her footsteps seemed to echo, adding a staggered beat to the wooshing autumn leaves.

A ragged, tired voice, called out behind June, barely louder than the Boston Oaks. "Why weren't you at Del's?" With his track record of terrible timing, June shouldn't have been surprised that Connor would show up now.

"I have nothing to say to you, Connor." June kept walking.

"We were supposed to go get lemonades today. It's their last day of the year. We talked about it all summer. It was your idea."

"Enough, Connor. I'm the town idiot and you never said anything! I've never felt so stupid in my life. How could I even think you were my friend, that you were capable-"

"That's not fair. I told you I had no idea people were keeping secrets from you. And I didn't."

"I don't believe you."

"The fuck's that supposed to mean?"

"Maybe you were in on it the whole time, Connor! Maybe you just acted like my friend so I wouldn't dig for the truth."

"Are you fucking kidding me? Who was there for you when you begged your dad to change schools? Who was there when the mean girls, whose ass you now kiss, told everyone you killed your own mom? Remember when you thought no one fucking cared about you and you'd be better off dead? Who talked you down off that ledge?"

"Then why didn't you tell me my dad was a fucking bear, Connor? That he was an ancient God of Persia? Why didn't that ever come up? That everything in town is just jizzing magic, and I was walking around blind to it?"

She didn't even know where to aim her anger, arguing with a disembodied voice. June couldn't take it and stormed off.

"Because I was fucking jealous, okay?" From his voice, June could tell Connor was crying now. "Because I hate this fucking town and my fucking family and all I've ever wanted was to run away with someone cool, somewhere I could be myself. And you have everything, June. Everything. So what if the girls at school make fun of you? It's high school. High school sucks for everybody.

"But you have your dad. He's cool as shit. You're gay and he still loves you. He's given up whatever life he could have had to move to this shitty small town, hold a shitty job where everyone treats him like shit all for you. You treat him like shit and he still loves you. And the both of you are the most powerful people in the whole town, maybe the whole state, and not just because of whatever ancient magic. But because you have each other's backs and you can make it through anything. Because you have made it through everything. And you don't appreciate what you have.

"So yeah, I had one way in my tiny, miserable life to have one up on you. Because you're too blind to know what you've got. Not magic, but a fucking family. And I don't. I just have you. And if keeping a secret about your dad's position as a Persian God or lying to you about your royal Pixie powers meant I could keep you as a friend, then it was worth it. Even if we're never friends again, it was worth it to have somebody to talk to, someone to sit with at lunch, so I wasn't always so fucking miserable and lonely all the time.

"And I'm sorry how you found out about it, and I'm sorry you're upset, but it was worth it, and I know I'd do it all over again, lie to you about the magic all around, the magic in you, just to have you as my friend, Nipslip. I'm just selfish like that, I guess."

June didn't know what to say. She was just so exhausted, she couldn't probe his words, couldn't search for the manipulation, the angle he was taking on behalf of the town or the elders or whoever was behind all of this trying to control her. She could only hear his words as he spoke them, accept them at face value.

Connor had always been so unhappy, so depressed. And whenever she felt bad, he felt worse. But together, even if they didn't feel any better, at least on top of everything else, they didn't have to feel alone.

She kicked at the ground, looking at her Doc Martens, and asked him, "You're not going to try to stop me, are you?"

"When have I ever tried to stop you from doing anything, Nipslip? I wouldn't even know where to start."

They both almost laughed, which was a welcome departure from the existential dread June had been feeling since planning a jailbreak this morning, which seemed like years ago. Connor spoke after a pause. "So what are we doing?"

"Going to kill my dad?"

"What?"

"It's a long story," she said, not looking at him, but hooking her arm in his. "I'll tell you on the way."

"Okay, I guess? Your make-up is on point, BTW."

"I know, Connor."

####

Taking a deep breath, attempting to act normal after the absolutely numbing past few days, June stood at her door of the giant, night-darkened birdcage, building up the courage to walk into her own home. In the bushes, Connor gave her a thumb's up, which she returned before inserting her keys and walking inside.

Zippy and his smell greeted her at the door and he was... soaking wet. The enormous pony-sized dog licked her face with his forked tongue and she scratched him behind the ears and around the horns, all six of his eyes rolling back in ecstasy at the attention.

"Dad?" she called into the darkened wood-slatted cage of a house. There was a rustling, a thudding of heavy steps. Within her coat, June clutched the vial of poison, and with a deep breath, she strode pushed through the swinging kitchen door.

The overheads flickered on, the only source of light in the gloomy house, and she immediately noticed the jagged glass around the coffeemaker, the globe of the pot with a chunk missing. What had happened?

From the cabinet, she pulled a couple of pint glasses with the URI logo, where Mom and Dad had met. From the fridge, she grabbed the coffee syrup and whole milk. Admittedly, she was parched, and her body craved the drink. That made this infinitesimally easier.

After coating the glasses with Autocrat coffee syrup, she pulled out the vial and uncapped it, pouring the contents into the glass with the big blue ram painted on. The thick, sweet coffee scent was eclipsed by the Christmasy smell of evergreen needles and dried flowers. Arnica and Juniper.

She filled both glasses to the top with milk, took a spoon, and stirred. Instead of the nutty the Autocrat that she adored, she only smelled the stinging poison. But Dad's veil should shield him from the acrid odor. Should.

"Why are you home so late?" Dad's booming voice demanded.

His sudden question from the other side of the kitchen shocked June, and her hand tipped over the blue ram glass. Her other hand shot out and grasped it, spilling only a little of the poisoned coffee milk onto the counter.

"I texted you," she pouted, turning to her father with a glass of coffee milk in each hand. "I had to work the football game."

But Dad was no longer Dad. The big teddy bear who'd always treated her so gently with love and bad jokes was gone. Alit in his fiery aura was Dobiel, the ferocious bear god, his animal shoulders bristling with fur standing on end, his beastly head as tall as the ceiling, his eyes burning bright white in the low kitchen light. When Dad spoke, the bear's mouth displayed its enormous canines, gleaming, dripping with drool, jawing along with the man's - no, not man's - the cursed god's words, "As punishment? What did you do this time?"

She shrugged, controlling her breath as best she could. "Someone scratched graffiti onto my locker. They figure it was me."

"Was it?" her dad, Dobiel the bear god, snarled.

"No," she said dejectedly before adding, "but I guess I'm suspect number one these days." That was easy to say; that wasn't lying.

He thought about it for a moment, and June's mind raced for an excuse if he continued to press her on the issue. Instead, he said simply, "I'm going out for a meeting."

Blinking, June betrayed no reaction, "Now?"

"Some citizens want to talk to me about replacing the mayor."

The words hit her ear like a wrong note standing out in a pop song. "Replacing the mayor? As in soon?"

"There are people unhappy with his work as of late. Think I

can do better."

"Oh, okay," she said as if the news were no surprise. Thoughts rushed to her. Who would want to replace the mayor? Did someone else have control over Dad? Was the mayor innocent?

Suddenly, she had to pause this plan and think about it. If the mayor wasn't the killer, if he wasn't the one behind all of this, June had to regroup. Was it possible she was wrong? Was she about to kill her own father for no reason?

She felt dizzy, sick. Behind the calm veneer, she wanted to scream, cry, and vomit all at once. But she couldn't. She was frozen in fear, face plastered with an unsurprised expression. Hands still gripping two freshly poured glasses of cold coffee milk.

Dad's big mitt reached out and grabbed the glass closest to him.

She was just having second thoughts. Right? No matter who was behind this, no matter who the murderer was, June had to save Dad from these curses. This is the only way. She had to stick to the plan. June's chest froze. Her guts clenched. For a moment she couldn't remember if he'd grabbed the poison one or the other. But no. She'd held the poison one out. And now Dad, Dobiel the bear god, the man who cried five times watching Moana while holding his daughter's hand, raised the glass of poisonous coffee milk to his lips.

Why don't I just slap it out of his hand? But June was frozen in panic, only able to watch. This is the only way.

Then Dad paused, raised an eyebrow, and asked, "You're not surprised? About the mayor?"

"I guess..." June had to force herself to talk, pushing her voice to keep it from quivering, pulling her eyes away from the glass to look at Dad. "I kind of expected it from what you said the other day."

Squinting at her, searching her words, he again brought the coffee milk to his face, sniffing it, his bear mouth scrunching in time with his thick round nose. June held her breath. Would he smell the poison? Did his bear-self have an acute sense of smell that would surpass the veil?

"You know," he said, putting the glass down on the counter, as June exhaled, desperately keeping eye contact, "a mayor couldn't send his kid off to school in the next town. It wouldn't look right. You'd have to stay at Miridical Prep."

His hand wrapped around the glass again, and June pretended to look deep in thought as he hefted the coffee milk up and held it in his thick, bent arm. His eyes searched her face, and when she was certain he wouldn't move until she responded, she managed to eek out a quiet, "Okay."

"Okay?" He was suddenly gruff and placed the glass back on the counter before stepping towards her. "Months of begging and pleading, now you're in the principal's office constantly, and when you can't go to the school you've been hounding me about, all you can say is 'okay?'"

Holding the angry gaze of his half-man-half-glowing-bear eyes, she again felt the urge to switch the glasses.

No, this is the only way. So she let loose, letting go of all the feelings that her father's disappointment and distance had stirred in her. To get everything off her chest. She let go of the anxiety, anger at Connor, feelings for Chelsea, the whirlwind her life had become. She inhaled in choking staccato sobs, but had no more tears.

"I'm just tired, Dad." Her voice had the rough edge of rock on vinyl. "Whatever you want to do. I just want to go back to the way things were when we were happy, and you were proud of me."

She pushed past him, as if to run out of the kitchen and into the hall, but instead she stopped at the end of the counter and spoke without turning around...or looking as she placed her glass of plain coffee milk down. "I've just been so angry, and I guess I took it out on you, and that wasn't fair. You've done so much, sacrificed so much after Mom died."

As she faced him, tears now streaming down her face, she unburdened herself, "And I was so caught up with being mad at the girls at school, and, I don't know, mad at Mom for dying and leaving us that I never actually thought about what you were dealing with and...and...I'm sorry, Dad."

They stood on either side of the kitchen, the space between them spanning not only a few feet of cold tile, but two years of emotions since Mom had died. The aura of the bear, the fiery outline of the powerful beast that was so pronounced tonight, faded, and June could see her father's face more clearly. Soft, tired, sad. He opened his mouth to speak, but was interrupted by a knock at the door.

Another quick breath and Dad seemed ready to say something, but instead lifted the glass to his mouth, tilted it back, and chugged the coffee milk down, down, down.

Her feelings and face raw, June couldn't gain enough control of her body to gasp. Her fingers curled around the air that once held the poison drink. He finished, wiped his mouth with the back of his forearm, and the bear growled with him as he burped, growing brighter to its former luster. The empty glass landed as punctuation to their conversation, and Dad said simply, "That must be the sheriff."

Stunned as he walked past her for the door, all June could see was the empty glass, viscous brown streaks running down to the darkening tan milk pooled at the pint's bottom.

The room spun. June's joints felt cold. Her dad's footsteps boomed toward the foyer, even once the kitchen door closed after him. But June barely noticed. All she saw was the empty glass. All she thought was, "He's dead."

In the other room, the front door opened and Connor's voice rang out. "Hey, Mr. S. How are you? All that extra weight looks good on you. Just kidding. Is June here? She left her phone at the box office."

"I'll take that Connor, June's still grounded."

"Totally get it, I totally get it. How you feeling? You look tired. With all the chaos with the animals in the square today, I'm sure you were a bit harried."

June knew Connor's overly loud pun was for her benefit, but she was beyond laughter, beyond feeling, beyond caring about anything except the poison in her father's gut killing him from the inside. She stared at the coffee milk running down the glass.

"Well, I appreciate your concern, Connor."

"I was just wondering if I could check on the lil' Nipslip? She was feeling really down about arguing with you recently, and I know it's none of my business, but I'm just trying to be a good friend."

"Connor, she's on restricted privileges."

"Totally. And I totally respect that. I would just like to check in and make sure she's okay."

"Goodnight, Connor."

"Mr. S., not to push the issue, but I need to make sure Juniper is fine and isn't under any distress."

"What are you saying, Connor?"

"Not that you would ever do anything to hurt her, sir. But I think one of the reasons you respect me as one of her friends is the fact that I would stand up to anyone to make sure she was safe." Connor's usually dopey and theatrical voice lowered. "Anyone."

The pause was deafening and stretched forever. She could feel the tension from the next room, and June was so thankful not to be in the middle of the high pressure stand-off between the two.

Then she heard the front door creak open a little, and Dad grumbled, "Come in, then. But be quick; I'm expecting company."

Connor's voice grew louder as he walked inside, "Mr. S, you dog, you. Kidding. It's none of my business. Juniper? Is she in the kitchen? This place is so dark."

"She's..." he paused, as if pushing out a belch. "She's in the..."

"Mr. S, are you alright? You seem a little stagger-y."

"I'm fine, I-"

"Woah! Have you been drinking?"

June could picture her father struggling, Connor holding him up, and all she could do was close her eyes and calm her breathing.

A commotion broke out, Dad's bulk falling around the hall. He staggered into the door frame of the kitchen, Connor calling out from behind, "Coming through! We need a chair here!"

Forcing herself into motion, June grabbed a tall kitchen chair, spun it around to the middle of the floor. As Dad stumbled precariously, his bear aura lolled, unsteady on its back paws. Dad let out a belch, shaking the fog off his head, blinking hard and struggling to focus his eyes. Reaching unsteadily in front of him, he pawed at the air in an attempt to grab the back of the chair.

His eyes blinked hard again as he continuously licked his lips, drool running simultaneously down his human and bear chin. Crouching and turning to sit, his hand swatted once more to hold the chair, missed, and his entire bulk rolled back, falling into - and through - the chair, breaking the wood with loud cracking noises, tumbling onto the floor.

Beyond words, June just watched, slack jawed, hands out as if she could do anything to catch her enormous father. Her enormous dying father. Before she could form any words to say to Connor, or vice versa, there was a loud knock at the door. Dad lay still on top of the remains of one of the kitchen table chairs, like he was passed out, but he was so still.

More knocking. Aggressive. Impatient.

Sprinting for the foyer, June closed the door to the kitchen, leaving her invisible bestie alone with her dying, maybe dead father in the room behind her, and turned on the hall lights. She cleared her throat, tightened her ponytail, and took the deepest breath she could, which was wholly insufficient to calm her in the current situation, before opening the door.

June thought Sheriff Marrock was scary before. That he'd be canine was no surprise to June. His thick-jawed under-bite was more pronounced with canine tusks jutting up out of his mouth. His ears were tall and tufted; one was notched like his human ear had been, only now it was decorated with metal rings of brass, steel, gold, and titanium that jingled as he walked. But the most pronounced difference were his eyes, now jade green. Not the iris, but the entire eyeball, from one lid to the other. And the lids were absolutely inhuman, the slit running vertical. Weird green-alien-vagina eyes. The sight of it turned June's stomach.

"Juniper Szmydt," his deep voice purred. "Is your daddy dead yet?"

Chapter Seventeen: Samhain, Too Close to Midnight

Hackles raised, Zippy kept a safe distance and growled as the lupine sheriff stalked into the room, standing on his hind paws as his claws scraped the hardwood floor, his leather bomber jacket with the sheriff's badge and trappings tight with muscles and fur. Stunned, June could do nothing but watch. Of all the magical creatures she'd seen, the Sheriff's enormous stature, musty urine-soaked wild dog smell, and bear trap of yellow-fanged jaws, frightened her more than anything. Sent shivers down her spine, eliciting a primal gut reaction, her legs tensing, aching to spring into flight, anywhere, just away from the beastly man.

Was the sheriff somehow actually the murderer? Had the lawman pack leader kept Dad entranced these two years? Had June been dead wrong?

As June tensed with that fear specific to tiny, shivering prey facing a predator of such magnitude, the giant Lycan strode past, reaching the closed kitchen door. A foreboding rectangle lit from within, the very sight of the door turning June's blood ice cold. It was the lid to the vessel that held her late father's body and the best friend who was very much alive. Glistening slobber draped from the Sheriff's maw as he asked through articulate canine lips. "May I?" He gestured to the swinging door with his enormous hairy pawed-hand.

Paralyzed, June couldn't answer, which the sheriff took as a yes, pushing through into the light.

"Spellman, boy, I ain't seen you in ages!" His voice was deep with a low rumbling buzzing, like a go-cart motor with a New England lilt.

As if compelled, June followed him into the kitchen, though every fiber of her being told her that was the last thing she wanted to do. She wanted to run as fast as her legs would take her, steal her dad's car and drive until it ran out of gas. She wanted to burn the house down. She wanted to die. That may happen soon enough, she thought as she pushed the door in.

The giant man-wolf crouched on the tile floor over her father's body, running a furry coal-black paw across the bubbling foam pooling next to Dad's mouth. Connor stood flabbergasted on the other side of the room, keeping the kitchen table between himself and everyone else in the room. The giant demon dog stood, touching the creamy substance bubbling out of Dad's dead body, then rubbing it between his thumb and forefinger. The sheriff licked it. "Hmmm, Arnica... Juniper...and Autocrat! I love Autocrat!"

With a flick of his sickening jade green eyes, he noticed the pint glass still full of coffee milk that June had poured for herself. His clawed fingers wrapped around it, dwarfing the glass as if it were a jelly jar. Bringing the light brown drink to his under bite, he tipped it back, taking a swig, spilling most of it onto the fur of his neck. Then he slammed the glass onto the counter, shattering it, making Connor and June jump.

The giant wolf burped and licked coffee milk from his chops. Then his giant fanged smile turned on them, sneering into a growl. "Have you figured it all out again, girl? Little Shit? What was it my cousin Ray called you the other day? Nancy Jew."

Sucking in staccato breaths, she couldn't muster even a stuttering whisper, eyes down on the kitchen floor which felt like it'd dropped out from under her at any moment. She felt the monstrous sheriff's hot breath on the top of her head. She'd failed. She somehow missed something, a clue, and her dad paid for it. With his life. What the fuck was she thinking? She didn't even know what she was supposed to do to resurrect him. And now this dickhead wolf sheriff was going to eat her and her best friend.

Fuck that.

Without looking up, she spoke loudly, directly, and angry AF. "Connor, run."

Of course, June didn't say that to get Connor to run. Too basic. June knew if she yelled it, Connor would look at her for a moment. Before he even decided to run or not, he'd look at the crux of the decision involuntarily. It was human behavior. Just like the sheriff would look at Connor. Which gave her a window.

She stepped toward the big beast and swung. Overhand right.

It was the first punch June had thrown in her life. And she was starting with a seven foot tall werewolf sheriff. Her fist didn't connect. His big hairy black paw caught her forearm. The sheriff growled through a massive grin, leaning in so close that June felt the growl in her ribcage. He had her overpowered and helpless.

Just like she'd planned.

"Ow!" She fell, letting her legs go limp as she whimpered

loudly.

Which was all Zippy needed to hear. His growl shook the floor. Flames poured in his wake as he moved impossibly fast. Leaping in two strides across the kitchen to sink his jaws into the wool collar of the Sheriff's jacket, Zippy's teeth clamped onto the giant Lycan's neck.

The Sheriff let go of June and grabbed at Zippy, both of them stumbling back onto the kitchen counters, knocking the knife block to the floor. June fell to her ass, then nodded for Connor to make for the back door while she scrambled to get ahold of Dad's body by the armpits. Pumping her legs, she dragged him across the tile, using every last ounce of energy she had.

Zippy and the Sheriff tumbled over the stovetop in quite the fair dogfight, as the more human of the two was out-weighed twice over. The Sheriff grabbed the jagged globe of the coffeemaker and brought it down on Zippy's six eyes. Glass shattered, but the Hellhound didn't even blink.

June grunted and strained, but Dad was too heavy - until suddenly he wasn't. Connor pushed June over, grabbing Dad's other shoulder, and suddenly they slid the dead weight as fast as they could walk backwards. Over the din of pots and pans clanging and ceramic shattering, Connor flashed June an uncertain smile—sweaty, pale, acned, and awkward as ever. Her BFF wouldn't abandon her.

Their momentum picking up, June reached behind her, blindly grabbing for the back door to leave the kitchen the two mythological dogs were destroying. Not ten feet away, the Sheriff, his pants and tail aflame from the stove, bashed Zippy's head with their ancient microwave. Still, Zippy wouldn't release his jaws from the now red-stained wool collar of the Sheriff, who abandoned the oversized appliance and body-slammed the dog through the tall wooden kitchen table.

Avoiding the flak of splintering wood, June backed into the back door, her hand pinching closed, only instead of a doorknob, her fingers touched cloth. Clothing. Someone blocking their escape. Her heart froze as June saw her number one suspect looking wicked different. Mayor Orbison, in long grey burlap robes, all wizarded out in beard and a pointy black hat.

He snapped a ringed finger once and Zippy yipped, releasing his death clutch on the lawman, scurrying past everyone out the open back door into the dark night, whimpering and crying.

"Connor, run. I mean it," June commanded in a low, broken voice.

"Oh, that's right. You still don't know, even without the ghost veil," the mayor mocked her. He clapped his jeweled hands together, and Connor fell suddenly limp, dead on his feet, limbs relaxed, head lolled forward.

In a frenzy, June pleaded with her friend, "Run!"

A low bubble stirred within the belly of the wizard mayor, his face contorting with glee. Laughter, cruel and biting, teeth and bile, rising until he threw his head back with a triumphant jackal grin, his mocking cackling filling the room. "Yes, save your friend, Juniper. Spare him from my wrath. Preserve his precious life!"

From one knobby finger, he removed a ring, creamy white with a pale blue stone, matching Connor's complexion and hair color perfectly. Placing it in his palm, the wizard blew lightly on the ring, and suddenly Connor's hair and clothing whipped about like he was facing gale winds. Showing no fear, June set a grimace on her face, furrowing her brow, desperately trying to understand what the wizard mayor was doing.

Pressing a pile of napkins to the side of his neck, the sheriff got to his feet, or back paws, and limped to his place at the wizard's side, joining in with a cackle. The wizard mayor pointed a liver-spotted finger straight down at the ring and rotated it round and round, drawing imaginary circles. At the same time, Connor, still frozen and standing limp, rotated, spinning like some playable character in a video game. June couldn't understand the control the mayor had over her friend.

"Leave him alone," she croaked.

"Juniper!" the wizard mayor said with put-on concern that filled her belly with so much anger her fists clenched their knuckles white. "If I left Connor Spellman alone, he would cease to exist. Without my sorcery, there is no Connor. He is but my dummy, a tool I concocted to keep tabs on you. A golem spy."

It punched June in the gut, pushing her a step back. Connor wasn't real? No. This had to be some sort of trick. Her legs waved beneath her as she wrapped her mind around it. Chelsea had never met Connor. She felt sick. Connor only talked to her when they were by themselves. She clung to the kitchen counter as hard as she clung to reality. A whole town kept running by Connor's cousins.

Reality tore. Her world fell from under her, and June fell under the weight of the world. Nothing was making sense. She needed her daddy. She needed this to stop.

But the mayor continued, savoring the moment. "Surely you saw the care I put into the curses on your father's head. Do you really believe I would let you roam freely with nothing to keep you in check, save a flimsy ghost veil?"

Her eyes flicked down to her father - his body, that is. He

would fix this. Any second, he'd wake up and save them.*I believe in you, Dad, I believe in you, Dad, I believe in you.* Then June forced her eyes back up to the evil wizard's.

"You Szmydts are a dull lot, and believe me, that's natural. I didn't curse you to be dumb. It was in his name: Connor was a spell man!"

"You catfished me?" June fumed.

"I don't know what that means. But if it's insulting, it may be apropriate."

"I don't believe you. You're just..." June searched for a word in a reality in which she was alien. "Enchanting him! Let him go!"

A wide, toothy smile obliged her, and the wizard mayor held a pinched hand above the ring. Connor lifted off the ground like a marionette held only by neck strings, hovering as his limbs dangled lifelessly. The wizard's hand opened suddenly, dropping the invisible string, and her best friend's body collapsed to the ground. She flinched at the thud. Then, as the mayor brought his open palms together around the ring, Connor's baritone voice spoke. "Nipslip." The wizard's hands clapped violently together around the ring, and the blue-haired boy vanished.

"Connor." The name choked June.

She'd lost them both. Now she was alone.

In rage, she clamped her eyes shut, reciting anything she could remember from the prayer from her Bat Mitzvah earlier. If she believed in her father enough, she could resurrect him, right? Whispering under her breath, she moved onto the Lord's Prayer, mouthing it as fast as she could.

Again an evil laugh bellowed from the mayor's chest, and it was parroted by the wolf sheriff, jangling his earrings and the gun holster on his belt. The old bearded mayor jeered, "Resurrect him, child! Bring him back to life with your faith," he spat the word like it was derogatory. "Unless," he teased, "you're not a true believer? Surely, you are a true chosen child of Israel, you worship the one and only true God? It may be poppycock to someone like myself, but don't you faithfully study the covenant between God and his people?"

Her clamped eyes and whispered recitations couldn't block out the mayor's words, and she fell to her knees, scooping her father's limp hand into hers, mumbling prayers she didn't believe. What if Chelsea was right? What if the Bat Mitzvah wasn't enough? Eyes shut so hard they squeezed tears out, June whispered the prayers anyway.

Still, the mayor laughed and tortured her. "I would hope you're not some sardonic agnostic, or even worse, to falsely claim belief?" The mayor chuckled, affixing the Connor ring back to his finger. He strode past June and her father's body, taking in the scene of the destroyed kitchen, the broken sink shooting a stream of water that was insufficient to put out the little fires everywhere. With disgust, he flicked away a shard of glass from the pool of coffee milk on the counter. He addressed June without looking back at her.

"'Tis almost the peak of Samhain, girl, and the ties that obscure this town grow weak. I'd planned on killing him as sacrifice, binding the linchpin to the wheel, and save the good citizens and protect your neighbors. But if he's gone, your magical dead body will have to do. Come with me."

"You can go fuck yourself," she spat at him before leaping from the floor, grabbing the heavy bottom of the broken pint glass, and lunging to stab it into the mayor's back.

"Pry-dep-ee-yah." The wizard mayor's whispering voice

boomed from all directions. The power was awesome, blowing her hair like a storm wind. Compelled by the powers his voice controlled, June froze mid-stride, arm out and still brandishing the broken glass, blood leaking from her palm in a crimson trickle dripping onto the floor. In perfect stillness, her dry, puffy eyes searched desperately. She was helpless. She was fucked.

The mayor said, "Why do I even keep you around, Marrock? Jesus Christ, my back was turned. Would it kill you to stop someone from stabbing me?"

And then again, in that terrible hushed tone that echoed from all over the house, he pronounced, "Ca-pee-strah."

The glass shard slipped from her hand, and June fell to a slack, neutral stance, her eyes fixed on the Mayor.

"I can break her neck so she doesn't try anything else," the lycanthropic sheriff, one paw still applying pressure to his own throat, snarled.

That meant they needed her alive. Of course. With Dad dead, they needed someone to curse to keep their precious hold over Miridical. June wasn't dead quite yet.

Thinking quickly, June formulated a plan, then shouted, "Wait! I surrender."

The smile faded from his tusked mouth, the laughter replaced with surprise. Did they buy it, her giving up so quickly? Every dog in the sheriff's office knew June was a stubborn pain-in-the-ass; how could she make him believe she was really giving up?

"Just...leave Zippy alone." There was no way this was going to work.

The Sheriff's rumbling laugh returned. "The dog? 'I'll do what you want but leave my doggy alone?!'"

The Mayor chimed in, "Stupid girl, I have no need for a hellhound. I summoned Manticore to make your puppy dog tremble. Fine. Cause me no trouble and your Zippy is spared."

Perfect.

"I agree." June fell into step between her captors submissively, and they left her brown birdcage house.

As the giant Lycan lawman ducked to walk outside, steam billowed from his wet fur in the night air. He nudged June along in front of him, while the mayor, lifting the hem of his robe like he was traversing steps in a ballgown, traipsed ahead to lead them. With a giant claw resting on her shoulder, June searched the lawn desperately.

Without breaking stride or moving her head, she scoured the ground for her only hope, the reason she'd surrendered to the mayor and the monstrous sheriff. If the Lycan held her shoulder too tightly, the plan wouldn't work. When her eyes finally found what she was looking for, a simple rectangle of white standing out from the leaf-covered lawn, she purposefully slipped and fell, her hand landing on the slick white paper for just a moment.

"Get up, clumsy girl," the sheriff bellowed as he lifted her with one paw, then dragged her by the shirt collar in the freezing cold down the street toward Fortune Hill.

June prayed that her last-ditch plan had worked.

Chapter Eighteen: Now or Never

After about twenty minutes of walking up Fortune Hill, Juniper started to bitch. At that point, she didn't care what they did to her—her dad and best friend were dead, she'd be joining them soon enough, and she'd never get to bone Chelsea, so she was resolved that these assholes weren't going to hear the end of it.

"Oy, can we slow down a bit?" From here, all June could see of the sheriff was a furry chin sticking out of the taught and torn bomber jacket. The wounds from Zippy's attack were gone. Maybe just be fur covering it up, or maybe his kind healed faster. But he ignored her and his steady padding didn't slow, pushing her along up the mile and a half road. Stopping and putting her weight back against the sheriff's hold, she whistled. "Hey, slow down. Heel."

The growl was so loud and close, she shivered and clenched up, ears ringing. She continued walking.

"Bad dog!" she teased before the question dawned on her, "Hey, does the phrase 'guard dog' mean anything to you? Are you a guard dog? Know of any? Perhaps it was a college nickname?"

She was answered with silence.

"Hey Grand-elf," she called out to the mayor wizard, a good ten paces ahead. He'd gotten a walking stick from somewhere. Maybe he created it out of thin air, and now the end of it lit up like a fluorescent tube. "Can you conjure me up a Gatorade? Or maybe got any magic spells to fend off a wicked Charley horse?"

He didn't even acknowledge she was there.

Her Doc Martens had become untied at some point, and she kicked at her laces as they went up the hill.

"Can I stop and tie my shoes?"

Crickets.

"Grammar police, huh? I know I can tie them; may I tie them, please?"

Looking back from down at her shoes, she noticed the sheriff's gun. She was rather surprised it was still a gun, and hadn't actually been another magic wand or some such mystical object. A wand wouldn't help June, but a gun... June could fire a gun, she was pretty sure.

Her mind imagined step-by-step pulling the gun from its holster, aiming it at him, making sure to flip the safety off, then unloading a clip of rounds into his stupid wolf face.

As she peaked and planned, June occupied the Sheriff with more questions. "Hey, Jake the dog, how'd you get that chunk of your ear taken out? Street fight? Were you a rescue - is that how the mayor found you?"

But she couldn't get a rise out of them. Only a grumbling, "You speak with respect about Roger the Gray."

"Is that seriously his wizard name? My name is a better wizard name!" But they didn't take the bait, no reaction at all.

Her feet grew heavy as they dragged against the incline.

When did the hill get so steep? When did her legs get so weak? What was the last thing she ate? Her head pounded and her eyes stung with the heat that comes after sobbing. Her mouth was dry. Her makeup was most likely a mess by now. She wondered if it would hurt to die.

Then a stinging acrid smell wafted by. She recognized that smell.

Sulfur.

So she cleared her throat and spoke up. Louder.

"I'm still putting this together, but I'm almost there. Mayor Grand Wizard had Vernon Carlisle killed in the square to stop ol' Vern from releasing my dad from his curses. Had the librarian or one of hers to do the deed. And you, Sheriff, knew about it and helped cover it up. But LaChance witnessed your little wizard's duel, and the mayor sent the Hellhound Zippy after him. I can't imagine what kind of threat it took to keep LaChance quiet."

The Lycan sheriff roared a laugh. "And you're supposed to be so smart."

June ignored the beast man pushing her and addressed the mayor ahead. "My only question is...how does the sheriff betraying you fit into your plan, Grand Wizard?"

For a split second, the mayor's gait, his even plodding punctuated by his illuminated walking staff thudding on asphalt hesitated. He almost looked back. The Sheriff's furry grip on her shoulder tightened momentarily, talons digging around her collar bone.

June smiled. She had them.

"Because getting the patsy, my dad, to come to your little playdate of the elders would have been easy. He goes anywhere the mayor says. So why did Sheriff Marrock try to get my dad to come up to the meeting first, before the mayor arrived? And why has he been convincing Dad over time to replace the mayor?"

"Cut it out!" barked the Sheriff. The wizard mayor kept trudging ahead, but his gait felt more deliberate, forced. The giant Lycan complained and explained, "LaChance was supposed to lure Carlisle to talk, then move the body when it was all done. But he got spooked and ran. Made the deed messier, but the mayor handled it. Like he always does. Holding this town together, keeping the blind man out of the library, takes a lot of power, a lot of energy, and before the linchpin secures the wheel, I guaranteed your father's loyalty so the Roger the Gray could rest. You and your father are so gullible, sweetheart. So easy to manipulate."

Anyone picking on her father really irked June, but being called the pet name sweetheart absolutely got June's blood boiling. She took a shot.

"Is that why you checked out that library book about how to kill immortals, Sheriff?"

"What?" The fingered paw on her shoulder loosed.

Ahead, the robed wizard stopped. So did the constant push of the Lycan sheriff. So did June's breathing.

They stood about thirty feet away from each other, the wizard mayor still looking farther down the road and June with the giant wolf Sheriff Marrock, all halfway up Fortune Hill, the very spot where Zippy collided with LaChance's car, below prayer point and overlooking the lit up yet empty town square.

"She's lying!" the sheriff growled.

"No, I'm not. I saw you leaving the library!" June had always been a good actor when she needed to be.

The heavy canine hand snatched at June's shoulder, spinning

her to face the fanged sheriff, furiously baring his teeth. "I'll kill you!"

June flinched, the sheriff's cavernous maw spreading open, coming down on her, enveloping her.

"Enough." The Mayor's whisper echoed from everywhere across the hill.

Frozen in a flinch, June couldn't help but realize she wasn't getting eaten. She opened her eyes to see the enormous bear trap that was the sheriff's mouth still open and around her head, but spellbound and stationary.

And it stunk in there in that mouth. Garbage breath, fishy and cheesy.

There was just enough room for her to duck down and clear her head of his front teeth. A swirling tangle of sparkles and embers wrapped around the sheriff, holding him just a few inches off the ground, completely frozen mid-leaping bite. The Lycan's vertical green eyes still furiously trained on June.

"Do not underestimate my power. Either of you." Far ahead on the darkened road, the wizard stood, emanating the whisper and a soft blue light, alive like it was reflected off the surface of water.

But then instantly, the wizard blurred and ended up closer, not five feet away. June's breath caught. Chills ran down her back.

"I'll do it here," his whisper boomed all around them. Then instantly he blurred to within an inch of her face. She could feel his hot breath. She whimpered and cringed back, but then he was safely thirty feet away again. "If I have to."

Both his hands reached for the night sky and impossibly black flames burst from beneath the old road. It raged taller than each of them, even the floating Lycan sheriff, hot enough to blast scorching air onto June's face fifteen feet away. She felt the force of the blast of the flames, pushing her back off her feet.

No. It was something else. It was magic. An invisible grip tightened about her waist and she saw the wizard mayor's hands ball up as if gripping something - gripping her. His hold was solid, firm, and pissed June off to no end. Kicking and flailing and grunting, she hoped she was landing some hits onto the mayor's hand, but she didn't pause her hysterics to check. All the angst and anger and sadness and loss sustained her once all the strength in her body left. By the time she was out of breath, beet red all over, and sopping wet with sweat, she slumped limply in the mayor's magical grasp.

The giant wolf sheriff still hovered, frozen in a leaping, snapping motion. The rustically robed wizard mayor held his ringed hands in the air, twitching various fingers about. He spoke out loud, but not to either June or the sheriff. "Just walk down the hillside. Don't go all the way down the road, that's a couple kilometers!"

The mayor's hand, the one not holding June about her waist (which was still aggravating AF), wound about as if beckoning someone, and a giant wooden cross, like some intersection of telephone polls, floated down from Prayer Point. Moving gently and softly, the heavy cross headed straight for June. Not slowing down as it closed in on her, the cross didn't appear so gentle or floaty, but rather deliberate and unstoppable. The butt end, the bottom of the cross, bore down on June's head like a mallet about to drive a fat, Jewish nail into the dirt. The post lowered down onto her head as she flinched, so close she could see the wood rings.

The cross passed over her. It settled behind her, and the

mayor's fingers splayed. June was thrown against the wood.

About this time, bitching and moaning while sliding and falling on the leafy hill floor, the rest of the elders emerged from the trees. Principal Donnelly, who was evidently an orc or a dark gray ogre or troll, the severe librarian cloaked with a small bird of prey on her shoulder like a falcon or a peregrine or something (whatever it was, it looked cool), all materialized on that hill, plus others June didn't recognize, but maybe that was due to their magical forms. A satyr, a horned lady, a skeleton, someone green, someone blue... There were eight more in all, bringing the total number of Elders to twelve. Thirteen, if you counted Carlisle.

Dusting leaves, twigs, and dirt from their robes, the various figures pulled up their hoods and circled around the black fire in the road. Reaching their places, they all fell into a pose in unison, each mirroring the mayor's gesticulating hands. After she gave up on pulling away uselessly away from the cross, June sniffed at the air, beyond the burning of the black fire, trying to pick out a scent beneath the crisp autumn air and stink of forest rot. Trying to smell sulfur.

June could really use that dog's help about now. Or Dad's. Or Mo's. But none of her plans worked. No one was coming to help. She'd killed her father and pissed off the bad guys and planned herself into an early death.

With a snap, the wizard mayor released the lupine sheriff, who lowered his ears, eyes, and snout to whine before the Greybeard as the lycanthrope loped to his place at the fire's circle, then turning to bare teeth and growl at June. The elders, whose blue, green, furry, horned, or oversized heads-sic-skulls were now exposed, raised their wands - craggy, knotted, twisted wood crackling with potential energy.

They hummed. Low at first, then building and building, and at some point opening their mouths together to join in a full-throated ohm, while their wands, shaking, vibrating, sparking, even distorting the air and light around, all pointed to June.

"Wait."

The group singalong chant trailed off abruptly and awkwardly. The wands, which had only just now seemed so much cooler than the magician kit version that belonged to Mr. Carlisle, sputtered and petered out. Principal Orc's even went limp, hanging from his fist like a scrap of rope. Muttering and whispers gave way to a staring stillness only broken by the unnatural fire. Once all the elders had stopped and faced him, Wizard Mayor Orbison Greybeard spoke without his mystical echoing voice, but with unflinching command. "Before we begin, I demand oaths of fidelity from each of you."

The seed of doubt had sprouted. June hoped discord between the sheriff and mayor would buy her - and hopefully Zippy - some time.

After a brief pause, the elders looking about at each other, most shrugged, and most everyone broke into some makeshift oath, saying a variation of "I swear my undying loyalty to you, oh great-" blah blah blah Dungeons and Dragon-Master, first of his name, whatever the Hell.

Taken down a few notches by the lack of pomp and circumstance in the oaths of fealty, Greybeard flinched, lips spreading flat in sour distaste. "Not what I had in mind, but it shall do. Except you, witch. You did not speak. Swear."

The falcon flapped its wings and adjusted its perch as the severe librarian bowed, her witch's hat pointing at the wizard mayor while she hissed the words, "I pledge my deeds, as long as I walk Miridical, to the mayor."

"You qualify your oath, Witch."

Oh, shit. June didn't know what was happening between the witch and the wizard (it didn't feel like sexual tension, unless it totally was?), but the rest of the elders held their breaths while awaiting the witch's response. This librarian witch, she was the real murderer, the one who finished off Vernon Carlisle for the Mayor. She, or someone under her control at the library, had the angle to fire on Carlisle. Just like Connor said.

Still tipped forward in a formal bow, the witch tilted her head up to lift the brim of her conical hat enough to look the wizard in the eye. "My absolute devotion is spoken for. I have my master."

Some elders gasped.

"And if your master were to command you to attack or usurp me?"

Still holding that bow. The core strength on this old broad! And it wasn't lost on June the witch didn't curtsey. "Considering He's never given me a direct order before, I would obey absolutely."

The elders looked nervously to Greybeard.

"Have you ever been compelled in any way to work against me?"

"No."

"No, what?"

"No." The witch spoke through teeth clenched in a fake smile. "Master."

The rest of the elders breathed and relaxed.

Greybeard shifted his commanding focus to the Sheriff. "Marrock."

"Yes, my Master?" The wolf's ears pointed down and back, and the beast-slash-man bowed his head.

"Swea-"

But the Sheriff shot him before he finished the word.

Hip shot. Deafening.

The elders froze in place. The falcon screamed as it flew off. June fell from the cross to land on her feet. Her ears rang. Sheriff Marrock holstered his firearm and flipped the safety. She'd turned them against one another, but it was all so sudden.

June hadn't caught her breath when all Hell broke loose. A couple of Elders vanished into thin air. Poof. A few flew away, two or three took off, launching like rockets to arc across the moonless night sky. Several ran away screaming.

Seven stayed in all.

June stayed frozen in place, the ring of the gunshot only beginning to fade in her ears. It had been so easy. With all of their spells and conspiracies, these guys still died with a well-placed bullet.

Latin spells sounded dumbed down in the sheriff's rural Rhode Island accent, much less the wolf muzzle. But with Marrock's words, Greybeard's corpse stirred. His hands lifted straight up, his head lolled, and June was ready to freak out if the murder suspect she'd been right about came back from the dead as a zombie. Zombies would be too much.

Then, small objects freed themselves from his hands and his arms dropped. Necklaces broke from around the dead wizard's neck, and the shot cadaver lay still again as jewelry, rings, amulets and bracelets floated over to fall into the sheriff's paws. He closed his furry fingers about the jewelry.

The Sheriff's eyes glowed gold. With a bone-breaking crunch, twin spires of goat horns twisted up from his temples. A hissing snake, undulating hypnotically, rose where the Sheriff's tail before had peaked through his khakis. Power flowed out from him like a fountain; the Lycan sheriff was totally feeling himself.

Super-Marrock raised an elongated taloned paw-finger to point at June. Her breath caught at the sudden attention back to her. The rest of the Elders again raised their wands and built a hum up into a communal voice as all around them, screaming power coiled and built and tightened.

And then once again, June was floating. Toward the darkened fire now. Arms outstretched to her side, her body controlled by magic and her voice gone, the string of smart ass comments and curse words June let out were muted to mere breath. She settled back against something hard and flat. The wooden cross. Like quick snakes, heavy rope coiled around her forearms, tightening them against the wood.

If she had the energy, she'd laugh at the visual of the only Jewish girl in town strapped to a cross.

But no one was paying attention, as Principal orc, the Lycan sheriff, and the rest of the Pagan Avengers now moved their attention to the black fire. The sheriff led them, mumbling some phrase quietly under his breath as he raised his other paw. The others joined in with their hands raised, and the wind picked up, whistling through the trees. Beneath her, the cross shuddered and jolted, then she dropped for only a moment, her body released by the magic, but catching on the ropes, hanging her painfully by her arms.

Drenched in sweat, her muscles screaming under her own weight, June felt the cross rise in the air. Seeing the town from this height through the magically black fire should have been beautiful, even breathtaking, but June was numb. Like she'd taken Nyquil and was watching everything unfold on an old TV.

She'd been wrong to turn the sheriff and mayor against one another. To annoy the old wizard enough to bring up the oath. Marrock would have turned on him, eventually; why did she have to try and outsmart the situation? And why hadn't she run when the wizard mayor's hold on her broke? Why hadn't she done something? Anything? Now look where she was.

The whispered mantra from the seven sorcerers echoed across the hill, and wind whipped the fire high into a frenzy, sending crackling sparks and making June scream. As the fire grew near, heat from the black flames scorched her cheeks and nose. It was too hot to breathe. The air burned her eyes, even after she closed them. Her tongue dried and swelled so she breathed through her nose into searing, raw lungs. This was it.

For reasons she couldn't explain, June thought of her mother. The way Mom sang and danced when she made spaghetti and meatballs in the kitchen. The way her death felt like she'd been replaced in all the photos by a vacuum, and June and Dad and anyone else in the picture were just sucked in a couple feet.

She remembered meeting Connor, all gangly with big eyes, bad skin, blue hair, and sass for days. She thought of that kiss. Chelsea's mouth, her perfect smile, her supermodel lips, the way the kiss felt like liquid electricity.

But more than anything, she thought about Dad. Big smiley, dopey, Dad. Her face screwed up as the tears came, and she wept openly, remembering the big dumb guy who only wanted to love and protect her and for her to laugh at his corny jokes, but she was just too busy being cool to love him back.

The fire, so close now, heated her tears, and she wondered if she would feel them boil as she died.

Chapter Nineteen: Time to Die

The impossibly black flames licked up at her as the ends of her now-dry hair singed. This is how Juniper Szmydt was going to die. Burned alive like a witch by a bunch of white dudes. And she never even got to use magic.

Suddenly, a sound shook the ground and cut the air. A roar boomed, vibrating the wooden cross, rippling through June's ribs, and chattering her teeth. Sparks and flying bits of ember erupted from the fire. The Slenderman lost his balance and toppled in an avalanche of elbows. The rest of the elders stumbled, dropped their wands, or generally lost interest in levitating the crucified Juniper Szmydt. She fell, crucifix and all.

The tree line rushed up around June. She scrunched up her face and held her breath, ready for the cross to tip back, crash against the hillside, and break every bone in her body. Only it didn't. Something caught her. She and the cross stopped falling. Someone placed the cross down gently on the rock, still angled up enough for her to see across the black fire at the sorcerers, all panicking.

A bear crashed through the woods. Not any bear. Dad.

Enormous and white, not like a polar bear, but like a glowing Grizzly, a white so bright the man within was indecipherable. He galloped into the clearing, reared up on his hind legs and shouted triumphantly with Dad's voice, "Le Heim, mother-fuckers!"

Relief and happiness and you're-all-fucked-now glee filled the cavernous emptiness in June. Coming down from standing, Dad, the Persian bear god, swatted the Slenderman's head clean off, life a golf ball off a tee. Running away while pointing his wand, the principal orc screamed, "Don't let him get to the library!"

Immediately, most of the Elders peeled off, several leaping through the air hundreds of feet, one literally sprouting wings and flying off. June almost laughed.

"Stop, you idiots! His blindfold is gone," Super-Marrock howled, but nobody listened.

Principal Orc kept sprinting for the trees, but ran into another figure emerging from the woods, this one with dark features, a black suit, and a white shirt.

"Mo Tilden." June didn't know whose voice said it, but she sure was happy to see the man.

His begrudging frown of a smile became visible in the light of the black fire. "Could be," he said. He'd distracted the orc school administrator just for a moment, but it was long enough. Dad the Bear God rushed him, clamping his jaws onto the principal orc's thick black neck and flinging him about like a rag doll. The cracking of his spine was audible and June looked away, swallowing back bile.

Behind her, Zippy appearing and started gnawing the ropes to free her other arm. He'd caught the crucifix like fetching a stick then lowered her safely to the ground. She couldn't hug the Hellhound hard enough as she stumbled off the cross.

"You fucking idiots!" Sheriff Marrock barked, either at his fellow sorcerers, or at those that had interrupted the ritual. He was all alone, surrounded by a bear god, a Hellhound, the girl he'd tried to sacrifice or whatever, and Mo fricking Tilden.

Super-Marrock, now Grand Wizard (was he technically Mayor now, or was Dad?) made a couple of fists...he put up his dukes.

June couldn't believe it. This idiot is going to fist fight his way out of this - against a bear gone Super-Sayan. But then his fists lit up. The dead mayor's rings, now magically fitting Marrock. Just as June saw the ring with the broken blue stone, Connor's ring, all the jewelry grew blindingly bright, then Marrock, screaming in pain, sprouted wings.

He wasn't putting up his fists. He was harnessing power, pushing himself to change. Moist, leathery, freshly grown bat wings stretched outward, a good ten feet to either side. The winged super-wolf leaped into the air, flapping his wings. He flew in a twisting, swimming motion, and his lupine body elongated as he corkscrewed across the night air, down the hill, and into the town square.

Overcome with emotion, June ran to her father, or the giant bear that was him, unfazed by his beastly form. With Dad's arms open, she collided with his furry mass, hugging him and burying her face in his chest. His enormous paws fell to her back and gently rubbed her. "Junebug," he said softly.

It was definitely Dad, alive, furrier than ever, and back to his loving self.

"I'm so sorry, Junebug."

"It's okay, Daddy. You weren't yourself."

"I hate to interrupt," Mo Tilden said, grimacing something

close to a smile.

June took a guess, "Stopping the goat-serpent-wolf sheriff?" June wiped her face. Oy, her makeup must've been such a mess.

"He is a lupine trickster demon. Amarrock," Dad the Bear God, now unshackled, unveiled, and without a hint of a human body said.

June gave him an incredulous look. Marrock was the fake secret name Amarrock could think of?

The bear shrugged. "I know, I know. There's a lot of weird stuff I remember now."

"So let him go. The mayor's defeated. Your curses are lifted."

"No, bug. He's taken control of the elders, control of the spells that bind Miridical's magic. He'll control them completely at midnight. As long as those spells exist, the people here aren't free."

"So what do we do?"

"'We' don't do anything. I have to get to the library, depose the sheriff, and find some sorcerers to reinstate the protections over the town. You and Bargeist are going home and locking up."

"No." June pushed away and stood firm. "I'm coming with you."

"No." Dad snarled with authority.

June thought of arguing, but was just too tired. "What's Bargeist?"

Zippy answered the confused June by sidling up next to her and nudging his head under her hand. "Oh. I'm still going to call him Zippy, though," she said, petting him behind his tall tufted black ears.

"Lord Dobiel, we should get going," Mo Tilden said.

"Wait, he gets to go save the town?" June asked about Mo.

"Can he even use magic?"

"June…" Dad warned.

"Juniper Szmydt." Mo wagged a finger at her and nodded as he spoke. "You are such a force. You outsmarted a council of Elder Sorcerers collectively thousands of years old, and summoning me was pretty clever. I will personally make sure your courage and wit are sung throughout history." He smiled, really smiled, then turned to Dad. "Lord Dobiel?"

And then the giant bear fell to all fours, nudged his muzzle against June's face, and stepped next to Mo Tilden. The short Persian in a suit climbed onto Dad's enormous back, and the luminescent ancient bear god bounded down the hill toward the square, where the demon Amarrock was coiling about the library tower.

Zippy, or Bargeist, under her hand, she tossled his fur and said to the hellhound, "You know I'm not going to listen to them, don't you?"

In response, Zippy lowered his ears and whimpered.

"IDGAF, Zippy," she said as she climbed onto the giant dog, legs straddling perfectly between the spikes in his spine and behind his furry shoulders. "Let's go save the town."

And in a plume of sulfur, June astride Bargeist "Zippy" the Hellhound vanished into the cold November air.

####

Teleporting back and forth out of Hell sucked dick sideways. It was the goddamned worst. The stinging stink of sulfur drowned out all of June's other senses as she heaved, cried, choked, coughed, and anything else her body could do to reject and clear out the acrid smell of sulfur-ious smoke. Then she collapsed onto a brick floor, face planting back in reality - this reality - realizing she could breathe again, that Zippy was by her side licking her face, and that she just shit herself.

"Holy crap, Zippy. Let's not do that again anytime soon."

Her awareness came back to her slowly. It was cold, and instead of a ceiling, the heavens were full of stars. No lighting dome. But the moon. What a moon! A big, sexy globe taking up a chunk of the dark, light pocked night sky.

But she heard noises, the strangest noises, like the inside of an arcade - buzzes, beeps, zaps, crackles, and warbles. Plus screaming. In the distance was the beating of war drums, literally a slow, steady percussive BADUM-THMP, the symphony of sounds kept in time by a beastly roar that June had come to recognize after recent events as her dad.

Over the remnants of sulfur, June smelled fire, like burnt ozone and charred wood, but also thick, dusty air. As she moved to get up from the brick, the ache of fatigue hit her body. Her legs sore from an abundance of running, stinging stomach muscles from retching, pain in her arms from rope burn plus the strain of holding up her entire body. Eyes, nose, throat, lungs, burned raw from heat and chemicals. It took some convincing to bring her body to sit up.

Then she realized where she was. The roof of the sheriff's offices. Hidden by the rectangular parapets lining the edge, she could look down over the entirety of the square, lit up in a frenzied battle. It was like an anime armageddon.

BADUM-THMP

With eyes of shining gold, Amarrock, lupine demon that he was, coiled around the tower of the library, the macabre bone-brick structure which shone a sickly yellow from the square's streetlights. Guarding the library doors were unrecognizable beasts, slightly smaller than Zippy. Miridical's lupine sheriff's patrolmen took up the stairs. Flanking the sheriff, perched atop the library roof, the librarians crouched wearing flowing black robes and pointy hats or wings or long prehensile tails.

Along with the surviving Elders and a few related Miridicaliens joining them, the sheriff's side shot all colors of beams, streaks of lighting, pulses, waves, and blasts aimed across the town square. At the other end, Dad, the bright giant bear, was flanked by the witch sisters making hand motions to throw up invisible shields on which attacks landed in sparks and sprays. It was a sea of magical fireworks.

BADUM-THMP. The distant drums were drawing closer. Were there reinforcements Amarrock had summoned?

So Dobiel had to make his way to the library with the most powerful magicians from town in his way. With a series of spell and gestures, Amarrock drew glowing red symbols in the air to swirl about him and the library tower. With everyone's focus on the giant bear, perhaps their leader was left vulnerable.

June slipped out of her shitty drawers, grabbing some khaki sheriff's patrol officer's clothes that had been abandoned when they were turned into a chicken earlier.

BADUM-THMP.

She pointed at the library, pulling the Hellhound's focus with a headlock to the landing at the library entrance. In recognition, Zippy growled at the two beasts at either side of the sheriff.

"I need to get up there, Zippy." She climbed back on him, held her breath and shut her eyes.

They disappeared into sulfurous smoke. When she felt the ground beneath her dog again, she hopped off before opening her eyes and breathing once more. Either she was getting used to the Hellish stench, or she'd figured out how to travel without dry-heaving.

Getting her bearings, she realized they'd materialized behind the bushes next to the library steps.

Standing on Zippy's back, she reached the stone railing above the steps, climbing up to slip under the roof-perched librarians.

BADUM-BADUM-BADUM-BADUM-BADUM. The drumbeat quickened, and a rushing noise, like a thousand footsteps, surrounded the square. The trees framing the buildings swayed and shook. Whatever was coming to the beat of the drum, it was close.

Up the clock tower, the big wand clicked forward, hitting one minute to midnight. They were running out of time.

Claws like cold, wet knives clamped down June's already-sore arms and then she was surrounded by the scaly lion creatures with fierce, expressive eyes and hissing snakes for tails. There had been pictures in some of the witch sisters' books of these monsters. Manticores. Or was the plural of manticore 'manticore'?

The manticore, with its claws on Juniper's arm growled, guttural and low. There was something familiar in its eyes. A tuft of white hair on its chest, mottled black around the fur of its eyes...June gasped. The wildcat in Dabbit's forest.

BADUM-BADUM-BADUM-BADUM-BADUM

Dad was being driven back by the Elders and their magical fireworks, and even though they hadn't seen her yet, June was deep in manticore territory. The clock was ticking and Amarrock confidently had control of the library entrance.

Then, there she was. Striding like a savior angel right down the middle of Main Street, blood dripping down from her exposed shoulders to her fingertips was Chelsea, waving her crimson-covered arms in ritualistic motions as blood red fire shot out to encircle and protect Dad the Bear God. The bloodfire encircled the witches as well, keeping the embattled Elders from advancing.

In June's gaze, the young Bloodstone moved in slow-motion precision. Hands spread, she pulled her arms out, coursing the flames out wider. Clenching her fists, Chelsea pulled her elbows in before triumphantly throwing her arms up, and the fire exploded, reaching skyward. Wet hair flinging about in chunks, her lithe body exuding energy and strength, she was a vision of beauty drenched in blood. But now was no time for lady boners.

Suddenly, the hairy serpentine Amarrock slithered to get in June's face. Eyes, glowing gold, he whispered in the omnipresent voice stolen from the wizard Mayor Orbison. "Pray-lee-gay," magically lifting June. Now used to the sensation, June levitated without struggle to stand before the library front doors, held by some giant invisible hand that pissed her off to no end, like being helplessly restrained as a child. She plopped onto her feet between Amarrock and the wildcat manticore, whose black-mottled face had surprisingly human features, albeit grotesque one.

Within the town square, Dad and his allies were advancing. The defense of the witches and Chelsea protected him as he plodded forward, pushing against the onslaught of power the elders poured on.

BADUM-BADUM-BADUM-BADUM-BADUM

Still in a golden trance, the horned Lycan sheriff placed a padded finger on his other paw, running it over the dead Mayor's rings. June eyed Connor's ring. Amarrock said another spell, whispered it into his rings, and from his paw poured blue smoke. Blue like the color Connor's hair had been.

Billowing and spreading down the steps off the library, the blue settled into a mist covering the street. Smiling his canine fangs at June, Amarrock snapped, and figures arose from the mist, the street now full of people, all with identical features - gangly limbs, curly hair, pale skin. They all looked like Connor. An army of Spellmans. They faced their enemy, faces blank, then charged the bear god in his magical force field. They were slaughtered. June found herself gasping, sick at the sight of it.

The dozens of Spellmans, collapsing once in contact with the witch's protection, or Chelsea's fire, or simply trampled by the giant bear, met their demise. But more rose to their feet in the road, standing in the mist. Dozens, then hundreds, sprinted to their deaths, the Spellmans hitting Dobiel's magic in an explosion of blood, like bugs hitting a windshield on the freeway, only in extreme close-up. Individually, the Spellmans had no chance. But as more and more came at them, they drove Dad and his allies back.

June could barely watch through the tears in her eyes. The Spellmans were nothing to him. Connor was nothing.

BADUM-BADUM-BADUM-BADUM-BADUM. Retreating in frustration, her father snarled.

BADUM-BADUM-BADUM-BADUM-BADUM. Amarrock's growling laugh squeezed June's diaphragm.

BADUM-BADUM-BADUM-BADUM-BADUM. The trees surrounding the town square erupted with a horde of at least a hundred zombies coming down from the hill.

Chapter Twenty: Midnight on a Moonless Samhain

The steady plodding of the army of the dead met wave after wave of Spellmans. The sight was sickening, all the pale Connor-faced humans crashing into dirty, rotting skeleton-people by the dozens. It was difficult to watch. It was both nauseating and tough to see what was happening at the point the two sides collided.

"I can conjure Spellmans for all of eternity, but eventually, those zombies will be dust." Amarrock's voice had taken a calm quality, now that his whispers reached everywhere at once magically. He was still a swamp yankee redneck, though. "And that bear's pretty badass, but numbers always win."

BADUM-BADUM-BADUM-BADUM-BADUM

The swarm of undead plowed into the square full of Amarrock's golems, running them back and into the Elders, whose colorful sparks of magical attacks were dulled by the rush of grey decomposing corpses and pale white Spellmans.

And leading the undead, beating a barrel drum slung to his hip, stumbled Evens Bonhomme.

BADUM-BADUM-BADUM-BADUM-BADUM

Amarrock snarled in laughter. "Without a blind man to reach the library, I've already won!"

Then Evens threw down the drum and rushed to Dobiel. June couldn't be certain what he was doing, but she had a guess. If Dad was going to have a shot at making it to the library, June had to get the slithering wolf demon out of the way. She locked eyes with Chelsea and held a hand out by her side where the Sheriff couldn't see, pointing her finger then recoiling – firing finger guns. She prayed Chelsea would understand.

And then came Dad.

With his now-signature roar, the great white bear galloped through the fading bloodfire and witch's shields, barreling across the town square, ramming and stomping Spellman, zombie, and Miridicalien alike, rushing straight for the library.

The low bubbling cackle of the Sheriff sounded strained behind her. "Look at him go, sweetheart! Is he gonna save you?"

Then June noticed why Dad was storming through all the fighters, even the helpful zombies – Evens had cursed Dad. Again. With another ghost veil. He was blindfolded and headed straight for the library.

Beside her, Zippy appeared, growling and lunging at the Amarrock's shaggy legs. With an easy flick of the paw, a swipe of magic tossed the Bargeist to the side, sending him sliding across the library entrance and landing with a yelp.

But it distracted Amarrock just enough.

A small circle of finger-painted blood appeared on one of the columns, and from it a soaked red hand. Chelsea's hand reached for the Sheriff's belt and pulled his gun from its holster.

For more distraction, June mustered all her energy into a

ragged cry. "Zippy!"

Still laughing, Amarrock spun her hovering body until she again faced his glowing horned wolf visage. "Dumb-ass, smart-ass Juniper Szmydt, what are you gonna do?" Larger-than life jaws of teeth bared at June.

The big hand of the library clock clicked over to midnight, and the bells bellowed.

Roaring, Dobiel swatted at the dog cops as they pounced all over him, biting and tearing fur. The giant bear god, glowing, veiled, a funnel cloud of light touching down on him, fell to the side and rolled across the library steps, crushing dogmen.

June couldn't help but gasp. Since finding out who he was, she'd thought of Dad as physically unstoppable. But even bear gods had limits. As the pack continued to pile on, relentless, June didn't wipe away the tears, glad her vision was blurring.

Amarrock leaned in close enough for June to again smell rank breath pouring out of his yellow fangs. "I am Alpha of a pack of cops. Alpha of a town of wizards. Alpha of the Elders and unlimited Spellmans. Your Hellhound can't defend you. Your girlfriend can't protect you. Your father can't save you. And you, stupid little girl." He was close enough June knew he couldn't see her hands. He sneered, "You can't even use magic."

Through another blood portal, Chelsea handed June the Sheriff's sidearm. With one motion, she flicked the safety off and aimed the barrel between Marrock's glowing gold eyes.

June smirked and said, "Abracadabra," as she squeezed the trigger.

The gun fired.

Amarrock's horned wolf head exploded into blood and viscera just as the veiled bear god plowed past.

Beside the decapitated trickster demon, June fell to the stone landing while the giant bear god burst through the front doors of the library. As the golden glow of the Amarrock's body faded, she clasped his dead, black-taloned paw.

Ahead of her, through the new hole where the library's double doors had once stood, Dobiel reared up at the old, browned Miridical map and swiped a giant paw, scattering all the dashed and dotted lines, streaking the surface with jagged claw marks. He roared in triumph, his color returning to chocolate black though he grew in size, nearly twenty feet tall, a halo of gold wreathing his head, while the library's clanging bells rang gloriously.

June lay looking in awe as Zippy nudged his head under her arm.

Slowly, the roar of the crowd of combatants faded and the odd orchestra of magical forces being unleashed subsided. Arms that had been aimed dropped, as did glowing wands, crystal balls, talismans, staffs, and one enchanted PlayStation controller. The cascade of impossible colors dissipated as everyone in town moved their focus upwards.

The night sky was changing, filled with a sea of stars to accompany the milky moon. Everyone's breath became visible, a heaving wave of steam flowing from upturned heads. And then the dark heavens cracked.

Jagged light fingers of lightning, fissures in the night sky, appeared as though some invisible veneer over the town was breaking. A murmur spread over the crowd, but the sight was too immense, too foreboding for anyone to put words to it. June's mouth hung open, breath paused. Cracks in the atmosphere grew and connected like a snow globe under immense pressure.

Then the sky shattered.

Instinctively, June screamed and covered her head with her arms.

An invisible globe that had ensconced the town fragmented. The clear dome exploded outward, shards flung up and out flying forever into space.

And intermingled with the ebb and flow of steamy breath, a greenish blue mist drifted up from the mass of Miridical citizens. Like an aurora borealis seeping from people, the colors wavered and sparkled and reached up to the sky.

"What's happening?" June could barely whisper before people began falling.

The first to collapse were Evens's zombie horde, crumpling into heaps of corpses. Then a giant or two keeled over. Wizards, witches, and warlocks all buckled and fell to a kneel. The staffs, talismans, crystal balls, and PlayStation controller, which had still been alive with energy and color, faded to dull neutral.

The Boston Oaks stopped dancing, freezing mid-sway. The glowing symbols hovering over buildings waned. The bright auras and flaming force fields about the town square were extinguished. For a few seconds, the only movement were wisps of smoke and small fires around the square.

Then the Sheriff's patrolmen, the dogmen whom June always knew as the Marrock family, ran off to the woods. But not the oaks of Dabbit's Forest. The cops ran into the birch of the White Woods. The citizens who stood with the Elders screamed in anguish, prayed desperately to ancient gods, and shrieked in denial into the night as their powers ebbed away into the great wide open.

"The magic is gone," June murmured to herself, eyes agape in horror. Under her arm, Zippy whimpered, the plumes of sulfur that rose from his tufts of fur dwindling.

Lumbering over, her giant bear of a father collapsed to sit next to her, resting a paw on her back, roughly the size of her torso. The funnel cloud above him had dissipated, and his veil had been lifted. In its place, a shiny gold halo.

"My magic no longer protects the town. The Elders were using me to trap power, to bind it here, tether it to the town and its citizens."

"What will happen?"

"There will be a whole lot more magic out in the world."

"And less of it here?"

"For some. Now they'll have to hold on to it the old fashioned way. Through work, study, and spells. But for others, their enchantment will have a chance to bloom for the first time."

Raising an eyebrow, June asked, "Is this some kind of reference to puberty?"

The bright faced bear God smiled down at her. "No bug, but your pixie dust is coming in."

Chelsea's hoarse voice broke as she approached, calling out to June, "Damn, girl, you looking fly!"

Wiping away whatever horror her makeup had descended into, June stood at the top of the decimated library and managed a smile, "Thanks, Chels. I'm sure I'm a wicked mess right now."

Her smile shone brighter through the crimson mask of blood. "Sorry, dude, but your wings are amazing."

"Wings?" To June's side, Dad's enormous paw gently stroked against long, gossamer dragonfly wings extending from June's shoulders, reaching out twice as far as her arms and flitting with spasmodic twitches. "What the fu-"

"Recessive genes," her Dad cut in. "From your mother's side." His bear face then rumpled, eyes narrowing incredulously on Chelsea as she climbed the library steps. "And who the Hell is this?"

"Oh, Dad, this is Chelsea Bloodstone, my...um..." A smirk grew on both girls' faces as their eyes locked. "Girlfriend?"

The bear's face fell open in mock surprise. "Girlfriend? Well. Nice to meet you, Chelsea."

"Hello Mr. Bear-God Szmydt."

"You can call me Daryl." Then the massive haloed bear scrunched his nose and tilted his head in that very Dad-way and asked, "Has anyone told you you look just like..."

"Don't say it Dad." June laid her forehead in her palm, shaking her head.

"My favorite artist..." Dad was savoring the moment.

"I am so sorry," June whispered to Chelsea, exhausted in every way humanly possible.

The bear smirked Dad's smirk. "Taylor Swift?"

Chelsea nodded and smiled. "Some people say that, Daryl."

June was too embarrassed to look up. "Oy, Dad, you're the worst."

THE END

Reader, if you enjoyed this story, please help it find more readers! Reviews are amazing and so helpful to indie authors like me, but word-of-mouth is the most help you can give this book. So if you thought it was any good, please tell your friends. Recommend it for your book club! Give it as a gift! Shout it from the rooftops! And if you don't have any rooftops handy, PLEASE post about this book on social media. Thank you again for your time and brainpower reading.

   -Z

www.ingramcontent.com/pod-product-compliance
Lightning Source LLC
Chambersburg PA
CBHW010843190726
48286CB00012BA/2971